P
A
W
N
S

By

Steve Shapiro

ISBN 978-0-9848133-1-5

www.steve-shapiro.net

This book is dedicated.

SGS

PREFACE

This story has two privately held never before revealed factual events that may open a door to understand the city of San Francisco, with a tie-in to the Rosenberg executions at the end of WWII.

The Rosenberg couple did in fact negotiate to sell brother-in-law Greenberg's stolen A-Bomb secretes, and another never solved murder make for a somewhat revealing character: the City of San Francisco.

CHAPTER 1

A dead body lifted on hooks, drips red in color by reflected setting sun light and cold air all of which bodes poorly for war torn west and through the San Francisco Bay.

Water drips off the tweed suit, unusual for a Chinese bookkeeper, who appears as one in a piece of this port side puzzle of malevolence, as evidence of this is hauled in by uniformed cops. Amongst those in the scene stand plain clothes detectives. This scene appeals to no one on this ominous San Francisco night. A local victim during an international incident. World War II.

No one knows it's the last year of it.

San Francisco has lots of neighborhoods, loads of people, and where nobody cannot avoid anybody is not at all a city. A sophisticated event like this happens only once in a life like a town and equally unusual for this, The City.

Nobody knows what can happen next in San Francisco.

The City, 'a town' Mr. San Francisco, Herb Cane, the boy from Sacramento, the ultimate society columnist would later call it. With ethnic diversity stitched together as ethnic eccentricity, the people of San Francisco appear to join in a crazy quilt, a copacetic play, a theater where in all these peoples dance their own dance to the same tune. Its same tune for sure, though no one wants to admit the tune is the same, for each of the players dance to different instruments.

Nobody in San Francisco melted in one pot, they all stitched themselves into one bigger than life crazy quilt.

Because San Francisco was born out of a port or pier into the Pacific Rim that brought the final peoples of Asia and the Orient in one place for each to join the American frontier.

San Francisco was christened a city on the edge of a continent of expansionist villages, towns that could not grow without rough stuff, pistols, and tight restrictions of deeply personal controls. Along the path toward municipality, past the Sheriff stage, tenaciously unruly even with US Marshals in place, and the same with U.S. Army, military control; San Francisco was a bawdy hitching post town at birth and when it grew it stayed the same, it just got bigger. It was bigger than most frontier towns, and so it became known through-out the frontier as 'The City.'

Downtown Chinatown in San Francisco most times with empty streets, now, 1945 during the Great War in twilight this neighborhood shows The City for the unique character of itself without any fog, or interrupted interpretation by the presence of any people. The twilight city character of Chinatown shown in what was painted on the walls for anyone to see.

"Chinese cannot build here."

Here, secretes only the adventurous would discover while the paint on those walls flakes away with weather and time, as anywhere in the Far East, arose discoveries by researchers about the true nature of the people found painted on the remaining brick walls, and reported into history not without some courage.

The quick draw artists gone, barkers and swindlers locked away, Vigilante white coat cowboys melted and forged into the citizenry, The City on the West Coast resounds with merchants and brokers dealing anything for a bigger place under the sun.

Like a freshly sunburnt tourist, 'The City,' looks bleached at sunset, fagged out by sunset light off the east side of architecture painted in eternally mysterious oriental reds, yellows, greens and brown-black. A particular architecture that brings to mind a distinct ethnic interpretation of its peoples that history has marked as subservient only on this side of the Pacific Rim. In The City, all the people have been subservient to a great war, in this day, this town, San Francisco is The City, and it is filled with nothing but Pawns to play war. But, the war is not a play, although they call the fight over the hump from The City the theater, the Pacific Theater.

Amid the dance, within the play, underlying the plot of subservience to some great foreign power fought out by allies and greed, patriots and players, the prop holding all the characters to their role this day and in this age is the gun. The great weapon is yet to be discovered, or better to note, yet to be announced to the world.

In this town, which simply is 'The City,' there is a West Coast elite who drive a syndicated economy, and as it profits with traits and trappings of an ethnic eccentricity where there exists more than one single syndicate, no one knows what's next.

With syndicates separated by 3,000 miles between banks, 15,000 miles between currencies this bastion of fortunes draws other syndicates to mussel into what may well be the cookie crumbs found in the fortunes of war within The City.

No taller than six stories, and perched on the edge of western European culture, those drawn to search out the crumbs of fortune that has become a characteristic fear, driving force in this town since 1849; in the dirty streets of San Francisco smiling and wearing the latest suits signs of profit since back then and more so during the second world war. While the Great 'Quake' leveled San Francisco and restricted height in The City, it remained now during the War, World War II, The Great War a fear of the Manhattanization of San Francisco with skyscrapers that could topple.

Financial control remained the syndicate style of domination an East Coast fact and those who live in tall buildings back there, those who leverage fortunes with an advantage of residence close to the Greenwich Mean Time, as those who would know ahead of those in The City of San Francisco which way the tides of fortune would swell. West coast fact.

What this Manhattanization means is
different for all the swells, some of them
into Real Estate, but only a few who know
all the differences about growing cities
control the big money. Apart from the war,
knowing that about growth and development
would be top news in The City.

For even since the Civil War, San
Francisco had a tough town reputation.
Tough and dirty, with ruthless men who
traded bullets on the streets, tamed after
the age of the Stagecoach, the Frisco Kid,
Gentleman Jim who was arrested here. Later
the Hearsts brought big western money,
Jewish families Knickerbockers,
Flischakers, Swigs, and Quowks of the
Chinese Six Companies, all syndicate bosses
of distinction from criminal to patron,
Protestant, Catholic, Jew, Chinese The City
in parts has been under a syndicate of one
ruling class of distinction or another
since inception at the end of land growth
and them facing the sea.

Such economic distinction in a
western frontier town depended upon
cultural shipping trade from the Far East,
and with the sun rising in the east coast,
business and trade closing upon the same
economy endeavored to somewhat victimize
financiers on the West Coast. They call it
the east coast deal that had dominated as a
'sure thing.' And, in the west three hours
later, even within the richest syndicate,
they depended upon the existing finances
out West tapped into Manhattan for the
saying was that the 'east coast deal'
rules.

Only one thing brought confusion to this system: pawned in between Real Estate in San Francisco, the East meant not only New York City, but China.

Any sure investment became 'an East Coast Deal.' But in the know, those tapped into the East Coast deals, were those who could prosper without the old American Barons. The Chinese came to financially establish a foothold amongst resistance of an ugly sort, an ethnic resistance. Laws were family law of an ethnic sort that brought about restrictions from all sides, on all coast lines.

At this point in time, the Pacific Rim that opened the far east for port of call San Francisco, the East also meant Japan and at this moment with the war in the Pacific in the 1940's Japan seemed all too close. At this time, in San Francisco 1944, The City rattled of featured traffic with cars driving on low light, covered headlights, and very slowly. Lawed during the war with brown-out rules to avert attraction from overhead by an airplane, perhaps due to this war time possibility would be fueled by the fear of invasion from Japan. The atmosphere was somber, classically romantic.

As an American ally, China was dependent on the United States for support in their war against Japan. An idea of allies and ass holes was a bar room version, not far from the truth over what was going on across the Pacific Ocean from just outside the naive, baby girl San Francisco front door.

Near the district where tourist trade flourishes, on this one night, along the even numbered wharves side of the Embarkadero, uniformed POLICEMEN and PLAIN CLOTHES MEN including one Irishman, LT FABER watch as the fog lifts and the unusually tweed suited CHINESE MAN'S body that is fished out of the water.

FABER has been a lead detective in San Francisco since his days at Saint Ignatious High School where the ultra honest Catholic boys went, and as a son of the son of an Irish Cop, he was once an officer in the High School's lettermans' society and that made him the school constabulary. Successful as the guy with the hub for gossip and advice, a confident for all, mostly, the beauty queens of all the catholic high schools, and prominent in the school's DeMolay; FABER was marked for law enforcement in The City. As a young adult, police academy was in his future and finally, a man who rose through the ranks with claps on the back by his superiors, fellow officers and friends who remain near him and keep him in the know from back in the high school days. To say FABER has not strayed far from the town where he grew up is to heavily discount that fact which makes The City one of few on the map of international cosmopolitan contributors.

He spent several sabbaticals overseas lending expertise to the Indonesian, French, German (before the war) and Scotland Yard --police. Not at all a fuzzy pussy willow, but an expert marksman and a one punch street boxing champion. His

adversaries rarely remain standing, either
physically or mentally. FABER is a guy who
is always in the know on all the laws.
For, in San Francisco that meant Catholic,
Jewish, Chinese and the Constitution of the
United States, state and local.

The one police detective is not the
police, but he knew. He knows who owed the
Chinese money, and who had the bookkeeper
killed.

Standing in his stuffed raincoat, a
well fed Lt. FABER and showing it with
additional warmth in the form of a heavy
lining that makes this Irishman appear more
of a stout man as he stands, than as he is.
His cigar butt fizzles from the rain and
gets short from his fingertip puffs. The
big man is not one to affect smoking
cigars, but to love them. He wastes not
time with personal enjoyment, for on the
job he lives for the facts. This policeman
is one for gossip as he waits, he looks
around for a voice to fill his ear.

Standing face to face with his half
body turn puts him full in front of
reporter DON DAY, who just finishes his
notes, puts the small notebook and pen in
his pocket and leaves. Just like that.

Once a local Burlingame High, San
Francisco Peninsula Lothario, DAY fits the
profile of a journalist. He covered social
events of the Circus Club in Atherton,
auctions for seats in the social yarn about
the yet to be finished War Memorial Opera
House; he sat in visitor's chairs in San
Quenton's gas chamber, and famously upon
stools in more than four of The City's

famous former speakeasies or what are now
known as 'bars.' Not the legal
organization, though in San Francisco often
confused as . . . .

The reporter knows, too. He knows
Faber will never tell. The body drips
bay-water for awhile and the congregation
all looks upon it. Nobody sees what the
City boys already knew.

Neither man nor woman, San Francisco
holds the cards and steadies the skids up
and down hills famous with secretes never
to be revealed.

So, meanwhile, reporter DON DAY finds
himself driving up the sanctimonious
Chinatown streets, down through alley ways
where night falls fast upon everybody. Any
mystery in The City remains 'um-known' by
those few who are always knowing what it
is. These law men, newsmen, and even the
news makers have been knowing what goes on
in The City since high school when they
were all in it together. Different
schools, patched together by the same
stitches.

Something happens and they all know,
all of them say with a shrug that does
little to interrupt their conversations,
little at all. When they all say they read
the newspapers for the funnies, it happens
to be the fact; only some read it for
confirmation of what they heard tell, and
already know.

Filing through the thin streets,
newspaper reporter DON DAY drives from the
scene at the wharf in his blue Dodge sedan,
headlights covered but for slits. Driving

during the 'brown out' nights, DAY sits
comfortably behind the wheel, fedora square
on his head, black raincoat covers his
tuxedo; for in this wardrobe, reporter DON
DAY is ready for anything. If he should
get picked up by the authorities, if he
should get corralled by the society
gadabouts, ready for anything that goes
during a war. In every case, the tux will
surely get him more respect.

In a San Francisco Chinatown alley,
Waverly Place, in secrecy, a sapphire
necklace is slithered into a man's suit
jacket pocket just as at the same time a
pin striped suited man slim, hatted, and
shifty eyed --one FRENCHIE JOE climbs into
a taxi. His pointed toe crocodile pumps
pick up off the street, out of the gutter
last when his rear end is, swish, covered
by the raincoat before it hits the taxi
back seat.

Reclined onto the base of his spine,
inside the taxi, FRENCHIE JOE is carted off
into the depths of The City.

With lights dim in respect for the
brown out, enforced cautions during the
Pacific theater, World War II, the cab
slides through the city, up steep streets,
along level boulevards and pulls up to the
Opera house. And with the fare offered
that includes a tip to the driver, Frenchie
Joe gives him a note on folded white paper
and with instructions to the CABBY about to
whom the note is intended before he hikes
it into the War Memorial Opera House that
is swallowing the swells in toppers and
fur.

There are very few people in any part
of the City on the street at this time of
night, mostly older men and women, and a
remarkably few young men. Unbeknownst to
the world, it is nearly the end of the
Great War, the Second World War. The war
that claimed as many young men as were made
by the high skirts and quick marriages.

Meanwhile, the POLICE congregate by
the coroner's station wagon at the wharf.

"They-e's not to be anybody knowin'
about him trying to collect from our Jewish
boy." LT FABER says with utopian
authority. "Gamblin's against the law
anyway."

When one of the uniformed police take
FABER's arm, he shirks him off and says, "I
saw Day standin' there, and believe you me;
he saw me."

Suggesting there is no intimacy in
this town, the Newspaper presses keep
rolling in the Mission Street basement of
oldest San Francisco newspaper The
Chronicle.

"I said nobody's to be know-in'."
FABER's deep voice gives anyone within ear
shot reassurance that it would be an inside
story to know there was ever a murdered
Chinese Bookkeeper in the city of San
Francisco that day.

Additional newspaper presses roll off
the news in a small format, weekend
supplement.

HEADLINES: WAR CONTINUES -- 3 YEAR
REVIEW IN PICTURES . . . and there are,
many pictures.

It is 1945 and typical of most of the

front page news, dramatic front page photos
of large munitions' battles like Midway
(June 3-6th 1942). Stills, photos of men
loading the massive ships' guns with shells
and casings piled on decks keep readers
interested in the rag, fish wrap, the black
and white, the local newspaper.

For as in any town, the newspaper has
a life of its own, and it sustains the
town. The City is no different, the San
Francisco Chronicle is The City's crusty
life blood with its blue and gold seal, and
character of The City's own, Emperor
Norton.

Inside the news room of the San
Francisco Newspaper, even at night, the
activity indicates that the paper is about
to 'go to bed' with STAFF rushing last
minute changes in copy to make sure it gets
to the street before the sun comes up. As
part of an ongoing city life inside the
great hallways, over speakers in the old
newspaper building resounds the latest
locally playing Opera intermezzo that keeps
the all night workers in pace with what may
be going on outside. The San Francisco
details that keeps night time workers
loving their work place and maintains an up
beat in this, for everyone, the
sophisticated city.

Dodging desks and janitors, REPORTERS
chase the CITY EDITOR to get final
approvals.

One handsome reporter, Irish and
dressed in a messed up Black Tie, pressed
to shine smoker, DON DAY partially unshaven
and partially weaving in his 'Hi Pal'

attitude, but probably acquired from
consistent 'serious' drinking, is about to
land the exclusive attention of the CITY
EDITOR, who suddenly and in natural pace of
his job picks up a phone, no bell, but with
light blinking that calls for his
attention.

A COPY BOY hands DAY a note. The
same one from FRENCHIE Joe to the CABBY out
front of the Opera House. DAY's casual
expression changes when DAY opens -

The envelope with penciled notes and
sees an -

Opera ticket within the folds, which
he looks over and on the back is written
with brisk strokes, in Frenchie Joe's voice
it reads, "Come backstage for promises
about Big Bang info. Manhattan Project,"
and signed in paradoxically refined bank-
teller like scrawl --FRENCHIE JOE.

DAY stands at the desk of the CITY
ED. and tries to interrupt him while he is
on the phone.

The reporter's intent for permission
is genuine, at first. Then, the dawn
breaks and DAY sees the opportunity to get
his job on a faster track and takes
advantage of the boss' immersion in the
many activities in The City.

"Sol Davidal's big munitions deal,
Chief." DAY says with some urgency. "I
need a few facts, and some bribe money.
It'll sell papers."

Every newspaper has an Editor in
Chief who carries the point of view from
the General Manager, from the Board of
Directors; and with this Chief SCOTT

NEWHALL, notably a serious man, comes all voices wrapped up into one. This time it stands wrapped up in a guy who went to high school on the San Francisco Peninsula, originally from Livermore. He stayed with an Aunt to attend an all college preparatory, public school and finished his University back east at Colombia.

A big belly with a quick wit, a former football player who could have gone professional. The lure of $40 a game versus a three figure weekly salary came together in the head of this University graduate, and so as City Editor he stands up for the girls and boys of the San Francisco Chronicle.

The City Desk where all the stories come like the open end of a funnel houses this City Editor, the CITY ED. and CHIEF are the names he accepts and with no one using his given name, no one claims more privileges than any other one with this particular position.

This paper has the good fortune to have a serious student of the news, of writing, of current events, politics, the law; SCOTT NEWHALL comes from a family that had read the Chronicle when it started as the more costly of the papers. He takes this paper and the news seriously and for a good reason, his best and most profound love . . . The City of San Francisco that has his heart, his hands, and his head. His father, a doctor, had its health and he likes to leave it at that.

But, in this historic era, Newhall is the Chronicle.

Standing with phone to his ear, striped shirt, no tie, suspenders expanded by a prosperous belly, the CHIEF is only half listening because of the conversation coming from the loose tulip part of the phone against his head, and he routinely initials a chit.

His frantic waves of the hand tell DAY to sit down and wait, but DAY continues, takes advantage of the diversion, his trusted seniority, and the fact that he has his chit initialed.

"Thanks, knew you'd be okay with it," and DAY cuts away.

CITY ED. tied up, now frustrated on the phone, because he can't break away and stop DAY, who has walked away with a chit for almost one month's salary.

With mixed emotions, DAY saunters through the half full news room. His wallet filled, but his heart half empty for he sees his friends on the line busy typing on their sturdy Underwoods. The idea that there are arms on the street, during war in two hemispheres, and him needing a drink has his conscience frazzled.

Momentarily unconscionable, DAY walks out, filling in the editor's chit himself with a ball point while he walks, and he leaves the CHIEF stymied, stuck on the phone and now angrily frustrated, because DAY's almost gone, out of reach.

"If you can't find who's callin' in those false sightings," the CHIEF bellows into the long handled mouth piece. "Rent a plane and fly over their heads yourself!"

The CHIEF hangs up the phone and in simple silence stands alone amid the confusion. He seems frozen, dark on both counts, the why from the phone conversation and the what from tuxedoed reporter DON DAY. In futile desperation to hang onto any semblance of authority, the CHIEF calls out across the room. DAY has stretched the distance.

"What's it gonna cost?"

DON replies from across the room, "Look there's a hot story beyond those munitions rumors, coming from Port Chicago."

"<u>All</u> munitions shipments are hot. And they <u>All</u> come into Oakland harbor: Richmond, Port Chicago."

"There's gotta be fire behind all that smoke." All DAY shows is the back of his tux, waving the chit, and disappearing down the end of the room with his raincoat slung over his arm.

He throws out a comment in passing one of the girls at a typewriter nearer the door to the hallway and elevators.

"My Real Estate broker friends are into something big with munitions. Or, something with big munitions. The only ones with big money.

"The question is: What's it gonna make them?!"

His voice resounds from the shadows at the end of the work room before the opaque glass door opens and closes. "Profit wise."

Red faced, CITY ED in desperation, calls out for the entire night staff to hear, "If you can get me the lead to a story about a munitions deal, SO BIG that it'll scare the daylights out of me AND the Japanese -- I'll print it on the front page. IN RED!"

Through the door closing slowly on its hydraulic slam proof hinge, DAY finally exits the large room without looking back over his shoulder, and happily turns to the first security guard at the doorway to the hallway to share his achievement with a smile and a wink before the door closes and frees him to the outside world.

His smile was only somewhat limited by a small seeping guilt.

Not so much the money, he had absconded with an unlimited or open chit; but what staggered his joy was that which he might find out about his friends. His Jewish friends who may have put a Chinese man in the drink over money. But what would he find out about their arms dealings? What could they do to the country, vulnerable during war, and headed for the drink, too?

He wondered what it is about the Manhattanization of The City his friends are concerned about.

"I got it." He waves his trophy, the chit. "Whatever it's gonna be."

CHAPTER 2

Somehow feminine Pacific Heights, where the members of society brocade a lush tapestry of proper Victorian art in architecture, men in tuxedos with tails, and women in furs dangling their precious stones nervously all dally as generously insistent MEN offer one another ration tickets for gas, and they share parking tips with their drivers standing outside their polished cars and limousines on the plush Broadway street.

One or another awaits their companion as they all wait, for groups gather on the upper crust street unafraid of what might come from over their heads for a night on the town.

While curbside, in front of his High Victorian Gothic mansion, alone SOL DAVIDAL dressed in a black unborn lamb roll collar top-coat, enters his Cadillac limousine assisted by his CHAUFFEUR, a burly dark hair Greek.

The head man in what now seems to have become a Real Estate syndicate, the large SOL DAVIDAL, who has by default become owner of the 'large' and, high on mighty Nob Hill the Fairmont Hotel as it perched for decades on top of the tallest hill in San Francisco; and that it commands amongst the highest rates of any hotel in San Francisco its owner rolls alone into the night in his chauffeur driven brown out town car with only a clubba clubba noise of tires across tar stripes that resound on his ears off the boulevards of The City.

It was by a fluke that he owned the Fairmont. His partner and he held listings for two hotels, The Fairmont on Nob Hill and the St Francis on Union Square.

One day in the St Francis tea room, across the tables seated with clients, each of the two Real Estate partners signaled each other that they sold the hotel. Unfortunately for DAVIDAL he sold his partner Sax's listing and since they both sold the same hotel, the St Francis it was the noble thing to do -- SOL DAVIDAL got stuck with the Fairmont, as he bought it on his own. As if he were The City personified filled with guilt driven pride.

This is a non sectarian Jewish town. These two big Jewish moguls roared through The City with each having back door successes.

Just like it was with the gold rush tailor Levi Strauss and the shipment of light weight, white canvas he got instead of gabardine. The material he 'got stuck with' because it was too light for making tents that he used the newly patented rivets to hold together the waist belt looped overalls he made. He dyed the white light tent weight material blue to hide the dirt and the new 'blue jeans' brought in such a fortune that later, as the history of California in song says, his family famously supported the University of California's cornerstone.

In San Francisco, the city of Saint Francis d'Assisi, patron Saint to all animals, DAVIDAL was the first Jewish man to meet one on one with the Holy Pope of

Rome. He successfully presented the idea from his own heart and became founder of Boys Town. He himself made it possible for orphan boys to learn to participate in a government model of their own with Boys Town. And it could hardly be said of anyone in The City with a bigger heart, no one could have known.

"PAWNS," mutters DAVIDAL to no one in particular as he recalls the shenanigans of the gadabouts down the street exchanging ration tickets.

That same night, inside Curtis Deuitch's home, furnishings dominated by a Woman's touch, very frilly with walls painted mostly in white and decorated in Hepplewhite furniture; the owner of this Broadway mansion, the man lurks.

Light fixtures glowing against filigreed walls and dark solid black-out window coverings, CURTIS DEUITCH, full of guilt, talking over his shoulder to his WIFE getting dressed, seen through a series of mirrors behind the man while he searches for something inside his daughter's room. White with pink and certainly a room not filled with adult finery, he pokes with paternal familiarity within antique French bureau drawers.

A consummate partner, never a syndicate chief, CURTIS DEUITCH just as dominant with numbers as his boss with connections, a bookkeeper and as a gourmand with barrel chest and belly so as to be seen with same prominence of presence in person as a might be a chef. A big man, hardly one to be called fat, but powerful

in presence. Soft spoken of firm
convictions by insightful perception and
assured pronouncements, the syndicate
accountant of San Francisco's most
important investment group having been
sharpened by having to raise a daughter
with exceptional IQ and creative talent.

Dressing for his singular, weekly
personal night out, CURTIS DEUITCH, whose
voice reverberates with the reflections off
the mirrors proclaims with no one in direct
eyesight, "I just told the bank to transfer
five thousand ... uh ..." CURTIS says.

In that other room CURTIS -

Happily finds and he immediately
pockets a sparkling diamond necklace, taken
from the French bureau that is filled with
among other things, some lacy woman's
undergarments, a panache purse, topped with
gilt framed photographs; and he glides out
of that room into a sitting room while
first passing through an elaborate hallway.

CURTIS continues his dialogue with
the wife in yet another room, "for a
project with Davidal."

"That's nice, Dear," MRS. DEUITCH
replies from not too far off. With a guilty
pride to mask a gambler's greed, CURTIS
straightens his tie and pulls his collar
tight around the back of his stout high
academic downtown San Francisco public
school reputation, Lowel High School,
Stanford football scholarship athletic
neck.

He walks deeper into his home where
his brilliant artist daughter DONNA, a
voluptuous major teen in tight lace blouse

and skirt with soft leather pumps at the
end of white stocking covered legs savoring
gum in an extra large languorous wad is
seated by the phone, her lips glossed with
sumptuous gum chewing saliva, she slouches
reading a magazine.

Although of a vintage Old World
style, MRS DEUITCH fits into a sheath,
evening dress of an opulence that has
passed through The City leaving few with
any remnant of such 'joie de vivre' as
perhaps the Cuban dancer, Carmin Meranda.
And with the club star style of gown her
own personae, too, proud of an almost lost
athletic figure the MATRON DEUITCH poses to
admire herself in a free standing full
length mirror, her jewels, her powdered
face do her well with a justified Hungarian
pride.

"Your mother's trying on gowns for
the Opera tonight, you ever going?" CURTIS
talks, already put on his coat, stops,
looks upon his seated daughter. "You might
try on something if you're going." Because
she doesn't answer, he comes back to look
at her.

"No, thanks, Dad." His daughter DONNA
replies without looking up at his face,
"I'm not going anywhere, until Kit calls."
She unconsciously fingers her neck,
absentmindedly looking for her necklace,
which she apparently wears frequently.

CURTIS pauses, adjusting his
collar, sympathetically guilty searching
for the same necklace in his pocket says,
"You just waiting by the phone?"

"He said, 'wait for my call,' and I

said 'I'll be by the phone until you do.'"

"You don't have to take everyone literally, sweetheart;" CURTIS says looming over her in his shaved lamb and cashmere black topcoat, "and sit there <u>by the phone</u>."

She just looks up at him with puppy-dog eyes.

CURTIS with warm smile repressed by self carried guilt at what went into his pocket a moment ago quickly continues out the open door.

And in the cold downtown as with every mid 1940's downtown, Market Street at a movie theater with a line outside this Friday night is no exception.

Pulling on, and closing their long top coats PATRONS of the movie exit, while CROWDS of mostly women in pairs and small groups each wearing gloves and veiled hats, wrapped tight in their cloth overcoats wait in a line on the street to get inside.

Inside the dark and comforting movie theater, Movietone News flashes on the screen with the glare of a marching band sound track that tends to bring the patrons to the edge of their seat. Perhaps planned that way, as flashes of inspiring patriotism in pictures, loud band music, and News recapture clips of: Tokyo Raid -- Jimmy Doolittle aerial motion picture shots show our first mission of attack on Japan after Pearl Harbor April 18th 1942, when thousands of bombs being dropped graphically display how that city is now victoriously shown to have been devastated, as the ANNOUNCER declares:

"Three years into the war since Doolittle's raiders leveled Tokyo. In the White house, President Harry Truman deliberates: How long can the American people endure this costly war?"

The Movietone News ANNOUNCER's voice seems to reach through the San Francisco streets. While the few people on the street look up occasionally with suppressive fear and a solitary longing for the enforced frugally of war to be over.

Until the sounds hit walls that protect the inside of The Happiness Fortune Cookie Company from revealing a plush, secret Chinese Gambling Parlor, which looks vulnerable from the outside at night with the green light outside over a discreet stooped door, but stands up for privacy to any one, weather, or spontaneous police investigations. Even inside no one fails to respect the night formalities in their evening dress indicated by the men clean shaved and women wearing green eye shadow, casually glowering at the flash of money in clips, posturing in black patent leather pumps and high gloss shined shoes.

Big money, large bills silently slide on a green felt covered table and cards that follow as,-- Baccarat the Internationally big money game is played here.

A card game for the very rich with big cash money. One player controls all the money in the game called 'the bank,' the house merely the dealer and takes a toke from the pot. 'The Bank' owned by a lead player is at the standard fifty thousand dollars and all, always in cash.

The point is nine, and whomever comes closest wins all the money. Face cards are zeros, and the smaller amount of cards wins over a large number of cards.

The DEALER softly beckons players.

"Buy the bank. Who owns the bank makes the play."

His unborn lamb top-coat now hung in the club's obscure coat room, SOL DAVIDAL, dressed to the 'nines,' seated and slumped over the card game shows his over sixty-year age as one man who supports the weight of the world.

He makes his play with the mandatory fifty-thousand dollars.

"I'll play the bank, if nobody wants it" SOL has the deep keel of a fully independent soul. With the sound of chips in the background, he pulls the almost silently dealt cards now in front of him off the felt. "This could go on forever."

He turns over the two cards: a four and a five.

Twenty thousand dollars appears on the felt.

In a glazed relaxed stare of a resolute man slowly surrounded by dilettantes, SOL pulls a card from the shoe. The 'shoe' is that wooden box with fifty decks of shuffled cards, offered to the player by a dealer, more of a clerk.

"The game is played for the point of nine. One card or more, the point is always nine."

One of the GADFLYS remarks from behind his twenty thousand dollar bet.

"This is a game for the 'nines'."
Someone chimes in to solicit giggles from
the satiny dressed debutantes and black tie
gadflies, there. A couple five thousand
dollar bills fly onto the table.

"I'm in for ten." A faceless bet
from the dark green light off the side of
the table.

Continuing up town society steps out
on upper Laguna Street, Pacific Heights
while the bank is played in Chinatown. The
dark night is relentless in the mandatary
brown out as the grey car that carries
CURTIS DEUITCH into town rolls forward like
a sperm cell through traffic by a chauffeur
who knows all the lights.

"I got the bank at one-twenty
thousand, now."

On his stool at the table, SOL folds
and pockets his cash reigns sovereign at
the club, says to no one who cares to hear,
but for all to hear though ever so softly,
"My bank. I bought it up."

He collects the two fives from the
table. His nine, jack is 'up' against an
ace and a seven.

Though DEUITCH is driven, and sits
inside the back seat of a grey Chrysler,
sounds of the tires on cobblestones, shards
of a bygone era later blotched by asphalt
match the sounds from inside the gambling
parlor and that clash of clicks from the
chips as the general quiet of a residential
neighborhood otherwise persists outside the
games, and as SOL rakes in the chips and
some bills from his winning at the not so
far away baccarat table DEUITCH continues

to make his way through The City into the
club. Both engrossed by the same beat and
clatter.

SOL's sinister laugh seems to echo an
effect throughout the city.

Wearing the beaver fur collar shaved
lamb top coat, style of the wealthy at this
time, CURTIS DEUITCH approaches in a
chauffeured car by himself and enters
through the club door held open by his grey
double buttoned full length coat chauffeur,
black cap uniformed driver. Some other
major players enter hats in hand.

First CURTIS had to remove his own
hat in order to fit out of the back seat of
his chauffeur driven Chrysler, and now
without him inside the car on the sidewalk
his driver takes off to find a place at the
curb to wait outside.

Inside at the Opera House, the
powdered faces of The City's social sphere
bob and sway in that conversational dance
which continues even during times of war in
a center box. Always inside of it, the
clique of the mostly ladies present
politely reserve their poise, while
imagination serves what the gossip can
contain, certainly little about the war and
Hitler's march through Europe and Africa.

In here, Episcopalian mix with the
Jewish dowagers, the Catholic matrons as
the wealth in San Francisco is seriously
secular.

The orchestra tunes up, and several
LADY DOWAGERS including Mrs. DEUITCH are
leisurely seated, although last minute and
by USHERS.

The young wanna be's of the music world of long hair and classical musicians take voluntary positions as ushers to simply get into the Opera House for each performance. There is no 'seen it already' in these children of the prosperous vocabulary.

More it sounds like 'can't see it enough.'

Some of the LADIES busily wind up their chat queued by the music. MRS. DEUITCH seems concerned with her second row box seat as the orchestra finishes their tuning-up, she looks around to see who may have become upped her into the front row box position she held for decades.

"I guess it was that investment and Curtis didn't pay our renewal in time." MRS. DEUITCH mutters to herself, remembering her husband's last comment to her before he left the house earlier.

Once seated, she relieves frustration to notice that all of their seats have been changed. She vaguely recalls an echo of her husband telling her about some sort of re-appropriation of their money, '. . . a $15,000 investment but it was with Davidal, he'd said.

"Oh Well, that's life in an Opera box." Says Mrs. Deuitch to no one in particular, who continued her inner conversation out loud, and from whom no one reacts.

Inside another form of war time society, inside the crowded, smoky Chinese gambling parlor, inside the secret chambers of mysterious Chinatown, VARIOUS

CONTINENTAL MEN in black tie and tuxedos,
LAVISH looking WOMEN in slinky-slit and
satin dresses play roulette and card games
in the hushed din of another opera, one of
Chinese elegance.

Places around the various tables
change, seats around the Baccarat table
change, no gossip around the gambling
parlor changes anything. But the powdered
faces and lipstick painted mouths continue
a gossip and chat into the nearest ear,
most not caring whose ear it is. Those who
bend the ear of their intended get a wide
eyes stare in return for their comment or a
burst of laughter.

Meanwhile, in front of the Opera
House in the night of safety lights, no
headlights in respect for the brown out, a
cab pulls up and drops a PENNY, the
formally dressed, young, blond city society
girl. Inside, music resounds onto the
outside streets as the Opera begins.

One of The City's 'smart' girls.
PENELOPE BURTIS, a Katherine Dahl Burke
School girl, a finishing school for young
'brainiac' girls to ensure they would stay
that way; when she dressed to the nines she
can get herself into or out of anything.
Any event is open to her, any home might
balk at allowing her inside, but she was
never interested in the inside of just any
home. She remains one of the girls who
always thought a true successful woman
should have two secretaries, one for
business and a second for purely social
affairs. The operative word, open to PENNY
any time is 'affair.' Focus on the one

facing her now, as PENNY's heels clack clack on the cement steps. No swish of her dress, tight as a second skin and as revealing except for the loose top held in place with thin spaghetti straps and made private by a roll collar mink coat.

Proud of her position as a hometown little girl of The City and with athletic charm, she climbs the stairs for the opera without a second breath and into the Opera House as though it were her own secret club house.

Harbored in the back of her mind is her father's fame for having been the last of the gold miners to bring his donkey into the St. Francis Hotel and that reputation oversaw her growing up, getting down, and at times saved her when she was being dirty. Only everybody who is anybody knows about PENNY BURTIS.

At the same time, another opera outside in China Town's Waverly Street, the one luxurious alley way in a culturally suppressed development of Chinatown.

The Davidal Cadillac limo from Pacific Heights turns around at the alley corner and pulls up a mere twelve yards forward as the big tires spit some loose stones across the narrow street against the curb on the opposite side of the street of the cunningly disguised Chinatown business entrance to the Happiness Fortune Cookie, Co. in order to make room for DEUITCH's Chrysler in front.

Time, like a dream lapses into the opera's finale, and at the Opera House, back stage after the performance as the

tunes from this French Opera ends and
subdued crowd noise tones the scene . . . a
social opera in The City continues there
with so many faces of society who paid for
the performance, and the sets, and the
curtains. Now, mingling with performers,
they no longer have to pay for the
champagne . . . uninhibited, they drink it
up, for they paid for it already in
overpriced subscriptions.

PENNY enters the behind the scenes
melee, pushing the respectable and
respectful crowd aside by her sensual
entrance.

As any beautiful blond in a slinky
strapless gown, bare legs, spiky pumps,
PENNY knows her advantage and pushes the
limits. A woman of fine family heritage,
as always, commands respect in San
Francisco, but this one also of daring
beauty parts the seas.

THE LADY DOWAGERS, Mrs. DEUITCH
included are in conversation with various
OPERA SINGERS embraced in contemporary
celebrity --status that permits them
ignorance of any miracle of heritage or
accident of birth like beauty -- for their
conversation penitents over seat changes is
a material concern and for them that counts
in tally of the most 'coiter' points in San
Francisco society. Meaningless
conversation, drivel.

Mostly the women who remark through
newspaper facts in one liners like coits
tossed in a back yard game on the grass at
some San Francisco Peninsula home, make the
toss onto a peg and the mere ability to

toss facts in group raises the pitch in conversation, as voices respond to follow each other as they show off that they have given some of their time to know of what the real world holds most of the time.

Like the young PENNY, Mrs DEUITCH attracts attention amongst those in the know, as she waves with familiarity to newspaper reporter DON DAY who appears, standing in the back of the crowd.

Prestige becomes the old dowager in knowing a newspaper man. DAY tosses off the acknowledgement from this rich and influential, as more waves and high-signs compete with Mrs. DEUITCH, because DAY is preoccupied with more important stuff. He has a following. He has the luxury to be knowing, so as his job influence gives him that and he can ignore these rich people who in fact need him at their breakfast table, and they adore him as much as for what they get on the radio quoted out of his column after dinner.

Day stands firm in his fitted black tie smoker, with obfuscating conversation. He looks for his messenger, while talking to -- An ITALIAN BARITONE while -- acting the charmer by rote at each socialite talking and simultaneously look around at different attractions in this circus of prestige.

The messenger, FRENCHIE JOE, thin, a nattily dressed Italian-French mafia type sidles his way toward -- not DAY -- PENNY, and pairs of eyes zeroed in on by a third party DAY not too distant, who crosses the room.

DAY, who at the sight of FRENCHIE and PENNY, approaches them through the crowd that gathers and disperses in circulation around one of the lesser Soprano STARS. This cotillion, which leaves PENNY and FRENCHIE daringly exposed to the astute, invites the approaching reporter, DON DAY.

DAY hears, but pretends he hears nothing, and so stammers his approach to gleam all he can through the crowd. Frozen in the poise of absence, and abstinence of conversation not his own his presence is a magnate directed at what JOE had for him as inferred in the note.

Because FRENCHIE asks PENNY, "Did you get any more stones?" PENNY replies in an ineffectual hush, adjusted for the din, "Can you get me any more money?"

It becomes more interesting for DAY to allow himself to be cut off, manipulated a little more by the crowd, and with his skills to eaves-drop on what FRENCHIE JOE and PENNY are going on about.

"Look, I told you, those stones can't be cut." FRENCHIE replies anxiously, "It's a one shot deal with sapphires. You got the paste, I got some money. You ... made out all you could." He sees DAY break the pose of absence and cuts short his commentary.

PENNY in her pretty-girl wine, "Well, what it is to me and what it is, is what it is. Isn't it?"

In the fast shuffle with conversational partners there's a game in this casino, a game that pulls FRENCHIE JOE apart from PENNY and pushes -- DAY closer, between them.

WHEN ... because DAY gets closer . . . kissing distance from PENNY. Over the shoulders that create a distance between them, FRENCHIE quickly plies her, "Try for another piece. Fence's comin' in from Detroit soon and we can, you know ... do it again. I have one over on your sugar daddy, Davidal. A dead chinese bookkeeper." With DAY right on top of them, not quite next to them in a shuffling crowd , PENNY pouts, "That's all he needs to hear."

Her head motion announces DAY, who approaches. She snickers at FRENCHIE's parting comment to DAY.

Because in the middle of her barking banter to FRENCHIE, FRENCHIE flicks his head to remark directly to DAY, "She's your ticket. I sent you."

With some difficulty reaching across the bodies of patronage, DAY passes him the note, which he acknowledges by taking it from DAY's hand but crumples it up immediately and drops it onto the very crowded floor.

Unabashed, suave DAY has been glibly announced, as FRENCHIE allows himself to be taken back into the melee by the tide, "Penelope, darling. I didn't know you were such an Opera fan."

PENNY seems startled at the refined voice of DON DAY, "I get around. You got a reason?"

They both take another glass of champagne from a tray circulated by a WAITER. The white tie crowd seems to class

out the black tie of DON DAY. FRENCHIE JOE
and DAY now more distant exchange signals.
FRENCHIE JOE holds up a piece of note
paper. Message retrieved from the floor.

"There's always a story here." PENNY
interjects into DAY's comment.

"'course there's stories here, this
is an opera house. People pay for stories.

"I'm looking for a war-money scam."
DAY continues, "All I see, though, is great
gams."

She bats his hand away from trying to
lift her skirt. Although he stands looking
into her face with a mischievous smile,
PENNY becomes instantly nervous,
suspicious, "I thought you were a War
correspondent?"

DAY drives his curious point, "It's
about a War Lord and his 'Tart,' I heard .
. . " he makes time with an emphatic pause
as he looks her over. "No one pulls one
over on Davidal. But listen, does
Rosenberg sound familiar? A New York
Trotskiite, friend of Davidal's maybe?"

The resonance of the back stage bell
to signal time for a closing comment and
get the patrons out of the place falls on
the dumbed ears of this serious
interjection of great political bent, and
one yet to become an historic post war
event for which neither of them would know
at this point. For, the war is raging in
both Europe and the Pacific. DAY and
PENELOPE are neither raging nor at war.
With considerable effort, PENNY feigns
relief.

"Every city is an Opera, full of

Operatic characters." She sips champagne. "Told ya, the stories in an opera cost money."

DAY defends his intent, "Only if you can make out the differences in the Mikado."

"The Mafia?" PENNY becomes nervous again.

"I said nothing about the Mafia." DAY keeps driving, but softly, "Frenchie Joe confuse you? Mikado means dream, opera story."

They look around the room, both in low-key admiration for each other.

Showing himself the consoler, DAY begins to wax philosophic,

"Life's a dream, Penny. It's all a Mikado."

His look lands into her eyes, though his own are fatigued.

PENNY resigns herself, "Go, tell. What's your story?"

DAY resumes, softly in his custom manner of pursuing business, the business of making gossip into hard news.

"I'm tracing this rumor I heard from two of my fiends in Davidal's syndicate that's about East Coast munitions deals."

"Source said PENNY's interested in anything that has to do with money, especially DAVIDAL's money," she hears what he says and puts her glass down on a passing waiter's tray. DAY takes her arm.

PENNY meekly asks, "Can you give me a ride?"

Playing the escort, DAY takes her arm, "Sure!"

Then they slide toward the door together. Both realize simultaneously this is better discussed outside.

Melting into his confidence, PENNY says, "Tell me ... I want to know everything about Davidal."

She looks, searches in his eyes, though he watches his footsteps and has no chance to see it, but hears her ask, "What do you know?

CHAPTER 3

Outside and mustering patience, without words DAY walks PENNY to the Opera House parking lot.

The night is as dark as in wild west photographs. DAY and PENNY get to his car.

DAY turns her around to face him, "I was set on an inside guy about fast money. Frenchie Joe. He called me to the Opera, and I saw you .... Overheard. Wanna blow me in on it?"

Blinking, she gives him a dumb dame double take.

"What's it to you? My boyfriend and how he gets his money, or the fast sign of good times [huh]?"

DAY stern face, says nothing nor is he weaving through any crowd consuming his concentration. They have made it to the outside and safely by his car. It happens to be night. They happen to be by themselves. While she leans against the car with her coat open, dress hanging off her body and him looking into her face, she sees his determination.

His concentration that rests on her eyes, not her body lines. "It's about what do you know?" She can sense a serious intent from him and takes him literally. He knocks out a cigarette from an open pack and she holds out her open hand, palm down, fingers spread to accept a smoke.

"Let's go to Chen's," PENNY says. "It's a sanctuary of confidences."

DAY helps her into his 1943 Buick sedan.

Seated inside, she fishes around in her purse while he walks around the front of this car, gets inside, starts the car, and tunes in a radio station.

She has a flask that she takes out of her night bag, besides some matches, and she takes a swig and offers it to him. He takes the flask and she takes the opportunity to light up her smoke.

"Let's us go ... Chens." DAY says.

He swigs while driving.

It could be romantic, in this low-light, Brown-out City that passes outside the car, as DAY responds in monosyllables to her vagaries about the 'boyfriend.'

Along the drive, subdued passing car lights flash by along the streets. A siren goes off behind them, vehicles veer to the side of the road and stop and the brown-out order is evident by cars' lights that go off in respect for the ambulance that speeds past them all. Search-lights reach into the sky, because the brown out is momentarily, and officially violated by a local ambulance emergency. The City is a polite one used to holding to the rules.

DAY puts up his PRESS sign on the windshield to catch the view of passing police that escort the ambulance, and everybody continues, brown out rules, with parking lights only.

She takes back her flask, as DAY has started giving an appearance of a dedicated drinker.

Resolved after the momentary crisis, PENNY resumes. "Sol gives me a chance to

be, er, stay in. In the life ... the life
My father wanted me to be sure to keep.

"My mother turns her back on all
sorts of responsibility. It's father who
pushes me. Mom doesn't know half of what's
goin' on in the world, and besides she only
hitched up with my dad for the money.
"Financial security" she said to me so many
times I had to believe that's love.

"I 'wanna' think she's too modest to
tell me all the details."

Brown-Out continues outside while
confidences begin to shed insight from the
dark car, but some lights come on around
them while they cruse through the City
where only the many sleep.

PENNY has taken back the flask,
continues now warmed up having downed a few
swigs, "They're in New York most of the
time. It's my boy-friend who's in control
... of all the whole thing." Her sentences
roll out with body language that displays
not only an emotional effort, but some body
parts in movement only a woman could
manage. She recovers a protruding breast
by pulling up the spaghetti strap on her
satin dress before she hits the flask
again.

"I don't know any details, and maybe
nobody wants to. It scares me. It's New
York!? They talk about Manhattanization of
The City. Maybe the money's East Coast,
they mean New York money, because too few's
got any here in San Francisco."

DAY talks for the first time besides
just 'uh-huh.

"You can help me out with more

details. The Manhattan project is a
munitions deal, I think."

When he looks at her, no reaction.
The silence pulls him into her problems.

"No. Real Estate."

She swigs.

"Jewish syndicate."

DAY goes on. "Listen, no one really
knows how long we have on this earth. The
world's at war, maybe this is what's meant
to be 'the new life.' Streamlined cars,
toasters, and a streamlined easy life with
a War front to eliminate those who can't
take, it.

I gotta know ... can Davidal take
it?"

At that PENNY straightens up, "Yeah,
take it. You got it. For me, too, get
it?" She says, "This is the end, so live
for life, right? Take it and give it up."

"Right?! All out, for what it's
worth." DAY goes on.

"This is it." He's confident though
vulnerable, merely imploring PENNY's
cooperation, getting her attention for
something serious. "This ain't cereal,
it's SERIOUS. They say there's a plan to
blow up the world or something."

She turns abruptly to look at him at
the moment he has to concentrate to turn a
corner. "No. It's a build up. They said.
I hear. Higher into the sky, like New York
. . . like Manhattan." After a moment of
serious driving, DAY resumes. "I get bits
and pieces, following the ordinance trade,
guns and bombs sales, but I want the
details. Help me. It's Davidal's East

Coast deal. Trotskiites, they say? It
ain't right, Penny. It just ain't right.
It's sellin' us out."

She passes the flask, pulls her
spaghetti straps over her shoulders,
nervously fishes in her purse for a 'stick'
to smoke. Lights it and smokes it while
DAY sips the flask.

"Yeah, sure, okay. It's about them
what's got it. Not tall buildings." PENNY
remarks, and now makes her sarcasm obvious,
asks, "Tell me, when the wars over don't
you think he'll still be rich?"

PENELOPE shows glimmers of a woman,
who's not some dumb dame. DAY keeps
driving, first up then down the steep hills
of San Francisco until he's finally at the
brink of Chinatown, then into the alley,
Waverly Place.

Finally DAY sums it up. "Rich!?
Davidal has it to want to own the whole
war. War means profit to people like him.
At all costs!"

"He's into Real Estate." She angles
her legs with the door popped to open, "He
wants no war!"

"Help me prove his character. Help
me find out what's gone into the drink and
by who. Let me in on it, and what else you
can find out."

Of course, there's no parking place.
He drops PENNY off and goes around the
block.

The Alley happens to be Chinatown's
crown Real Estate. They named the street
after and in hopes of that prosperous
street, Waverly Place, in Atlantic City.

When the Chinese arrived and settled
on the few streets that cross Grant Avenue,
one small alley was in effect pristine.
The plain used brick walls, flush with each
other and equally set back along a real
functional sidewalk had an air of
prosperity, a propriety of long lasting
that the Chinese harbored in a forecast for
their settlement. They were banned from
owning, from improving, building anything
in The City. Naming the street for the
icon of prosperity in Atlantic City,
Waverly Place when they got the chance,
they claimed the spell of success for their
own settlement. On this alley, or street,
rests offices for their powerful unity, the
San Francisco Chinatown Triad. In the
open, sort of. A fortune cookie company,
or what looks like one.

After all, with everything written in
characters, Chinese characters that reduced
the number of people who could tell what
was behind those doors, those walls; what
did it mean to have the Chinatown Triad
offices so openly proclaimed. It was,
after all for security. Scarecrows in a
farmers field that could come alive and
attack with silent weapons, more than
knives, more than secret moves. They knew
the real soft spots. The Triads knew the
shame everybody hid. They also knew the
Sicilian clans.

The Happiness Fortune Cookie Company
gambling parlor opens from Waverly Place.
Day or night. Now, it's night.

Inside and up stairs, her mink coat
draped off her shoulders PENNY heads

straight over to the big Baccarat table,
but she's stopped nearly there by a woman
with a little too much make-up, green eye
shadow, like a working girl on the night
off. A brunette with an Irish attitude in
a Chinese club surrounded by mostly Jewish
men. MARGIE is one private dick nobody
sees unless she wants them to see her.

MARGIE stops the private clock, she's
a young attractive dark hair brunette woman
who comes out from a corner of the bar with
other YOUNG WOMEN of a high fashion look.
They are extremely sensuous with powdered
faces all in doll like colors. For them,
this night out is the norm of nights out
with 'anything goes' written on their faces
rather than staying inside during a war.

Right out of the Catholic School
rebellion to public school discrimination
against honor roll students, a Sarah Dix
Hamlin School girl, sometimes the school
called the Van Ness Seminary,

now simply the Hamlin School that
moved to Pacific Heights,

Broadway to tower above Cow Hollow
where the mansions have one block
addresses. MARGIE HERON dropped into the
working girl category as a dedicated
patriot. As a woman of this stature, to go
to work, like to don the make-up of a girl
on the hunt, makes her a rebellious girls'
school drop in. Dropping in on the real
world instead of to slide into society
work. Finding a real man instead of some
trust fund baby, who might talk with a
fashionable lisp. She unconsciously claims
the prerogative for a real man, and this

has to be one of the few places to find
one.

Grabbing PENNY's arm, MARGIE
retaliates from what may be an old high
school conversation. Though from different
finishing schools, their hang outs remained
the same.

"Why do I come here? I'll tell you
why. I come to find good looking rich men,
and so do you, Penny. Don't deny it."

Like a heard of cats, ferrule,
foreign, and domestic, the group and
especially the brunette MARGIE slides near
the place at the table where PENNY in the
red satin dress with spaghetti straps that
can barely keep her slight breasts covered,
and she flippantly tosses her very blond
hair and comments, generally for the group
to hear.

In feminine defiance, PENNY remarks,
"Marge, you and I have only one thing in
common. We share the same shade of
lipstick."

PENNY gibes AGNUS in the ribs, a wild
looking French blond, who takes a stick of
marijuana from her night bag and agreeably
hands it to the half-closed eyed PENNY.

Detached from this countries' fate as
a refugee from her own home, AGNUS with
thick French accent sarcastically says,
"Look at those 'lugs.' Not one cares a wit
about what their baby's 'gonna' look like,
or who's gonna get a new pair of shoes.
The war makes them forget the future."

She seems more to be worried than
sarcastic or bitter for, what the most of
these ladies are bitter for, lack of money.

More plainly, lack of lots of money. Her family put her through Burke's School, too. She went to Paris to learn the language of her father's family and mother's skirts, but Hitler's army made a

change in plans, and put a French frown on her face, a pout that she keeps forsake of her heritage. She has money, and like most French girls she will probably take it to the grave.

Never to be outdone by sarcasm, MARGIE says, "They care about the future, all right. They all have futures in this war."

Even more so, this makes the AGNUS-es of The City lay out for the boys and what they can take.

PENNY stares into the room like a cat looking into oncoming headlights. DAY has planted something with his words and thoughts about the invasion of East Coast mentality, or what it was he wanted her in on it.

At the Baccarat table the money is piled high on top of the green felt. Most dialogue is muzzled by crowd garble, smooth HIGH-STEP PEOPLE gathered around the TWO PLAYERS, DAVIDAL and DEUITCH.

The girls approach closer to the table, and PENNY bumps up against one of the players. One of the losers, CURTIS DEUITCH is uneasy.

CURTIS takes a blue white diamond necklace out of his pocket. "I'll take a chance," he says, tossing the necklace onto the table. "Unless you have something that can raise this, I'll call you."

His opponent, SOL DAVIDAL stares at his challenger a moment. In a slow, soft, and slightly lisped pout, SOL replies simply, "Stinker! You can't do that!"

Some MAN makes an apparently demeaning comment close to SOL's ear. Then in a burst of rage covered by laughter, SOL lavishly throws the cards over his head and scatters cards and money off the table all over the room.

"You ungrateful Cow Palace resident," SOL bursts.

"I control your, whole fortune. I know what you've got in the bank. All of you!"

The chaos is cut short by the appearance of a crisply dressed Chinese man.

The 'club owner,' CHEN LAI appears from the black-out depths of the parlor. He is a young, small well groomed Chinese man dressed in a black three piece suit. In his hand, arms folded across his chest, rests the outcome of one main bank as he stares at the raging men.

CHEN is a 'knower,' that defines his position outside of ownership, outside of credit references. He knows who killed his bookkeeper and he knows that the Irishman, policeman wants to bury the secret with the body. He knows what these men do to be able to put big money in cash on his tables. He knows SOL DAVIDAL runs CUTRIS DEUITCH's life with the money he controls that they both revere as much as it supports their family above the streets and mostly above the law. He knows what the top dog, DAVIDAL does not know, that he loves DAVIDAL's daughter and she loves him.

A small well dressed Chinese man in black silk three piece suit, silk shirt and tie, CHEN LAI uses his presence alone and it settles the crowd.

Both SOL and CURTIS begin to breath easy after such physicality, heavily pacified with consensual judgment levied by hard looks against each other and juried by another person. A position of judgment that neither of these particular men can ever accept without this proprietary providence. They respect the proprietary ownership of property, of the money that all belongs to CHEN LAI; and they respect his ability to hold their blood, guts, hearts, their veritable lives his hands, or more likely his hand signals.

Reaching through the crowd, CHEN takes the necklace delicately in his hand off the table . "I'll keep this 'bauble' in the safe ... we'll straighten out the winner- by cards off the floor."

As CHEN eyes CURTIS, a murmur grows through the room with everybody curious about how he'll do that. CHEN turns to the two big men with the quiet assurance of a guy followed by three very big Chinese men, body guards who were looking on without contra move to the small powerful man who is their boss.

"Chinese are good with puzzles. They can figure this out by tomorrow," CHEN says.

"Now, everybody OUT!" CHEN had his patience tried, and he is not one to accept that.

Momentarily satisfied, THE CROWD, uneasy, mills toward the exit, coats are handed across the room as the three CHINESE MUSCLE quickly cordon off the card strewn floor.

"A problem has been created, here. I'll have my house EMPTY." Everyone's disappointed.

By his famously respected, silent command, out come various CHINESE in oriental togs and Occidental dress who guide the players out onto the street.

Suddenly outside in front of the gaming club's building, street level where secretes inside once innocuous buildings and plain store, factory fronts and polished brass plaque labeled offices seem suddenly revealed in the face of formal populace milling about in significant numbers on an ally pavement. Night time offers no comfort in secretes, outside nothing too hard to be revealed, so the patrons scatter quickly.

Finally having parked his car DAY, the reporter, saunters up to the door outside just as the crowd is leaving.

DAY says to no one in particular, "What the ... what's happening?" He gets filled in on the event by exiting PATRONS, and he gets the gist of a power play just as . . . . MARGIE exits, and she gets pushed, right into his arms.

A very pretty girl falls into his arms. DON says, "What's goin' on?"

The pretty girl is MARGIE, who answers with sarcasm. "God came in and

stopped the war. Said to all 'go home,' so
we did."

He laughs an admiring man's
comforting laughter.

A reporter, trained quick study, DAY
replies, "Chen kicked everybody out to stop
a fight, eh?"

"Hardly." MARGIE bumps him in a
gesture of familiarity.

"Think he ever completely closes?

She stands face to face with him.
She's attracted. "We all see what we want
to see, each of us in our own special way."

She begins to walk up the steep hill
and he falls into step.

She takes his arm as if they'd been
friends for a long time.

"You grab hold of any guy that's
thrust into your arms?" DAY asks without
wonder.

Her attitude remains undaunted in
their steep hill climbing. MARGIE says,
"There are no accidents. Besides, I only
live a couple of blocks from here. Walk me
home, I'll give you a story fit to print."

"DON asks, Why would I want a story?"

"You don't look like some poor Joe
off the street," she says and stops and
hands him back his own wallet. "So I took
a look ... saw your press card."

"Sheee!" he pushes an imaginary hat
back and looks at his wallet. He laughs,
takes his wallet back from her loose two
fingered grip and allows her to take his
arm again. She precedes to lead him to her
place. He secretly looks for the note from
Frenchie Joe while they walk and she talks,

relieved as he finds it in another pocket.

CHAPTER 4

From a velvet dark black-out the lights go on to reveal MARGIE's Art Deco apartment, mostly black enamel and polished brown wood.

She begins to undress and pulls down a Murphy bed all in one animated invitation onto the merry-go-round.

DAY doesn't wait to be invited, be begins to undress, only he stops to serve himself from a whisky bottle set with a pair of cut crystal glasses near her phone on the other side of the room from the bed.

Naked except for pancake make-up, seamed stockings and high heeled shoes, MARGIE comes to him, takes his glass, and after one hard swallow from it, covers his whole mouth with one kiss.

"Life seems short. Nights are too long. Nobody likes to be alone." MARGIE says.

They go down onto the bed. Lights out and from somewhere there are music sounds that mingles with rustling sheets.

DON whispers, "Not during a war."

MARGIE replies, "I don't guess so."

Intimate sounds dissolve into morning noises.

The setting sun creeps up the side of a California St. Nob Hill building into a San Francisco office. Afternoon and San Francisco is alive. The city folds up in lazy fear at night, but in daylight, by the time people are fixed into routine life they find their security in unrealized freedom.

With the sunshine on his back, SOL is on the phone at his desk in a very plush office. His is a desk covered with several papers. His executive success displayed on a leather blotter, a set.

SOL has a command in business as with his gaming. "I'm the one paying for all those bombs, guns, shells, ships, tanks, helmets the whole she-bang." He spits into the phone.

"We paid before delivery for enough 50 mm howitzer shells to stock every battleship and cruiser the Navy has ... out of Port Chicago." He catches his breath, "West coast money prejudiced, back East, now? We're not hicks!

"What good is any one's money if we loose the war, Bernard?" He leans more intimately into the phone. "I've got control of all the units from the community in my office, and I'm no looser when it comes to making good on the West Coast bank paper."

He becomes more bold. "I'm it for San Francisco. Bernard, don't count me out."

He listens to the east coast response, and argues his position. "We have the capital to go on all year and it's only February.

Now, that's a fact. From my mouth to your ear."

From the east coast, something makes him laugh. "O.k., o.k. I'll stay "shut-up" on this Manhattan bomb project I told you about, and you can key me in, as if I don't tell you first." Something said

pauses him, "... a Megaton. You go that
large for us, Hell, we'll bomb Tokyo again
for 6 months this time. We have 'groups'
here that can stand up for that kind of
profit."

Again, with pleasure he pauses,
"Good. I'm glad You can see

finance doesn't stop at the Eastern
seaboard."

He hangs up and immediately an
intercom buzzer beckons.

His SECRETARY chimes in on the
intercom. "Mr. Davidal, you

have another call. It's Mr. Chen on
line two. Greenglass from Virginia is on
line three."

"Thank you Rose. Please have the
transcript of my meeting with the Pope
about Boys Town on my desk by the end of
the day. Start with: Sol Davidal, the only
Jewish man to meet with the Holy Pope of
the Vatican in Italy, one on one. Thank
you Rose, and tell Greenglass I'll call
back later."

He picks up after another "thank you,
Rose."

SOL picks at the button on his phone.
"Hello?" He recognizes the voice. "Yeah,
Chen." He listens, "Yeah, yeah. My cash
is all tied up, but I'll pay off. I always
have, haven't I?" He continues all in one
breath, then after a pause growls back,
"You loose a bookkeeper, lately? Give you
any ideas?"

Inside Chen's office, it presents
very Chinese with a second floor window
open to the noisy afternoon streets of

Chinatown.

CHEN sits at his big Ming styled, curled end heavy burl wood desk with a CHINESE MUSCLE type looking on from a chair situated in front of it.

CHEN has a direct, soft piercing tone in his voice. "No threat. You know Chinese, they don't listen to the stock replies from businessmen. No matter one might be in the Bay. You can't tell them about money being 'all tied up.' Sell something."

On the other side of the world, though just up the street SOL replies, "You're tellin' me I'm a loser? Well, you son-of-a-bitch, I can put a round American through a square Chinese ... Peg Me!"

Not one to back down, CHEN says, "I'm not telling you that puzzle didn't work out in your favor. Right now you have to pay for that card. No bookkeeper shenanigans. Whomever goes 'banko,' wins or loses the bank. When the money's counted, then, there is a winner and a loser. Could be it's all nines. Could be sixes and sevens. You're not a loser, Mr. Davidal, but in order to continue, and you control the bank ... It is the best 'deal' I can offer ... one card, pay it, or lose the bank."

Having been clued in on the outcome, a position that makes SOL's 'used to that' makes him comfortable. "Alright, all right. You tell 'em I'll put up my part tonight. Or, tell 'em they're going to stop bullets ... for the war effort, that's all there is -- I got Jewels. Just like

Deuitch. Try that on the new bookkeeper."
CHEN continues to soften confidence.
"Jewels and precious stones are always
negotiable with the Chinese, Mr. Davidal.
They have channels. Into every family,
there's channels."

Ever so slowly CHEN hands up the
phone and looks over the shelves that
surround him in his office. Small bottles
and ancient opium pipes all with detailed,
multicolored yellows, reds, blues, greens
from another world that lend comfort to his
statement about 'channels' and families
that have not merely immigrated but
migrated from China. China, only a
sailboat voyage away.

While up the hill in DAVIDAL's, his
entire office is a tribute to a potentially
great, and powerful man. Office walled in
on book shelves where he shows his
trophies, mostly with Jewish symbols, a
gold Hanukkah Menorah, a small bottle of
oil for the seasonal flame without candles,
several dreidels in various sizes and
duo-tones mostly blue and white, a
statuette with the Star of David, an
unusual picture of DAVIDAL with the Pope.
SOL DAVIDAL was the only Jewish man to meet
with the Pope in Rome shows him next to the
holy man in his fish hat. An enlarged
newspaper story, with the dream come true
explained on a framed newspaper front page.

Seated behind a big burlwood desk,
SOL'S mouth slams shut having heard what he
needs to know from CHEN that satisfied his
wonder and completed his speculation in
thought.

At an overly large desk, outside DAVIDAL's private office, sits ROSE a young pretty curly hair blond secretary, who is on the phone, chewing gum inside DAVIDAL's front office. This afternoon, she has the phone to her ear listening to a man speak in soft personal tones. Life for her is maintained on the telephone outside of this powerful office at the Fairmont Hotel atop the mighty Nob Hill.

"And then ... Yeah?" She responds. And then, "Yeah? Yeah, Oh yeah?"

The other phone line lights up and rings so she has to pick up. "I'll be right back, Jack." She pushes some buttons, "War Incorporated, West Coast, may I help you?"

When the day is over, ROSE, Davidal's secretary closes the office late. He has gone, and the office at the top of the hill, Nob Hill holds a particular strata of awe that she accepts and basks in slow ritual of leaving the room. She slowly wraps herself in a mink coat. Difficult for her to have acquired, but worth it to aid in other of her personally owned dignity, self assigned by her position in such surroundings.

While entering his own home, Davidal carefully places his unborn lamb coat in a closet and goes directly to his private home office. Even though the night has closed the City, there are some things left undone.

He enters the office from the outside hallway, takes the phone from the BUTLER who takes his hat, and scarf while he's talking.

SOL immediately starts talking without salutation. "Yeah, yeah, the money'll be in the bank tonight Greenglass."

SOL stands up with the phone and narcissistically faces outside the office, through the open door, out into a hall mirror at his own image.

He likes doing business at home. An extension of his power, a city dwelling of imperial magnitude. So, while talking, looking at ideals far far away that remain under his control, he slowly removes his shoes with his toes. Right shoe, left toe, left shoe with stocking feet, and he shuffles softly back into his more modest office with comfortable chairs and soft lit lamps.

SOL continues the conversation after a self admiring pause, "I told Barouche. Fifteen thousand's nothing. I'm tellin' you. I got that on one card out here in The City." He listens, "Okay, I'll letter the bank on GNR from me, then for this -- what do you call it? Pitt machines ..."

He makes notes on a pad at the desk while taking more instructions. "... the Manhattan project, the plans for an atomic bomb. We're in for sure, so fifteen thousand to you in a draft for Rosenberg by tonight. I heard. Send it to the dentist. Shut up already!

"No? Okay." He continues talking, still writing, "They'll get it tomorrow. You and I have a deal, closed. Final!

Tell
          Rosenberg you got fifteen thousand
from private finance and get the plans into
the doctor's office for transfer from New
York. I'll see that the Russian account
will back it if I have to use our own money
and leave Armand Hammer out." He slams down
the phone. To see himself in the hallway
mirror he merely looks up to enjoy his own
severe, self satisfying, determined
independence.
          Inside his lush San Francisco Home,
in the dining room this night is no
different from other nights.
          Seated at a large formal dining
table, SOL and his WIFE face a serving each
of food. That is to say, the food sits in
front of them, they face each other. SOL
is the first to speak.
          "Got a line, and finalized a bid on a
big big bomb deal."
          The TURKISH SERVANT enters, wearing a
fez, carrying a covered silver tray, which
reveals another helping of potatoes for the
plump MRS. DAVIDAL, who takes the potatoes
onto her plate. Their formality in dress is
almost a costume, a revelry in respect to
the era of that time when San Francisco was
born out of the mudded streets from a
burgeoning frontier progressed by Eastern
Europeans who loved bringing a luxury they
only learned about was absent, so for them
it was a notch above the mudded streets. A
notch relished in practice of the formal
rituals, like dining at home, together.
          MRS DAVIDAL says without effect,
"That's nice dear. Don't we have the same

pair of seats this season at the Opera?"

SOL continues to eat.

"Something I should I look into?" He stops eating, sympathetically. Then, curious for a split-second. "Where's Marisa, tonight?"

Unfettered, MRS. DAVIDAL answers him. "Paris, dear. She's getting ready to go to Paris."

SOL expresses concern, "It's the middle of a war there, for God's sake."

There are some refined Chinese restaurants in The City, where the dining room hosts a very stark decor for the night time patrons. There, the kitchen is out of sight and out of ear shot. Here the company is discreet, quiet and intimate. All Chinese. Not the chop suey joints most tourists, and people from the Peninsula rarely think of this elegance when thinking of Chinese restaurants.

The formality through-out is intimate, private, forsake of the large room and the remarkably few tables and softly lit ambiance, with favored service of three servers for each table as CHEN entertains the only one Caucasian beauty there surrounded by few Chinese families, MARISA DAVIDAL.

Formal and straight backed, CHEN, a well known local business man sits next to MARISA not across, in anticipation of the serving that confronts them face on. He loves her, he shows concern, says, "Paris may well be exciting, but there is still a war going on over there."

MARISA stands out not only as a

Caucasian, but her high cheekbones, long
flowing softly curled dark hair. Her large
blue eyes and delicate hands, long arms,
boldly revealed to the near completely
exposed slight breasts. The epitome of a
high fashion

They are served by a CHINESE GIRL
dressed in the national costume. MARISA
patiently waits until the service is
completed. With an almost instinctual deft
ability with long dull ended chopsticks,
she tastes one of the delicacies off a
serving plate. Her symphony of movement
seems to lead the classical music in the
room.

"I know. But, we have ... I have
connections that will keep me well above
the street. Your concern is touching."

They share smiles of mutual
appreciation.

CHEN serves them from dishes of small
portions, rare delicacies served in
moderation, and he asks with affectionate
modesty, "Then it is true, you and I share
the desire for a long life."

Without a word, she expresses
agreement.

"Together," she says. He looks at
her quickly. "Desire for a long life."

Outside, the city air is crisp.
Traveling through the City on foot DAY
saunters as only one from The City on the
steep hill can manage comfortably, and
finally onto the Cable Car A sparsely
populated car, as this transportation is
rarely used in the late evening.

With daring abandon, DON DAY jumps

off the cable car right in front of
MARGIE's apartment just as . . . MARGIE
approaches with a bag full of groceries in
her arms.

DON surprises her, "Night shopping?"

"Golly! What a darling guy you are.
Off his trolley to save a lady."

DAY loving to match wits with a girl
who has some wit says,

"This city can make any man look like
a hero and crazy at the same time. I'll
take 'em, honey." He takes her bags,
ulterior motives hidden by the kind act.
"Say ... what-d-ya' know about Davidal?"

MARGIE gives him a sharp look.

"How'd you like me to pay you to find
out?"

She stops at the front door to find
her key in a pocketbook.

"I'm a Dick, you know."

It throws him until he realizes she
means, "Oh, yeah. Detective." "I'll take
you on, free off." She procrastinates
showing him her smile.

He's half weaving, standing there
dressed in his tux, as always. She lets
him in behind herself.

MARGIE continues, "I'll tell you, ...
if Don Won doesn't get a case soon, I won't
have a job with this 'dick.'"

The name is pronounced like the
Spanish 'Don Juan.'

Within the warm hallway, in Margie's
apartment the couple continues to talk, or
she does.

The couple in the hallway, headed for
her apartment door have an air of

complicity. Complicated by his now wanting
something more of her. Complicate because
of the acts they shared in this place.

DON has the tipped air of surprise of
learning more about his intimate
relationship, and he explores, "I thought
you worked
alone. What's this Don Won do for
you?"

The door closes behind them, but her
snicker is not muffled ... inside the
hallway, nor by his coarse laughter, she
exposes him with her brand of humor.
"You think my intimacies are
exclusive?"

He tries to hide any jealousy.
MARGIE's voice lingers in the dim
hallway. She tries to lead him on with the
savory moment of curiosity and a very slow
twist of her key in the lock.
"Not the Spanish lover, Don Juan.
Sweet guy though. He calls me his number
one daughter." She opens the door.
"He's a Chinese, a detective. Job's
are hard to find, for a girl who can't
type."

DAY's voice illuminates the hallway,
as he gives into complicity. "Well,
everybody's got a hustle." There survives
life outside, in San Francisco within the
Market Street area at night. Living
provided anyone willing to work, as in The
City these days, manpower without the bias
of gender is in demand.

From the Market Street movie
theaters, through the Pacific Heights and
Lake Street neighborhoods again, with signs

of a war going on few young men on the
streets. There continues outside activity
in the city . . . those Barbary Coast
street lamps converted to electricity
turned so low, they're almost off. People
driving, walking and playing in the night,
at the movies, in and out of the
restaurants that dot the boulevards and
streets.

Inside her apartment, DAY continues,
"Say, what-d-ya hear about Manhattan comin'
into San Francisco? One of my Real Estate
finance pals' at the club talks about a big
East Coast money project while he wets my
whistle. Sociable, but too many riddles."

Outside ... people all types getting
into limos, and shared taxis, driving
sedans. Even from their exclusive
neighborhoods, on the sidewalk two
NEIGHBORS share, and exchange gas ration
books on the street before going places
like Chinatown. "It's evening. It's The
City, for goodness sake." Somebody says
anonymously.

Privacy and solitude purveys inside
Sol's massive town house at night, and SOL
is the phone.

"Tell John, John Law; tell him it's
funny that I have an offer to invest in an
atomic bomb by a civilian machinist on the
New Mexico ordinance development project
and to wire money to a Mr. Rosenberg in
New York City. Doesn't the government pay
t=for this kind of thing? And, if Law, if
you at the FBI in San Francisco office
can't tip in with this, I'm a monkey's
uncle. Tell Hoover that's from me.

PERSONALLY! I'm Sol Davidal."

Inside and continuing through his own home, darkened by blackout curtains, SOL, in what appears to be his daughter Marisa's room, goes through a few bureau drawers. Shortly, he comes up with a large teardrop sapphire necklace encrusted with diamonds.

Its the same necklace she wore in the exclusive Chinese restaurant
earlier in the evening.

SOL whispers to no one but himself. "One card."

In the enormous hallway he confronts a young woman, sensuous in her slip style dress. Coming into the light from undressing after her dinner-date his daughter, MARISA appears. Self conscious, and without question, with inward privacy of her own she goes into the room he just came from. They both look back at each other in passing, smiling, but without inquisition or comment in shared familial glances.

Then, MARISA turns back. "Pop," she says.

He turns to look at her for a paternal moment before she runs to him and hugs him tight.

"I'll be in Paris, tomorrow."

"You kids ... Danger's nothing, to you. A war doesn't make any difference, does it?"

"Nothing to worry about."

"No. You're Jewish and Paris is full of Nazis." He turns on his way, "And I'm not to worry?"

CHAPTER 5

Morality seems continually abandoned during any war. This one is now an open ethnic struggle in Europe. But, for the free world Europeans with open banks, open passage, willing to help those of their same ethnic background, the adventure is of some second nature and danger is mostly unforeseen at this level, education, financial strata. For, at the same time inside the Gambling Parlor, more than currently meets the eye in this City by the Bay, ongoing plays expand the Chinese Opera, act after entr'acte.

At the baccarat table, CURTIS is raised by SOL -- with a sapphire necklace thrown onto the table.

There's a pause in the game for an appraisal. SOL gets up to stretch his legs, he's handed a drink and he drifts into the club.

From the front door, CHEN enters as the fog seems to follow him from outside and the night air of The City. He stops at the coat check room removing his top coat, and is met by his new bookkeeper who says something in Chinese that seems to smack him on the face. It sobers him immediately.

PENNY and DAY pick up with MARGIE at an empty Gai Pai table. Behind, MARGIE has her eye on -

DAVIDAL, who now has DAVID and PETER by their collars backed into a dark corner.

The dark hair eastern prep school boy DAVID SILBERSTEIN in snappy dark suit and shiny shoes is stiff backed by SOL and his approach. PETER's face falls into a sober look as a blond German, who by SOL's hard look has PETER's face flushed with some kind of embarrassment, a guilty sensation that seems to be lurking inside him as himself presenting the image of an enemy from that land what declared war on the whole world he knows nothing about.

Both native born Americans with guilt from two sides of Europe bred into their bones and hidden until some kind of social shock tears it out like weeds from some private garden. SOL knows the garden of this social sphere and knows how to take hold of the stem of their doubts, take hold of them by their collars with his mighty hands.

Tall dark and handsome DAVID SILBERSTEIN of New York City came to San Francisco, by way of Massachusetts' Andover High School glad to have found Roos Bros. in the west to keep him in a western interpretation of an English version of prep school wardrobe. With him, he brought a style of making money like his family in a conglomerate that falls copacetic with the Jewish boys' in San Francisco and their state of mind as their syndicate investment program. The Conglomerate thing that he brought with him through New York on his way to the western capitol of San Francisco from back east, where he stopped in Ithaca at the additional Colt factory to take up the overload from U.S. Armed Forces orders; his family thing included the colt firearm. He cut a contract himself with Colt, New

York for arms to the U.S. Army. It was part of a company in his family holdings that was bought out by the Witney's of Connecticut only a generation and one half ago.

Then in The City, he bought a small three story frontier era office building with his family money. Ensconced in the West, DAVID found PETER, one of his tenants who got him into the Jewish syndicate run by DAVIDAL.

A western family from Big Sky Country, Montana, while blond with the bluest eyes and a German name, PETER TEUTON is a Souix nation Cherokee like many of the German-Americans claim to be during this awful war. None the less, a member of the tribe, with a family name misspelled by the Indians who captured his family too long ago for written history, and not educated enough to have spelled the name for the mountain range ultimately named by the French correctly. He is in fact a blue eyed blond American Indian, and he too traveled after graduation from Teton High School, a public education avoiding private schools and the Indian school by his parents insistence for him to be raised as normal, he went east to find the origins of the Colt 45 bullet. That interest took him through Pennsylvania into New Jersey where at the cartridge factory in Patterson, New Jersey, and now a Wyoming University graduate, football hero, he cut a deal and signed a contract with Colt ammunition makers to broker 45 millimeter cartridge bullets for hand guns to the U.S. Armed

Services out of Port Chicago, Oakland with his offices in DAVID SILBERSTEIN's building in San Francisco. It was there they met while he was looking for an office, blessed their coincidence, and in short order the two of them became good friends. PETER would ensure delivery of bullets to our U.S. munitions depot and make a few percentage points in the dealings as a private arms sales, government broker.

Like magnets, these two boys attracted major East Coast arms dealing syndicates to The City and into the office of west coast syndicate heavy weight DAVIDAL, who has made some real money out of that unfortunate timely game for his true passion, Real Estate. And the building of The City has always gone on with outside money that just has to stay inside, as no one can take away the dirt, moreover their money stays once they put a building on their dirt.

Now, the way to go is up, but founding fathers of The City want no part in another earthquake clean up, so they refuse permits to take the buildings in San Francisco any higher than seven stories. At least they claim in the background that is a good thing, for while holding The City to some unspoken international standard reputation that gives them one more story than Paris' limitations. Meanwhile, it keeps The City apart from the concrete jungle Manhattan has become, and the prayer is for no Manhattanization of San Francisco.

San Francisco is better than Paris.

Only at this time with the Nazis goose stepping down the Champs-Elysees, while Market Street in San Francisco is crumbling under war time poverty the only doubt is removed by patriotism for free world democracy.

Behind all of them, looking over his shoulder as he crosses the room into his office deep behind the parlor, CHEN looks to find SOL and drills him, unseen, in the back with his sharp oriental eyes.

Dangled in his hand is the sapphire necklace. His thoughts on MARISA and her clandestine destination to help her ethnic counterparts in Paris get out of the trap of prejudices against Jewish citizens on dictatorial pretexts that are taking their lives. This thought flirts with the principles that are taking the Jewish families to the ends of earth's rewards, and here where earth's rewards are being taken from the same families. The Chinese can relate to that, can relate right . . . right here in San Francisco.

In this foreground of one dark place, SOL tells the young men of his syndicate with a severe grip on their very cloth, "I cannot let anyone know where the latest fifteen grand went, or for what! Understand? It cannot be known we independently supported GNR engineering in Virginia and an atomic bomb. Say nothing connected to Manhattan. Take that to the grave. When Rosenbergs sell high, we make out. Take my word, that we bought in low. Got it?"

"Sure, low down and dirty." PETER

smirks.

"Shit! So serious. Okay, Sol."
DAVID straightens his black tie. A
frivolous gadfly confronted with serious
accusation without having done anything,
yet.

"That's what you need to know. Get
it!"

Experienced distance onlookers, DAY
and PENNY, remarkably pale by the forceful
display, immediately go to the back, to the
lavatories. They have to discuss what they
saw, because neither heard anything very
clear, and neither knows that standing in
the open is the place to explore.

When DAVIDAL leaves DAVID, MARGIE
approaches him, but SOL pulls her aside.

SOL's coarse whisper ripples against
her earlobe. "You get too close, my little
Margie, you'll end up another skid on my
slide going down from so much pleasure you
won't know from love or money."

Stiffened by SOL's broad, rippling
grin, as soon as he leaves her, MARGIE
greets her friends. DAY, who reenters the
club from the back, and apart from him
PENNY, who also returned from the dark back
of the club, sees both stammering without a
doubt, frightened, emotionally on edge.

"What's gone on, here?" PENNY fluffs
her hair.

"We just see a 'fast hustle?'" DAY
asks while following SOL

with his eyes back into the room.

MARGIE replies to the both of them,
more than a little bit ruffled herself, "I
guess that's war, huh?"

PENNY, now tries to become an ally, "I guess you don't know what's goin' on."

Turning back quickly, hiding any fear DAY intervenes to protect his story, "Now, now. You gotta push the right buttons ladies. Let's all get along."

Successfully bringing himself down to a cool demeanor, DAY straightens his tie and rubs the two young ladies on the back.

It works, it calms them and they redirect their attention back to the action.

PENNY slowly drifts into the crowd. Approaching like hawks, PETER and DAVID cast a haunting glance back to MARGIE encased in DAY's one-arm hug, the other hand on a high-ball.

Locking her eyes onto DAY's face, MARGIE tries to get inside DAY's mind to push thoughts of PENNY aside. "She doesn't have to know anything. Those two gadabouts put money up for Davidal. They wonder about him here to cover his play with a sapphire necklace, No money? He called Deuitch's bet with a necklace? Go figure."

Back in control from the fear of an insider in an illegal den, DAY becomes curious with wonder. "A necklace? With his 'g's, it's tied-up war-money. This debauchery ... . With Davidal as reckless as he is, it might very well be the whole war debt on that table."

"The way they're playing that game you might think so." MARGIE agrees.

He ponders. She powders her face from a gold compact.

She warms up, and remarks for his

attention, "Hey, you big lug." To adjust
her garters, she pulls back her dress,
stretches out her gorgeous legs upon a
chair.

"Look at these ... worth Penny's?
You think I'm worth the time?" MARGIE
wants to get his undivided attention.

DAY is suddenly and whole heartedly
attentive. "Honey, you just gotta do for
others, then they do just right for you."

She continues to straighten her
stockings.

DAY says, "I can't see you're a waste
in my time when I look at ya'."

MARGIE responds reeling him in closer
with the ditz act, "I didn't know you if
had true feelings."

The group of younger GADFLIES and
slinky GADABOUTS gathers.

"Here comes Penny." Jealous, MARGIE
continues, "Don't you think you've had
enough of her, Day?"

"Penny's workin' Davidal ... time
enough for all of us." DAY continues
without letting too much be known.

Sensuously intimate, PENNY appears at
DAY's side raising MARGIE's grief.

PENNY leans secretly to DAY,
"Something isn't clear about the munitions
deal. Tons of millions or something called
megatons. The money seems so dinky. The
community's about investing in an
engineering company for only fifteen
thousand dollars each, from

David and Peter and that doesn't make
sense."

DAY seems surprised. "You mean, for

all his pain?" He scrutinizes the air,
"Just fifteen thousand?"

PENNY adds, "And all their stump.
Yeah. They're never in so small. That's
about all I got from Frenchie Joe for his
necklace.

And he, she motions to DAVIDAL, "Just
played it. My paste."

DAY's stymied. The word, 'paste'
rings in his head.

PENNY shrugs her pretty shoulders
against dangling, diamond earrings and
moves off into the parlor as the rest of
the younger set crowd around the aloof DAY
and jealously clinging MARGIE, and talk
about good places to go in the 'City'
rebounds around them.

Behind the action, DORIS bangs onto
DAVID and grabs him in the crotch area.

Always in a dark dress, DORIS is one
of those young ladies who always wears the
right amount of makeup. She always has a
dark loose fitting dress and champagne
slippers with custom heels just a little
higher than everybody else. So, with extra
pressure on the straps that always break,
and a larger than average bust line that
always breaks the straps on her gown, DORIS
attracts attention during any given evening
for the entire night and with that kind of
danger when the straps break one gentleman
or another is always the hero. Mostly, it
has been DAVID and he likes her ways.

He hugs her close to him and runs his
hand up her thigh, lifting the skirt of her
dress high enough to show her garters. It
seems to be his girl and his to show anyone

with eyes on the prize.

DORIS, one of the society girls who love danger says,

"Let's go down in the basement and I'll make a pipe."

DAVID, a man always into that danger says, "You sound like a french girl I knew in Paris."

DORIS continues beyond the pale, "I need the Chinaman in our basement to help me keep you attached."

She pulls him away from the group.

At the same time, and from the back of the room goes PENNY, who manipulates herself up to a BIG IRISH MAFIOSO, JOHNNIE, and tempestuously sticks her tongue inside his ear.

With that flirtation in his line of sight, SOL gets mad and

claims be can't concentrate on the game.

JOHNNIE MALLY stands out in The Sophisticated City, not as a Midwest gangster, but with his checkered tweed jacket and solid green tie, he looks the part of a big shot hiding his money with

bad taste. Except for the two 'bodies' nearby, his heavyweights deep in the shadows behind that follow his every move, no line on his criminal past is evident. His confidence bordering on arrogance will only be upheld by winning at the table. His bodyguards make sure few men can get close, and some of the GADFLY types are pushed aside as they angle to get close to the table to see better, or even to make a bet. As with PENNY, young ladies are a different matter.

JOHNNY, who instantly feels he has the upper hand, hand on DAVIDAL's girl says, "Go on, big man, play your bank. You gotta good thing goin'."

With naive indifference, PENNY buts in, "What's the deal here, Detroit movin' in?"

For a moment, all stops. While JOHNNIE got DAVIDAL pegged, PENNY nailed JOHNNIE as a Detriot heavy and the game freezes. But, just for a pregnant moment.

JOHNNIE tries to make light of his move into the city interrupts the ruffled Sol, "There Davidal! I heard about a secret project ... one about enough power to build up bigger than Manhattan. Or is it a blowup?"

SOL suddenly looking guilty wakes up to danger, "So, what's secret? They can't be Talkin' about 'The Manhattan Project' all over your town? Skyscrapers. Think we can't get San Francisco built up? Big growth, tall buildings. You got East Coast connections, Johnnie? Tall buildings, you know something I don't? Detroit got some money made there, maybe?"

"Pitt engineering, Sol, machines, labor.. With ships at sea ... planes... All material during a war goes through US intelligence." JOHNNY fluffs his cards. "What's private?

"That's all I heard about your sky high contracts. Here, it's the Jewish community and I'm sure you got no trouble with that and the war, Davidal. The government's got your every deal on paper or wire, because it's American, <u>all</u> dealin' here, Sol.

It's gotta be American.

"Most of you Jewish guys buy low and sell high. Simple business. Don't matter when ... when patriotism might get in the way."

"Here we got earthquakes to deal with. Detroit construction handle that?" SOL looks at him from underneath his eyebrows with the doubt of the world sages. "Bing-Bang, and all fall down. Can you handle that, Johnnie? I got a flag pole up there as high as any around."

Behind him. Four of JOHNNY's BODYGUARDS crowd in two by two. "And, no one to blame for any investments." DAVIDAL comments while looking at his cards. Maybe the presence of the heavies makes DAVIDAL hunch over and look at his cards with more intensity. Maybe he wants the gamble to build the bank.

DAVIDAL trying to avoid tough action adds, "We got no problem. Friends of some family back east need dough and sell a set of plans."

JOHNNY keeps on playing SOL against his group, right there in the room. "That's Rosenberg's, if I heard around right?" He keeps probing, "Same family as yours? The money stays in the synagogue for danger?"

"Earthquakes." SOL, visibly ruffled. "Somethin' giving up?

It's ours, already!" SOL makes for a diversion, as one seemingly trying to protect his unique investment in a

construction plan. "A small investment, big
build. Money enough to save starving
Russia they tell me. Pull out my heart,
Mally. Here, we wanna build up, but . . .
well, if you know. I already got enough
money for it. It's permits, that's where
it's tough." He looks up and into MALLY's
eyes. "Permission."

He throws chips into the center of
the table, gets a card. "Legal."

DAVIDAL, suddenly a winner. "Banko!
Pay the bank. Nine."

DAY, snoops around with MARGIE, both
ply the younger set for facts regarding all
mega-bucks deals coming down. Meanwhile
SOL rakes in the cash.

"You wanna join a family, the Chinese
need cash for China against Japan."

"I got a family. I'm Irish."

Easy to get the information,
everybody's feelings are on their sleeve
with the in-house big daddy, DAVIDAL having
beaten the pants off the outsider.

"You're fifty 'g's lighter, Irish."
He laughs a soft dominate huff like laugh.

Rumors flow. From PENNY at the small
Baccarat table, prying makes people more
frantic, eager to know about the war's end.

Apparently, DAVIDAL's rant got
through the crowd, even for those who could
no more hear or even have seen what went
down.

With the two GADFLYS on his elbow,
DAY moves and the ladies too, away from the
big table.

Satisfied he moved out of earshot,
DAY surreptitiously queries over PENNY's

shoulder, into her ear, "Is it a delivery or what?" PENNY, discreet in a tight crowd, edgy, nervous, "Sounds like just another development deal to me."

DAVID, too close not to hear, overtly calming 'lost cause' over his shoulder to toss off rumors, and stop the gossip floating around the room, he interjects to DAY with the girls, "It could be our investment to end the God Damn war. Build skyscrapers in San Francisco. Invest in a machine company in Virginia, Sol found out about it when he heard from Barouche about some a newfangled plan. Some invention to fail safe against earthquakes. A rivet, or a washer to fit bushings against the struts. Big-bang, to him is more than just money. It's Skyscrapers to me. I told you all that Don, yesterday at lunch. Manhattanization project."

DAY is not fooled. "Make sure, David." He says to Margie, "I know all about the Pitt book. U.S. Navy property intelligence log with all, guns, ordinance ... identification of enemy ships. We had it on board at Midway. No girlie pictures. It's armaments," and he turns to DAVID, "you said so, at lunch."

DAVID tosses it off with a nervous laugh, "Aw, let's get outta here. Day found a girl. Go to Izzy's. The boys here are crazy."

CHAPTER 6

Remnants of the Barbary Coast still remain in the art and architecture, the road and alley plan, and are exploited in the city by the bay as commercial hang outs. Remnants of prohibition dot the landscape, too. Outside this one, there is a sign shaped like a woman's leg, dancing the can-can, but just her leg. Sensuality accented with lights.

Inside BOOT'S BOOTY is a large open bar, a long hallway by the docks. The place is a wooden structure, warehouse type with a long bar down the center and filled with mostly down beat, unpolished men, and women of a loose virtue, all drinking beer in mugs heavy with foam. San Francisco Steam Beer floats across the hallway hand to hand amongst plenty of well worked hands off ships.

The smoke is thick enough to need a fog horn to get up to the bar. Crowd so dense the whereabouts of the bar is almost lost, but at the end of the room on a stage is a five piece string band with music mellowing behind a single clarinet. Smoky dark with bright lights on the stage dim as
. . .

. . . DAY and MARGIE, who enter just when the star, singer -- MAGGIE THE BOOT comes out.

MAGGIE is a heavy woman who wears 19th Century boots with purple stockings held up by green garters from a black corset and little else to cover her except for her flaming red hair, tasseled down to her mid waist. Up to her calves, loosely laced shine the pointy toed patent leather boots adorn her legs.

Both DAY and MARGIE's attention zooms in on a sapphire necklace, that sparkles in the now raising spotlights. The sapphire necklace is around MAGGIE's thigh.

DON DAY and MARGIE are stopped, maybe it's the crowd.

DON, stunned, says, "There's the jewel."

MARGIE is taken back, "Same necklace," and thinks DON is attracted to THE BOOT.

Then MARGIE tunes in and says, "That's the same necklace Davidal played just a few hours ago!"

When Day responds, the din drowns out his comment. "Said it was paste." He stiffens, "Someone got the original."

"That it?" THE WAITRESS, with a round tray and bouncing, mostly exposed breasts doesn't distract their attention "Two beers?" - both focused on MAGGIE and the sparkles off the sapphire necklace, while just above the thing around her thigh, a nearly exposed feminine middle holds everybody's attention as the lights highlight her every other move on an elevated stage that showcases the singer from underneath her dress, but she's not wearing a dress and what's there barely covers this remarkably attest able, true red head.

MAGGIE sings: "IIIII ain't got no boaww-dy" interrupted by hoots and hollers as she tantalizes the men with a jerk on her corset and a toss of her hair to completely expose one of her boobs that popped out from her movement.

Around he other thigh is another, yellow diamond showcased, diamond necklace -- the one CURTIS DEUITCH stole from his daughter DONNA and threw into the pot at Chen's; and when MAGGIE turns , seen - a jewel no one can dispute covers by attraction the family casing she exposes with every movement of her body.

DON suppresses his gaping. "Wow! She's really got the booty ..." The small spot lights open slowly to illuminate her on the otherwise dark stage. Strapped to her other inside thigh is a - Colt 45 automatic --fine argument for self protection with all that booty.

MARGIE stands agape, too. "And, the right to protect it."

"From the right company, too. That's a Colt!"

Singing all the while, she turns and does a strange strip tease, she pulls her panties up tight and jerks them inside her buttock cheeks. As she tucks and folds her clothes while drifting from one song to another, she reveals more and more of her otherwise private bounteous body.

By now, DAY has tossed five straight whiskeys and a STEVEDORE turns to MARGIE and DAY to make the comment known.

STEVEDORE comments though drunken breath that turns DAY's head. He says, "Booty's the word. She's taken it from every Waggin'

Dick comin' and goin' from this

town."

     The whole crowd gives a giant hoot as MAGGIE THE BOOT goes into a croon-duet with the clarinet and a violin that both try to crack middle 'c' in between her sighs.

     DAY belts another whiskey.

     The TOOTHLESS STEVEDORE adds, "Wait'll you see next week. She'll be wearin' an emerald bigger than your thumb."

     He starts to laugh, and the other STEVEDORE jams him in the Ribs "Wonder where she'll hang that?"

     From nowhere in the crown, a BIG BRUTE calls through the smoky din, "Hey! Keep your mouth shut." The din is so loud, what he says stays in secret.

     The TOOTHLESS STEVEDORE responds defiantly, "Yeah?! They'll have us break it up, otherwise, and sell the stones like he does in Detroit."

     "Shut up!"

     There's a shot, muffled by the din of hoots and hollers, and the TOOTHLESS STEVEDORE drops dead right next to DAY and MARGIE.

     MARGIE grabs DAY by the collar, whirls him around like a school teacher who grapples him out of an angry school yard, while on stage MAGGIE begins a sing-a-long to keep the crown from trampling each other.

     The outside night air hits them like a water balloon. Suddenly, they're wet with sweat in contradiction to the change in air from inside the bar to The City by the bay.

     The two of them have wandered down,

down the hill to a dockside street, the
Embarcadero, a quiet dangerous looking
place in the night.

MARGIE has DAY by the collar and he's
barely able to stand from the whiskey
consumed in the warmth now outside in the
cold, he wobbles, smiling all the while.

"You have to come down here to find
out what's going to hell and back." DAY
says, "Once in awhile."

MARGIE says, off to the side, "Make's
you wonder just who are the leaders in this
world."

Drunk as he is, DAY adds to her
comment, "... it's us." And, he tries to
sober, "Kind of makes you wonder."

Looking back over her shoulder,
MARGIE fails to notice just how drunk DAY
is as he fumbles open the car door for her.

Together, happy to have evaded the
crowd way up the hill, now infused with
police arrival, inside their car they are
off through the streets with his lights low
for air raid proof driving.

Inside DAY's car in the dark of the
night, a womb like sanctuary embraces the
tired reporter.

"Chinamen usually use a knife." DAY
postulates with his girlfriend.

"Must be some Italian kingpin."
MARGIE has become intrigued. "Irish." DAY
continues, "They're sayin' this town's
open, what with the war and all the
competition over the Manhattanization of
San Francisco."

He swerves to avoid a cat in the
street.

DAY is undaunted by the spirits and his command of a notion. "More happens, no one's to know. This is a fishin' town. The Italian community is so, ... too strong here."

"No argument." MARGIE agrees.
"Just, here it's not only the Italians."

"Said Irish."

The famous China Town alley of seemingly benign activity stands as merely an architectural showcase at this time of night. For after a few swerves through town they're parked curbside at Waverly Place, finally the car rests at the curbside of the alley just yards down from the night time casino, daytime fortune cookie company.

While exhaust fumes add to the slowly building fog, inside the car DAY'S got Penny's flask to his mouth between kissing and making more steam inside the car with MARGIE.

Soon, inside the car, behind the wheel of his Buick, DAY's passed out.

Down on and off Market Street, Buicks, Lincolns, Cadillacs criss -cross with their lights dimmed by headlight shields. Society does not stop in The City, especially not for war.

CHAPTER 7

Inside the Gambling Parlor above where DAY has parked, sexy people are gathering to leave, with their alligator wallets used to fish money for ... women in revealing dresses that take folded bills on the sly to tuck into their brassieres, and top of their stockings, and underneath their garter straps ... men wearing loose clothes, ties undone and tuxedos, whose ... women's hands are hidden in men's clothing at strategic places all migrate from the plush inside to outside -- some who left the building remain still, crowded around parked cars -- where departure is part of the party that seemingly, like the Great War, will never end.

The couple that just witnessed a murder stumble past the crowd to get back inside the club. Stumble because MARGIE has to navigate for two, as DAY is polluted.

In the chaos that has begun to erupt, MARGIE and DAY turn and sneak out of the club.

With MARGIE at the wheel and DAY giving directions, they find a parking place on the street at Broadway, below Kearny Street.

On Broadway sidewalk amid the jazz clubs and bars, tourist traffic spotted with men in uniforms, now DAY steers MARGIE on foot down the steep slope of Broadway in through frosted glass, double doors and before them a long wooden bar in low light. Andres.

This is a post prohibition bar, located way off the track on Columbus where commercial traffic makes parking on the street during the day a dare. Dangerous as a place not too often frequented by anybody who knows little about The City. Not a tourist stop. Not all that dark, but a place where patrons are rarely visible to the outside world. Frosted glass, low lights to simulate gaslight and the only feature is a great selection of liquor. This is the place where men meet their girlfriends, and the wife would never find out.

So, Andre is a quiet type who holds his mouth closed, but for a few good friends; and those get the inner circle, inside scoop on any social news. To hell with politics, in Andres, and for all those reasons this is where the real serious drinkers, the newspaper crowd hang out.

Inside, DAY with MARGIE slide up to the bar with ONE COUPLE already there. Stretched in a certain familiarity with Andres as their base, bodies across their table, they are who that never looks up to see any other couple, equally ignores the newcomers, for their conversation is too clandestine: "My wife would never do those things you do." The man pleads with the bottle blond to go across the street to the flop house.

"Gotta be a place with room service," she says trying to make eye contact across the table with a wad of greenbacks between her and the man with the gold wedding band, head swirling in closed eye appeal. Their intimacy stops them from doing anything, coming, going or counting the money in a big wad of cash on the table.

No clue given as to what side of the professional line they stand.

The man with a plain gold wedding band, fondles his drink, and with his right hand paws the woman's thigh and slowly opens his eyes to meet hers. They laugh together, quiet confident laughs.

A clean woman with tight clothes, revealing only in her smoky eyes, moist with provocation and frustrated silence in a solitary plea, no one nearby at the bar to respond.

As the BARTENDER makes his way toward the two from the outside now within the dark depths of the long polished mahogany bar, DAY remarks to MARGIE.

"Here we are. The get-away for San Francisco's reporters. A remarkable situation and I don't know what to drink."

"Is drinking something important?"

"You don't understand the Irish. Here is a day for me to remember."

"So, what do you Irishmen do? Try to challenge yourself to remember at all?"

He looks at her, leaning one elbow on the bar, head melting into his hand. "You're a vision in superb delight. You're givin' me a reason to remain clear headed."

His eyes water in a stare meant to dissolve her resolve, which gives her a chance cause to smile softly.

"And," he sings, "the bombs bursting in air, gave truth through the night that our flag was still there . . .

"It was 55mm howitzer shell coming from the guns on board of the Cruiser. I was on the bridge, didn't know if I would <u>ever</u> file the story. I flashed on the streets of San Francisco, California Street, the flower print wall paper on my grandmother's apartment, the lines at the bank on the Cable Car line. All those things of MY San Francisco, and now it's just a collage that comes out again with the drink."

After he stops for the moment, forsake of a pause to allow her to feel his reunion with his own city, ANDRE appears at their corner of the bar.

At first sight, ANDRE looks like a robust American with phony style made out to have him look like a Frenchman. The cravat around his neck, lateral striped long sleeve boat neck pull over. With dark hair and a mussel bound arm, he reaches over to take MARGIE's hand and gives it a kiss. Then, in perfect French, which proves his is one of those tough fighting Frenchmen, he tells her that she graces his humble church with the fresh air of a real women. Then, cold and matter of fact he turns to DAY.

"What'll you have?"

"Pabst Blue Ribbon!" inserts MARGIE. "That's just where we were at."

"Beer bar?"

Day says, "How 'bout a Singapore Sling?"

"Alright, make it two." MARGIE resigns.

"Something to help with a new vision.

A murder right next to us."

After awhile, the two of them with
ANDRE serving yet another drink out of his
silver shaker to the couple with locked
arms, intertwined and both slumped over the
bar in a discussion, recollection of past
loves and their lives.

"It was all I could to, to get away."
Day recalls.

"The boy stood on the burning deck .
. ."

"Thinking of lost loves and thinking,
'to heck . . . '" Day blends in.

"When all but he had fled . . ."

"With all those flames,"

"The flame that lit the battle's
wreck," MARGIE cooperates with the verbal
intercourse, but not the variations.

"And all those loves . . . "

"Shone round him o'er the dead.

They finish in unison, "To hell and
gone, to heck . . . ." She cooperates with
his invention.

DAY refrains, "Upon the burning, the
boy confessed upon that day, upon that
deck."

"Discernment from your father's
instructions; don't procrastinate or flee
from your conscience, Mr. Don."

In one instant, bleary eyes lost to
the place they both sit and while MARGIE
poised with her glass to salute an
invisible falling starlit emotion . . . DAY
falls off the stool onto the floor.

"Not really a Casablanca," she says
to ANDRE, "Doesn't remember the poem."

He having approached, concerned with

the reputation of his bar, and stern at the reporter damaging that sacred trust within, ANDRE asks, "You able to pay for those Singapore Slings?"

Casually, MARGIE continues to sip, and looks down at the now emerging DON DAY, a morose, silly drunk rising up off the floor.

"Maybe not old enough."

Taking the opportunity to talk to a pretty woman, ANDRE says to MARGIE, "I took on this bar to have something in the States. Yes, I'm really, truly French. And, now I'm part of an institution, here." He stops drying the glass, stops wiping the surface of the bar, stops everything but his address to DAY and his girl. "And the main institution I am *not* is a bank."

"I'm decked." Day giggles, slips and lays there on the floor. "Look, Andre. How long have I been coming in here?"

"Here begins the proclamation," ANDRE says to MARGIE.

"And, how many of my cronies do I bring in here with me?"

"What's it gonna be, Don?" ANDRE asks, "A story or a proposition?" "He's celebrating," MARGIE justifies his stall.

"We told him when we came in, remember?"

"No such thing."

"I gots no money, Man." Arm over the stool, looking at ANDRE, DAY continues. "I am what I am, and that's what I am."

The ultimate boss, owner and bartender looks at him with arms shrugged around his chest, coat lapels exposing

wrists that cause his watch to shine in the
under the bar light. DAY quickly looks at
the watch.

"I offer you this watch."

He takes his own watch off his wrist
and holds it out to ANDRE. ANDRE seems used
to this. "You better get up. I got no
license for beds."

"I come to your church all so often
that I trust it will be here when I shall
come into redeem myself -- and the watch."

Just at that moment when he passes
ANDRE the watch, he passes out, down again
onto the floor. MARGIE with ANDRE look
down upon him; she slickly sips the last of
her Singapore Sling.

"Surely he'll be back before the
war's over."

CHAPTER 8

Charismatic PENNY at Chens, and everybody near her are concerned over a 'rumor' about power to end the War now. "Why prolong it?" Clearly, one person heard something another heard while eavesdropping, and the word spread by one or more of them. The word around the club . . . motives for money, and war profiteering all makes for the guys on the outside to feel like suckers. They want to question what brings us into a foreign war, and that we have so much money to keep it going, why not stop the flow of funding and let it dry up and end. Forgotten is the despot who started the conflict with a 'Putsch' and with such a new term in our vocabulary, a new threat. Lost to this crowd, the idea of a government dispensation of ethnic diversity, disposal of anybody less than that found acceptable under the despotic law of the land.

Threat. That feeling of fear felt by individuals and drives us all to irrational and uncontrollable action. The push of a mob in a confined space that makes for a form of combustion that ignites without fire.

Smoking cigarettes one after another, Penny, a skinny, pretty blond nervous without her boyfriend or her mentor, and the crowd seems to look to her for answers.

Many express concern about the baccarat 'bank' and the banker/players; and now the War all of a sudden stirs fears held under the skin for so many years, here

in privileged company rumors make it seem
like it could be over already. If the big
men here are truly good on their bets, why
not good on the nations' threats?

A plan, big as Manhattan.

If it could be so big, could it stop
everything?

They mingle at the curbside, high
style society in paradox to the Chinese
commercial neighborhood, and they are all
calling for facts about financial power and
influence, right there at night in high and
tempered, sometimes shrieking voices in an
alley.

Their fates in question. Some become
argumentative, concerned for their country.
Some look around and question patriotism in
The City that flairs tempers.

The few of the 'inner circle' seem
'to know' they are in the company of men
who can make a difference. The rest become
uncomfortable and vow to leave and never
come back.

DORIS, in semi-desperation, "When's
it going to end?" She hysterically turns to
the faceless crowd. "Somebody Tell me.
Somebody, ask Sol!"

Edgy, CHEN appears at the door and
quietly ushers people out of the doorway
and out of the alley.

"Night's done. Game's over.
G'night, g'night everyone," CHEN says.

Inside the Chinese Gambling Parlor
the nervous crowd that collects around the
door make up people gathering their coats
and preparing to leave the mainstay of
clientele. This time they reluctantly

collect at the coat room, anxiously pushing each other outside at the exit.

For the loyal outside, with early backlit morning as night wants to be reclaimed by the new day, those who got out of the club calm and in control all filter outside slowly and homeward. These devotees remain faithfully resigned and accept that their government is doing the best ever possible.

Nobody wants, however to leave the collective, fear driven, gambling ridden group of clustered folks, those who feel comfortable in union.

From somewhere in the crowd, a gruff attitude filtered through the crowd when CURTIS says to SOL, "You of all people ought to know what that bauble I 'wrote' was worth, Sol? Damn it, arms broker! Don't you give a rotten boom-bang?"

SOL says back to him, "Come on Jew-boy, match the bank. You can't be goin' broke."

CURTIS replies, "You control it all, don't you! You do. You know."

Not just those two know how true CURTIS' comments ring, because he controls the books though DAVIDAL controls the bank.

There is no intention to win all the money, as much as CURTIS' intention is to win more respect.

Outside in the Alley, Chinese 'Go Boys' collect and solicit --as groups -- various services from some of the 'toughs.'

The young women are mingling arm in arm with the older men. The alley seems abandoned to SOL's footsteps.

Watching SOL in fact, lurking in the smoky fog strewn night are a slowly building group of YOUNG CHINESE, - Small PETTY THIEVES, like giants in this Chinese darkness, deny each other's presence as alley cats that might be looking over clean white mice in the gutter, as the HEAVIES exit. THE YOUNG PETTY CHINESE BOYS suddenly diminished in esteem and in numbers,

look for a tip-off, look over those who have slowly dispersed.

The whole collection in Waverly Place congeals over some insatiable desire to control one another and get more money out of it. The desperate ones have left, departed with empty pockets and holes in their collective conscience. They had seen the power and felt themselves to be less than pawns.

Down the alley, DAY with MARGIE driving come onto the scene as his car rolled conveniently into a corner parking place where the street seems mystical, more fog builds up over the curb.

Even those two, who have become bonded by crime and polluted by drink have no will power to stay away from the den of inequity where the common factor is to loose individual integrity. So, rich and poor alike descend to a depth of equality. All become lost souls to simply just return home and regain individual identities. Maybe that becomes the most difficult reconciliation during a war.

Inside his car, DAY is polluted. No one notices them, though MARGIE is passionately trying to hold him together. Maybe she feels some loyalty, or maybe she thinks she got a hold of something and it has become worth while.

INSIDE THE CAR it is a tender scene of regressive care as MARGIE finally stows him behind the wheel, and 'swipes' the keys from his pocket.

While trying to forget he had been stalking his friends. DAY is after the confidences of guys that have raised his spirits for decades, been there for him during times of concern, and for the community they all call The City. DAY drinks as a social convention to relieve the burdens of his prying, and his obligation to snoop in and around his powerful friends' personal business. His career advances by following their ambition, they put their financial security in drag to pull out the residuals of the community troubles. In their dilemma, they come to a point of save or salvage the problems of society by their sometimes sordid business, and DAY is the stop plug on problems that cause or resolve those problems. His responsibility bears pressure that builds up in him over how much he dare expose to bring his friends up or tear them down, for in his personal assessment he cannot know the extent of how much they hold control over the community destiny, or what he might effect in that control if he exposes them. So, he gets blotto .

MARGIE says, as she leaves him inside the car, "You better call me in the morning. Tomorrow, ya' find some love, maybe."

There may be the type of young woman, who during a war, immediate time of life, or under pressure for personal achievement want to grab hold of a man. MARGIE is not that sort of person who needs a mate. She has her job and hitched up with DON DAY as a matter off a joke, almost. He became a game for her and it pays off for knowing as an investigator to be involved with a newspaperman.

She likes the sex, but the intimacy that comes later may be the other side of living at home away from death and destruction during a foreign war. The young woman plays the field with her boyfriend not to open doors but pave the way further into her career.

And, within all that there remains his personal, emotional life. "What's man made for?" DAY says, fighting against his alcohol daze, "It is morning. I'm not that bad off. Hey! You had something' to do for me."

At the end of his comment, he passes out in the driver's seat, ambulatory behind the steering wheel. She closes the door softly in respect for his solitude.

DON DAY is not going along the way, or anyway not after a night of blotting out the game. At this moment she sees him not going anywhere, and she certainly cannot carry him.

For MARGIE, that under any circumstances is not in the cards.

CHAPTER 9

Outside the car, in the alley, as the light begins to filter through the foggy, dark morning air. DAY awakens and wiggles around, tries to warm himself while wedged behind the wheel of the car.

Cramped, he can't make himself comfortable. Seems to do it, and awakens fully by the discomfort from the car window that is open.

Awkwardly, he begins to close the window and notices the street activity in front of him.

He continues to roll up the window and slouch deep into the seat before he passes out.

He has seen in front of him, some seventy-five feet away; THREE YOUNG CHINESE approach the wall of the building.

They throw a hook to the window above the Fortune Cookie Company and climb up the rope.

In short order, while he is dazed trying to sober, to get comfortable, to look out of the car from under his deep drunken slump a muffled blast shakes the neighborhood.

Suddenly startled DAY wakes for a split second, still boozed, leans against his car window; and he sees -

The THREE YOUNG CHINESE drop from the window, snap the rope to pull the freed hook ended rope after themselves and make a get away, taking with them a black bag.

DAY stumbles out of the car to stand, weaving and 'pisses' against the nearest wall.

In the morning, sun creeping over the edge of the Chinatown buildings outside on Waverly Place, industrious people ignore the lonely parked car at the curb and half upon the sidewalk, for them the morning begins bustling with activity.

Matted hair and cold, the unconscious DON DAY again fallen asleep behind the wheel of his car that is rediscovered by MARGIE.

The faithful girl MARGIE who comes back for him where she left in the dark of the night, the dank of the club, and the drippy Dewey alley way foggy morning. She has more than the keys to his car, as he seems to have more than the key to her heart. Neither one has made any promises or pledges. She drives him and his car away.

Inside the warmth of Margie's apartment, the morning seems more optimistic although still a dark place.

She strips him. Getting the drunk undressed is not easy. "What's your hook, Margie?" DAY, the self effacing drunk asks. "I'm just an in and out newspaper reporter. What is it I do for, you?"

"You asked me to help you." MARGIE says, frantic encouragement, suppressed. "You're on to something ..."

He grabs her in a half coordinated way, and she reverses his ploy, smothering him with kisses; as she jerks off her own clothes while he tries to keep up, sobering, offering a return of affection.

He faked it. He is sober.

"... onto my case, now, reporter."
Margie begins to reveal his intentions by
uncommon intimate physicality that plies
his sense of obligation in a display
without words.

Their slow compatible movements seem
to overlap with mutual purposes, the
sobering intimacy at the end of their
lovemaking security after surly crowds and
strong drink. Here there seems to unfold a
reveal at the end of what surely became
more than a trick.

"The last time I saw Paris," DAY
says, "was only make-believe come true. It
wasn't as good as you."

MARGIE replies, "You were never
mothered enough."

DAY says, "I've had good experiences."

Day sits up in the bed. "I keep
having these visions. Like

last night, I saw these five gremlins
climbing the wall outside the Happiness
Fortune Cookie Company. They climbed the
wall like flies. There was an earthquake.
Then they ran down the wall with a little
black bag and off into the night."

She perks up, leans into him on her
elbow and looks at him. MARGIE emphatically
in agreement, "You were down in the alley."
DAY doubts himself, "It's just another
Saturday night Hangover." MARGIE reassures
him, "You're on to something. Important, I
bet." He's up and out of bed.

DAY resumed the pace, "I've got a
mundane walk to the office." Forever the
flirt, he continues. "I wish I had your
gams ... to walk to work ... to walk for

me."

"There was a murder, a burglary, evidence of theft big enough to blow up the sky in this city." She struggles into her bra, "It was one hell of a night."

Hot with stories, a crime to chase, they both dress in a flash, DAY still with his same tux, but a fresh shirt.

"I can't fit into your shoes, or I'd help you out," MARGIE says. He catches his keys, she flipped to him. MARGIE, encouraging all the while with the make-up out of her purse, rapidly fixes her face while . . . .

"I don't think you know. I bet you've witnessed the crime of the decade. A robbery."

They both know they witnessed more than a petty crime, more than bloody murder.

They are out the door, together.

DAY says on the way out, "The crime of the decade is WW II. Here, and I'm beginning to think, the big story may be a May-December romance."

MARGIE following the wry satire, "This is San Francisco, wanna know? Find what love is. Report on that one!"

They're out, following an altogether new line.

At the Newspaper, the news room as it bustles with activity, becomes spurious to DAY's love affair.

The Copy BOY comes up to DAY, who hardly notices with MARGIE's voice in his head, "May-December ... not news, here."

Followed by the young COPY BOY, DAY

who swaggers into the news room toward his desk allows himself to hear . . . the COPY BOY.

"This report was just grafted off the police scanner."

He looks over the piece of paper.

DAY objects. "Looks like a stock robbery not the City's war syndicate. Why me?"

The COPY BOY waxes poetic, "Like Churchill said about the War ... We've done so much, but there's so much more to do."

DAY, unmoved says, "He was talking about his supply of brandy." He reads further, looks up to comment, . . .

DAY says, "This isn't <u>my</u> story. God damn it. If it's not one distraction, it's another."

. . . But the COPY BOY is gone. DAY phones out.

"Ed?" DAY wants to know more about the Chinatown affair, " . . . and more on the murder, body fished out of the Bay . . . what about that barrel of fish, eh?"

"What happens in Chinatown is not on our docket. They're tellin' me we'll never know who put the Chinaman in the drink, and any robbery there will never sell papers, either. You get on this robbery, because Lt. Faber's willing to fill us in, and with more guns on the street people want to know how clean are the streets of what it's gonna take to wash their panties later in the week, not what's goin' on in Chinatown that'll break up their day."

"Guns, you say?"

"Yea! Read the fuckin' scanner! A gun shop was robbed." The CITY ED clunks the phone closed.

Stunned for a moment, DAY sits at his desk straightening out his thoughts about guns, guns, nothing but guns, arms, ordnance, his friends, the scene. Who does he have to turn in, to turn to?

Back to the high school crowd.

"Hello?" DAY gets on the story. "Lt. Faber? Don Day, from the Chronicle, how-are-ya'? I got something here about a gun shop robbery on 3rd Avenue. What's up? Oh, and by the way ... know anything about ... Oh, wait. You first. 3rd Street, okay, shoot." While he gets filled in he writes on the story: It's of a night scene where THREE MEN break into a Gun Shop on Third Ave.

DAY thinks, 'We never have the right pictures, and the story's dead unless I pull 'em out of my mind's eye.' He writes and listens, 'This is like writing fiction.'

Like rivets, sharp sounds of Day's typewriter build the story of the Gun Shop crime scene from the muttering of the policeman on the other end of the phone.

In his mind's eye, TWO THIEVES stand immersed in shadows, curbside on alert. THREE GUYS inside crazily grab guns.

All the while, over the action pictured in his head from the phone narrative, DAY writes.

'Last night shortly after two AM, logged by the silent alarm system, there was a break-in at a Third Avenue, San

Francisco gun shop where several small arms were stolen.

'The SFPD have a list of the stolen guns, fingerprints, foot prints and other evidences that lead them to believe this may be a preamble to another small crime wave yet to hit the City.' Day continues like a taking the voice off a Dictaphone. '"I've seen this sort of thing before," speculated gun shop owner, Jack Person.'

DAY takes his copy to the CITY EDITOR who reads it. Quickly.

CITY ED looks up at DAY, "Good summary. Strong mind's-eye. Work on the lead. Go on down to the station, interview Faber and the other cops, then go out to the shop and talk to Person. Get any details, possible leads. Looks to be worth a series. A running feature on Chinese tongs." He looks into DAY's face, and comments, "The small footprints, get it? You might get your lead into Chinatown yet."

He looks up into Day's face "Glad you fell onto this, Day."

With a 'me too' smirk, DAY thinks he might get his can opener into the Chinatown scene yet. How else could he begin without a lead to pry it open. At least his notes on the Manhattan project is building up in a big Chinatown firecracker. Boom.

With an assignment on Chinese Tong activity, and a self confident smile, DAY is about going out of the office, again.

DAY mutters, "Why me? Damnit! Shee ... I don't know what I'm fallin' into."

Sorting papers, walking past DAY at

his desk, CITY ED hears him and says, "You
know all the financiers. By the way, Lt.
Faber says you might have stumbled into a
Trotskiite spy ring ... what he got out of
Washington and he's tellin' me. So, if he
says so, get with it on that munitions
deal, and Davidal... with Faber. Guns on
Third Street for now, Day."

CHAPTER 10

The bastion of secretes, inside
Chen's Club and mostly at night hide the
action through-out The City. Not too
different from its Barbary Coast days, this
city by the Bay overflows with crime and
barely enough time behind the typewriter to
sell them all a newspaper.

Concerned, CHEN approaches to talk to
MARGIE at the gambling club bar. Nobody
buys newspapers, they have the network,
now. Most everybody has a plug in, in on
the inside, a portal into the activity of
the world, for at this point it all focuses
on the war in Europe and in the Pacific.
In The City the rumor mill feeds curiosity,
the newspaper only verifies.

"I want to talk to you. It's a
difficult situation with respect to the
'safe' in my back room. It must be
confidential." MARGIE, who is not
surprised, leads him. "A robbery, Chen?"
He looks at her, surprised that she
guessed.

"This confidence must be kept in the
Chinese community. Police don't care what
Chinese comes or goes through the Bay.
Even murder doesn't call them into the
Chinese community for resolution. I need
for you to have Don Won come to me." And
CHEN leans into her ear, "And, about
Davidal's necklace, KEEP QUIET."

CHEN knows. CHEN knows something,
but MARGIE cannot pick the right keys to
tap into what it is he does know. Of all
she saw that night, of what she knows DAY

had seen; and what she hears at the bar
that will be in the next day's paper she
has no idea what CHEN knows. She knows she
gave off.

Drowning in confusion, MARGIE
searches CHEN's eyes for more knowledge, a
chance to make sense of the bleak infection
of crime witnessed in The City. Her city
is soft and a comfortable place to fit as a
woman in hard times of war so far away
where lives are claimed for some ideal that
means little here at home in the land of
the free, with beautiful men sotted, and
submerged in the dens of inequity it stays
closed for them.

MARGIE tells him, "Why don't you ask
me what I might know?" CHEN his severe look
softens, says, "When the nightingale sings
by itself the song is beautiful. When the
bird tells its father, it's truth." He
cannot tell her that the bird never told
her father. He becomes stern, "I shall
expect Don Won to come through the basement
and resolve problems without causing family
scandals. Answers, I have already too many
that just come to me, so no questions."

MARGIE, suddenly concerned, says,
"Those War Lords represent a lot of fire
power, Chen."

CHEN, emotionally touched replies,
"As a nightingale, you sing truly
beautiful, Margie." Strict again, "No
scandals."

Querulous, she stands still, left
alone amid the hub-bub, and the BARTENDER
leans over to tell her something. She has
a call from DAY, "he says, that he's stuck

at the newspaper."

MARGIE takes the phone, "Oh, uh, sweetheart, I'm glad you've called." Awkwardly because withholds her side of story out of

fear. "I just had a feeling that you might have become distracted by something big."

DAY continues, "You're intuitive senses amaze me. I am onto something. They assigned me a robbery."

She stares ahead at the wall of bottles in a forced pause, as CHEN looks back at her. This private secret and all that comes to her mind from the night that just passed gives her belligerent courage, although confused by seemingly coincidental assignments.

MARGIE volunteers, "I might have a case, too. I must see you soon. There's certain danger."

DAY, over the phone, "Can't talk there? Are you clear on Davidal?" MARGIE thinking of her case, "No."

DAY holding on to the intimacy of the phone, "I thought so.

Will you be, tonight?"

MARGIE allowing herself to become absorbed into what will develop into a double intrigue, holding the intimate moment, "I'll grope for a short moment. Then, clear as cream. We're thick, pal."

DAY plays into her idea, "That's a Chinatown rum drink, you know, 'Two, Between the Sheets;' served in a long stemmed glass."

"I know it." MARGIE, with a laugh in

her voice, "Heavy on the Rum, baby."

She hangs up and immediately dials out.

Like rising blinds on their relationship, sooner than later, both lay still inside Margie's apartment. In the dark, DAY begins.

He starts with a moan, and she answers as though out of breath, as though having run up hill from the bar and with a hint of 'between the sheets' on her lips as a preview. Now opening a first act.

With Day, intimacy is a love scene, in MARGIE's in bed, already it has become a ritual.

MARGIE revealing and fishing for his psyche. "You have all the girls working for You."

DAY unknowingly defends himself with humor to continue, "I give them confidence, something to do. I always stand up for 'em."

DAY empties his pockets onto the bedside table, and fishes among his 'pocket-brack' to retrieve a 'rubber,' and runs his eyes down her reclined body.

DAY admires her, "You're always light on the long stems."

"I'Mmmmm ... for a stand-up guy." She feels the sheep skin takes it with sounds of wrinkling cellophane and pops into her mouth to soften the instrument of her safe pleasure.

While the sheets rumple and shapes change, she makes sounds that compliment or respond to his. No talk exchanged only sounds of pleasure.

Their mutual pleasure resounds softly outside their vibrant skin, while inside their individual thoughts rise and fall with erotic pulse until climax together and enervated bodies that lay in wait for the next time. While their minds juggle the events and evidences of the night before, the idea, the very idea that the power of all the world inside their bodies, mind and spirit come together and contain a beginning for what? An ending that remains outside of their grasp for a moment. This moment it remains within them, without frustration, for the full three act play finished well on the small stage. The big theater production had been put out of their mind.

CHAPTER 11

Back inside the gambling parlor.
Mild activity persists late into the night,
through the early AM.

MARGIE enters with DON WON and they
mingle. Within the character of a patron,
and with the ability to scrutinize the
people within this eccentric scene, WON
plays Gai Pai until . . . .

CHEN comes up to him. CHEN politely
acknowledges MARGIE and cordially motions
to some of her fiends.

CHEN says, directing MARGIE away.
"David is over there."

MARGIE replies, not grasping his
implication. "He'd never miss a night.
Doris? Penny?"

CHEN, now playing into her game.
"Big boys are not in tonight. I wanted you
to come in and talk about a possible
scandal, Mr. Won. I want to avoid,... I
must have investigation, and the utmost
confidence."

Chinese detectives are not really
rare. Since the Judge Dee novels were
written in the late 19th Century about a
real historic figure, all Chinese boys
could aspire to follow the mental puzzle,
unravelings of the famous Chinese master
mind and community public servant. Then,
there are the Charlie Chan movies that gave
more credence and possibilities for a
Chinese boy to dream of achievement in
spite of what the Caucasian world said
about the movie detective. From a family
of Won, the gentleman DON WON comes to San

Francisco with an education and some money. His education in China was in western law, but to follow that as a profession in the west is a dream no Chinese man could realize profitably, as mostly arguments in the western courts would fail in a sympathetic decision for any Chinese man.

Contract law, for a Chinese is a futile argument unless they had the Triad support, and in those cases there would be no need for the court. That is to say, there are no contract arguments because they have the Triad in Chinatown, San Francisco. A version of the Mafia, but open and settling arguments without legal contest.

No one wants to confront the Triad, registered and with offices also on Waverly Street. While it goes unnoticed, they have money and not to pay off the authorities, but to quietly resolve Chinese community conflicts. That seems just fine as far as the powers that be in San Francisco are concerned. Patriotism is a stitched concept, stitched into the quilt and fabric of the U.S.A. by each of the ethnic peoples in this unique port of call.

That means, DON WON, private detective is as much of a powerful man as could be found in the working class of professional and educated people who are not entrepreneurial, who are Chinese, mostly. The entrepreneurs rely on good detectives and that is what brought DON WAN, MARGIE's boss to the house of Chen.

CHEN subtly beckons WON to follow, and with MARGIE they go back to his office.

Enter into the Club, wearing a red, slit to the waist oriental dress, TINA, a new object of attraction for the GUYS, as . . . .

She is tall, Chinese, serine and aloof, a strident exotic sensation. This is a woman who has one attribute that is as attractive as a detriment to the rich boys of Chen's gambling parlor. She's Chinese.

What nobody knows at this time, TINA is DON WON's daughter, a crack shot, martial arts high ranking fighter, brilliant bookkeeper, and his aide in the office side by side with MARGIE.

Her eyes on the outside of the meeting in Chen's office are both a mandate for the business they will conduct, and a pleasure to behold.

She orders a drink.

While inside Chen's office. CHEN turns to WON, looks at MARGIE and then begins.

"Two of the most powerful families in San Francisco's Real Estate community now involved with deals of munitions and they have begun a gambling duel. One threw in his daughter's diamond pendent and the other became outraged. He had a good hand. No one knows what it was, who made him so mad."

WON is the sage Chinese detective. "A raging bull is mad because he sees red. Whatever put red in front of his eye is lost to the bull in the rage."

"He toppled the table, and everything on it upset onto the floor in a manner that created a puzzle so only a Chinese man

would even try to solve." CHEN, more
matter of fact, "His gambling is more of a
game for control than a desire to win. He
put one of my bookkeepers in the bay when
we called his markers."

"The boys in San Francisco don't want
to expose a Jewish family of means forsake
a Chinese man of nothing more than a chair
behind a desk."

"We know," replies CHEN, "The City
fathers simply don't want to get into it in
Chinatown."

"Not at all the city fathers, just
the Irish Detective, Lieutenant Faber." WON
looks up from his small stature into CHEN's
face.

"Faber knows how to keep a secret."

In an agreement of understanding, WON
and MARGIE simply rock back and forth in an
outward, resolute sign of agreement.

They all realize what CHEN deems
necessary is accepted.

He begins taking command of the
office, CHEN paces around to the back of
this desk. "Whatever possesses these men
to rob their daughter's purses can be
found, perhaps in the rage of war. The
jewels are always impounded in MY safe."

He points to the safe.

MARGIE makes herself known. "You
said, 'Their daughters'?"

CHEN continues with humility, "Last
night when I came into the office, the safe
was blown open and the books were gone. So
were the jewels."

MARGIE grabs the larger picture.
"Ledgers?"

WON slows things down. He grasps MARGIE's arm to still her curiosity. "This kind of curiosity is better reserved for wonder, in so much as the Chinese who present scandal prefer not to dwell on that, so the humiliation is lost to the passage of time and not built into any festering of sorrowful guilt for not having foreseen this grief.

"Case has been offered, my number one daughter. Men stealing from their own families, money to perpetuate war, perhaps. An involvement they might not want to face. ... their daughters with ... ."

CHEN recognizes a reluctant-to-believe young beauty's appreciation, so with a flick of his wrist signals MARGIE to go out.

Softly breaking from WON's grip, MARGIE follows his unspoken order. MARGIE walks into the gambling parlor, where one turn into the parlor first presents a mean CHINESE TOUGH on guard to protect the sanctimony of the main man's office, and MARGIE stops will full confidence in the shadow of potential danger. She talks to him while looking over the room.

"Is anyone asking for me?"

This act gives MARGIE stature, and in one way dwarfs the guard in his stand of implied importance.

He shakes his head "No." She sees.

At the bar now, DAY newly arrived, passes time talking to DAVID. DAY asks, "What do you know about Colt 45 automatics in the community?"

DAVID sluffs him off, "We bring in

that kind of gun into The City for the smaller shops, what we can't sell to the Army. That one is supposed to become the all Allied Officers piece. There are always excess in any shipment." Appraising the women in the club with DAY, DAVID is only interested in himself.

MARGIE sneaks up from the shadows of the office to the bar and lays a big kiss on DAY, which doesn't phase him in the least.

"If it were me, and the Allies wish for the same thing, I'd give everybody fighting a Colt 45 or at least use the same ammo. Peter sells the cartridges. He's my tenant and his prosperity gives me security."

DAVID continues, "We over bought you say. All the countries want to use the same bullets. Our idea. It's a tough sell, though."

She turns to TINA sitting unobtrusively at the bar with a drink that has a little umbrella sticking Out of the top. Eyes all around her falling onto her and away. As if nobody wants to resolve the temptation of a Chinese girl.

DAVID sits by himself with a highball, whose glance raises from his glass and now falls onto TINA, and rests there, as he continues to lust for her, whatever she might represent besides a raving beauty alone at the bar.

"Davidal's bringing them in like donuts for the Police, and sonof-a-bitch, Deuitch is nervous. They're both in it to the limit with gun deals." DAVID breaks his spell to mention that to DAY.

As detached as a hunting tigress, TINA watches all around her at what and who seems to be happening, since all parties in the place are paired and some in public display of affection. She lounges at the bar, eavesdropping on the gossip about munitions, surprising to be such open conversation at this club bar.

"To the limit?!" DAY speaks into DAVID'S face. "You want me to believe that?"

MARGIE appears and wrestles him down to a calm, grabs his arm affectionately. "I thought you had something to do at the paper."

From back where the door is now open at the office, WON approaches, eager to share. He savors the moment in this open privacy with such passionate relations around him.

When WON approaches, MARGIE seizes the moment. "Don Won, this is Don Day."

With her head, she signals and includes TINA with the introduction as the men shake hands.

WON enjoys the formality. "Margie, told me about you. I thought we might come together and be Dawn one day." He tries a laugh for himself, all that DAY can do is smile. When TINA acknowledges them, DAVID loses interest.

MARGIE never thinks of TINA as competition. "Tina, here is Don Won's real daughter and assistant."

WON ever polite. "Number one daughter is Margie, though."

TINA slithers up to him in full six
feet of femininity. "Hi." Close to his
ear she whispers, "I'm the one watching
over you."

TINA turns to lead their eye as she
claims her handbag at the bar and slips ...
her own tiny revolver -- hidden under the
handbag on the bar, back into her --
handbag.

At the other end of the bar, FRENCHIE
JOE slips his Buntline, long barrel colt
into a shoulder holster, in a manner only
the we can see. What it is and what it
was, nobody may ever know.

DAY is impressed. "Sheeee!" He downs
his drink. "Frenchie is a harmless tout."

"You think?" TINA speaks with
flawless clarity. In two well pronounced
words, you know she went to the higher
academic Lowell High branch near the lake
in The City.

On a bar stool looking off into the
club, DAVID, although nearby, never notices
the tension or the gun play.

WON puts it into prospective. "When
the bull is watched by vultures there is a
hunting party about to make a kill, or very
little water about."

"Plenty to drink, Won," DAY says.
"Allow me."

"Then it must be the men over there."
WON signals behind him at some stout
heavies watching over a few important
looking men.

He calls over the bartender to make a
drink for WON.

"One of those little umbrella drinks,

please". WON says to Day, "Thank you."

DAY, thinking they might work together, he might get a story.

Why else would Won be here?

"I might be able to owe you. I've been assigned to case a robbery. What're you doin' here?"

MARGIE and TINA grow tense.

WON handles his own. "Are you talking about a street crime?" "Plain talk? Yeah, that's right."

MARGIE and TINA relax.

WON diverts DAY with rare finesse. "With me it's always crime of the upper crust."

Uncomfortable amongst these prime high-steppers, TINA is being drooled over by DAVID. His attention has returned to the exotic beauty.

One of the table games closes amid some anxious groans. The vast array of patrons mill about with the bar as a hub.

Pleasant and focused, WON continues through the fray. "Maybe you could give us some of your 'street wisdom' about these round eyed people. Chinese people have a strange sense of humor. I can always use a man of the press."

Ever the jokester, DAY says, "To impress someone?"

At the bar, another intrigue polished with less finesse, as DAVID is put off and distanced by TINA's cool.

WON remains unflapped. "I need public insights. Any talk about Sol Davidal lately?"

They smile and hoist their glasses

before comparing notes.

WON recovers, "You brought him up," says DAY in sly delight.

This may be the team he had hoped would come together.

Recalling lots, reeling a little from the drink, but not too much to know WON was the one who brought DAVIDAL into the conversation.

Forming a half smile to bate the detective into more of a disclosure, DAY, disguising his own strength, says simply, "Yeah, me too."

WON turns to MARGIE. "Go, my number one daughter, find the raging bull chasing the red cape."

TINA follows MARGIE from the bar and they move through the crowd where the BOYS follow, interested in TINA. The two girls approach a third, AGNUS.

MARGIE has added strength amongst the girls of the club with TINA at her side.

"Agnus, what have you got to say about the 'boys' who are here tonight."

AGNUS answers MARGIE. "The big totes are missing. But, the night is young."

PENNY comes to join in. Day's friends become giddy like children over the choices of beautiful, now exotic women all together a few feet away, still in their view.

TINA addresses AGNUS. "And what's the action from those big 'totes?'"

Looking down a provocatively low cleavage, DAY comes up from behind AGNUS, a thick-accented French blond, who mysteriously leaves with TINA's question

unanswered. Only PENNY seems to notice
DAY's focus of attention, and that's the
reason for her smug, flirtatious smile, an
act that makes MARGIE uneasy as intended.
DAY remains cool.

MARGIE remains cool, while PENNY cuts
DAY away, "I found out that Davidal's
Manhattan deal is some small investment
with David and Peter."

"Well, they're arms dealers."

PENNY embarrasses DAY with the
intimacy right in front of MARGIE who
listens, quietly throws quick hard looks.
"Small money wise. Fifteen 'thou.'"

Then MARGIE no longer quietly through
her blast of a comment casts comment into
the group. "Manhattanization's what they
call it.

Then San Francisco Real Estate would
look like New York. Go, what's the big
news that could end the war?" With looks
from side to side, TINA cannot simply
remark from what she heard, there and now.

"What kind of money would get behind
that? You said fifteen thousand. Why,
that's not so much to shade the whole
city's sky."

The silence is caused by DAY and
PENNY staring at each other in what could
be perceived as flirtatious.

Infuriated, MARGIE glares into
PENNY's eyes and -

TINA silently pleas with AGNUS, who
as a diversion hides a marijuana 'stick,'
and out of her purse instead chooses a
lipstick to go over her mouth, says not a
word as she stashes the 'muggle' back into

the purse.

The mix of spoken and unspoken facts makes the all too curiously informed beautiful, volatile ladies frozen, absorbing for later gossip in a lipstick and powdered face moment.

Awakened with bright eyes that snap from glossy and frightened, PENNY comes to, back on to her assignment. "Oh, there's Sol, now."

She moves away from DAY without any disappointment from MARGIE to join SOL at the entrance.

DAY with grit, "These guys can't be trusted." He remains staring at them like a hunter. "It's the shell game. Who's hidden in which basement?"

Taking in more than he seems, sucking on a straw with the little umbrella poking at his nose, WON stays focused on the small party just a few feet from his position on the bar stool.

Light footed around SOL, PENNY swishes past the boys as the crowd, like a card shuffle, she eyeballs parts of groups from the various tables and collects around the one Baccarat table . . . .

Where the 'elite few' anticipate a crowd, so they all claim a

place to watch there forms a gallery. DAY makes a special place for MARGIE.

Some shuffle chips in their hands. Some make and pay off side bets while behind them a small game in progress winds down.

Disinterested, TINA wanders off to quiz PENNY, now behind SOL at the table.

"Give with some Information!" TINA tells softly and asks with a firm assignation, "Who stands to win more from gun sales, the winner of this game or the better businessman?"

Ambivalent, for personal security, PENNY turns only to look at her, then turns back seeking details of the game and to rub SOL's shoulders. SOL quickly looks down. The first cards are dealt, everyone's quiet.

Both ladies suddenly wonder if DAVIDAL heard her comment, her question to PENNY, the one with spaghetti straps falling over her shoulder.

PENNY turns to TINA and to get rid of her says, "I think Margie is over there."

Embarrassed by her horse whisper that fell, perhaps too loud, TINA takes the hint to leave without much to further convince her to do so and moves off to join MARGIE and DAY as they watch over CURTIS' shoulder. There, she can see DAVIDAL's face and watch his eyes that remain fixed on CURTIS.

MARGIE leaning for privacy into CURTIS, goads him, "Come on

Curtis, do tell. Do you stand to make more money on these cards, or the sale of diamonds like what you bet the other night? Or, on the Manhattan Project?"

Few who overhear laugh, but SOL becomes indignant toward CURTIS. SOL sputters, "Jew, you'll get fatter if you win. If you don't, you can begin to enjoy sardines, because, arms dealer, the war's going to be over soon. I've got the bank, remember! Big as Manhattan."

With that comment, the crowd's sympathy shifts toward him, and when SOL is dealt another card.

"It's as if you know something I don't, Sol." CURTIS retains composure. "I'm the one who counts your money."

"Word has it my 'bauble's' worth ten times what yours is; and I can raise you out of the room. Here, the bank's a game."

They look at the cards dealt each of them. SOL steals a glance at -

CHEN who discreetly nods an approval.

Under the table, a man's hand tries to sneak inside TINA's dress at the slit.

Not one to give into impulse, TINA, blushing and suddenly angry amongst the crowd of intense spectators, turns to face . . . .

DAVID, who just arrived at the table and is at the same time, kissing DORIS heavily on the mouth.

While TINA shocks him by grabbing his balls. "You better look at what your reaching into, I'm the serious type."

Lifting his attention, DAVID with deluded self indulgence looks down to see . . . .

Her tiny pistol pokes his ribs with the other hand. He backs off, leaving DORIS in her own swoon.

While he steps back from his embrace with DORIS, DAVID sucks in the hot air and leads DORIS around to the other side of the table.

To regain composure, TINA slides around by MARGIE and gives her a confident nod.

TINA says, "I get there's an underneath the table game, here." Enraptured with the card game, DAY stays back to watch DAVIDAL and CHEN.

"The Jews and the Chinese both know restrictions." DAY makes his observation to no one. An observation that will never make it into the newspaper.

CHAPTER 12

There are successful Chinese businesses of intimate personal formality. The Hang Ah tea room where they serve Dim Sum, little Chinese dumplings from the kitchens of emperors and queens. Little Jewels, Dim Sum are the dainty finger food like small bites of precious and savory exotic tastes from ancient China.

On this sunny, cool afternoon, TINA leades MARGIE into the alcove at the side of a tall building on Sacramento Street, where the entrance opens off one of the more steep hills of The City in the shadow of the Fairmont Hotel where Davidal's office looks over the rest of San Francisco not covered by small businesses.

They enter, leave coats with the mistress of the house, and take the three steps down into a sunken dining room of triple cloth covered round tables in sizes to fit the number of guests in any one party. The table for the two ladies is large for what one might think would accommodate six people, but as MARGIE would soon understand the table is meant to hold a vast array of small dishes. This begins a 'girls' day at lunch.

Their conversation is anything but superficial as it might seem on the surface to an eavesdropper. But, their run down of all the Gadflys expose one suspect after another, the accused of selfish and ethnically eccentric players during a war meant to open the community as one for all. So, that is no motive in The City for any kind of thievery, and especially a thievery that seems meant to create a vulnerability.

The target for debility, would that be Chen, or his clientele? After all it would surprise anybody except a San Francisco kid that the murderer of Chen's bookkeeper howsoever known, will never be brought in. The crime perpetuated by Chinese upon themselves is a Triad thing, too. Besides, who else could detest without hate, and in The City without prejudice, who could become the criminal during a war, anyway?

In this war, with no question about patriotism, duty, for cause seems to unite the whole world against despotism. No one would stop to think about prejudice, not until it was over in any case, because the whole of the alarm, call to emergency in defense of national security was obvious.

In her mind's eye, MARGIE sees Peter. MARGIE settles in on the boys. A tall blond, self conscious for looking like a German. Habitually in a blue business shit, who appears as if from behind the bar always handling his 'high-ball' unconsciously and taking a second to make a quick quip, before each gulp to drink in first one of several beauties at a time as he passes through the gambling parlor hiding his personal guilt for Teutonic good looks.

"There's Peter. He's an industrialist who inherited his father's machine manufacturing company. They build boilers and refrigeration units for large buildings. They were in a financial group that started consortiums called conglomerates. He collects small hand guns. Deals cartridges direct from the factory during the war, a profiteer. His expertise in foreign exchange.

"He's an American Indian from Wyoming."

Habit that illustrates his character while in the main room at Chen's, Peter stops at a Gai Pai table to respond to AGNUS' flirtations. She slides against him, and pecks his cheek nothing less expected from a French brunette in a sequined slinky gown showing more skin than sequins, anyway.

He leans to within inches of her face, challenging her to serious flirtation, tells her a joke to which she discreetly laughs.

Then she returns his back-handed stroke of her entire body and pat on the rear end with rolled eyes, yet without moving her feet one inch away from the table before being called back into the game.

Peter moves on to circulate.

"His passion is collecting Medieval armor. He used to speculate in the European Real Estate market. Guns and money from prehistoric German castles. Suspicious, with his natural, very blond hair and sky blue eyes. He calls attention about himself an American Indian though his attraction to Teutonic past goes to his looks.

"Those German castles in ruin are the same era as the Zuni Indian ruins, don't you know?" TINA seizes every moment to

ridicule Americans with their historical
lack of sophistication about their past.

Peter moves about easily among
Europeans at Chen's, cat like motion, back
to the Gai Pai table, and while he looks
over AGNUS' shoulder he tosses a fifty onto
the table for her to play. She gives him a
warm look, smiling her mostly lipstick
French smile into his all too Germanic
face.

"Peter may be faking something, he
seems competitive to the big boys. He's
generous, but not one to take advantage.
He plays cards and probably his life with
caution as though he's not using his own
money."

Listening with intensity, TINA
adeptly takes something, delicate from a
small dish, deftly manipulating her
chopsticks.

"These are Har Gau. There's a
secrete inside. They roll the chopped sea
food in these pasta sheets." She loves to
eat. "Maybe Peter doesn't like using his
own money."

MARGIE helps herself to the last
piece and TINA calls the server for more.

"Peter invited me over to his place
to see his armor collection. At the end of
the tour he stood looking at a French
tapestry from the Valois period and turned
to watch me go out the door. He deals in
the small arms sales to the Allies, bullets
for hand guns. If he can convince his pals
to get our Army to use the 9mm, both sides
would have the same guns and same bullets,
he told me. He brokers 45 millimeter

bullets.

"He watched me without letting me see it."

DAVID, a tall dark haired gentleman dressed in the black tie smoker of the majority of the 30 something patrons, moves through the crowd and stops at a black jack table. He places a bet, and immediately TWO BEAUTIFUL Revlon types are at each side. One offers him her drink, which he tastes and drinks in her face while swallowing the liquor; and the other puts a lit cigarette in between his lips as soon as he swallows his taste of liquor.

"There's David," MARGIE continues. "He's the economist. A real junior investor drop out from a large brokerage firm owned by his brother who lives in New York City. East Coast, West Coast investments that puts his family at the front lines. Their money is from long term bonds and Real Estate swaps in the East Coast recreation centers. They are called 'opportunists' behind their backs. Their family also began to trade companies as conglomerate owners. Mainly from those who are jealous without as much money or contacts as they have. He's always fighting jealousy from greed unrealized. It's his money that fronts officers' hand guns. Another war profiteer. This prep school pilgrim is, if nothing else, loyal.

"While he is Peter's landlord, who sells bullets. They found each other here in The City, though their families were connected in the same conglomerate. Peter's folks told him about a person in the company out here, but they never expected to meet."

While continuing in the theater of their mind, MARGIE sees DORIS, an athletic salt and pepper hair beauty in pink and grey satin, off the shoulder gown comes from another part of the parlor. Garrulous for a sophisticate, she gooses DAVID from behind. He turns to smile at her and they kiss in a greeting that tells the world they're in love.

Then she moves one of the girls out of the way to slide in at his side and help him count his cards. She leans in to tell him something about the dealer's cards. He reacts to her comment with a hand signal for no more cards from the dealer. He doubles his bet.

"David's considered one of the most attractive bachelors in San Francisco." MARGIE goes on, "His warmth makes him desirable -he'll do anything for a dame. He's been with Doris, though, since before serving two and a half years in the Army. He was in France during the rise of Hitler and left the service before the hot war broke out. Unflappable and without question takes whatever she wants to dish out and onto him."

The typical act in Chen's during any given evening would show DORIS who pulls DAVID away from the table after he looses. But he revisits her, and then turns back angered by her anxiety to 'visit' insisting that he came to gamble. She wants to socialize and leaves him to play.

"He comes to play. We have seen this

a hundred times, that within a few seconds,
ANOTHER GIRL is by his side to fill the
void."

MARGIE goes on, "He is, a player
despite his dedication to DORIS,

and then he asks the next beauty for
advice.

"She can't get on top of that one."

"He's a committed arms broker,"
MARGIE continues to draw the characters to
TINA. "Generous only in polite company.
Dedicated to Doris, but unwilling to admit
it. He loves playing the field. It's
almost as if he has no affinity , except to
his own country." "He's seen the war first
hand." TINA looks over the dishes.

"After that, no one wants to
pre-judge their fellow man."

At the Dim Sum table, the girls pause
to make choices. Chopsticks doing ballet
over each dish before making selections.

"David can be mean if he looses big.
I only saw that once. He flew off in a
rage and covered his selfish humility by
buying drinks, one after another and for
the bar, too. He doesn't want to be known
as a big power. Not until he takes a
bullet. He covers himself whenever the
spotlight falls on him for whatever
reason."

"Does he get involved in other
investments? Locally, I mean."

"I think so. I heard he had 'men'
all over the city doing little 'errands;
for him. But, with Sol controlling them in
investments to their max, I don't know what
exactly. I know it's never illegal."

"How do you know?" TINA shifts in her seat, "Is he in debt?"

"Johnny told me he was straight. 'Honest and clean,' he said. It's like he couldn't be tempted, they know, because they tried." "So, Davidal and his syndicate tossed off the Mob?!" They see JOHNNIE is a big barrel chested man, dressed habitually in a three piece suit, grey or pinstriped with a flounced floral tie. He strides through the parlor right to the Baccarat table where he hands the DEALER a fist full of big bills. The DEALER counts the money as JOHNNIE takes a seat. The game is in progress, but his heavy betting drives out most of the other smaller players; their girls lean over them and paw their men without the game to distract them, with an abundance of feminine offerings of smooth ecstasy in the subdued light of rich pleasure and demure intimacy, who's to make judgments.

"Johnnie is an older man who states whenever necessary that he is Mafia.

"He lives in a small tenderloin hotel he took over, where he conducts his business. His entrance is always proceeded by two bodyguards, and there are always two more by his side."

They see him in their mental theater at the gambling parlor,

behind JOHNNIE, a SLIM LADY edges her way toward him by pushing one of the big BODYGUARDS aside. She lavishly drapes herself over his shoulder and starts to kibitz. He shoves her aside, casually with a large abrupt stroke and oblique manner,

which hides the actual force. His 'BOYS'
behind him do nothing to support his act,
but their leers catch her falling off
balance enough to warn her not to do that
again.

"His 'city games' seem to be small
time," MARGIE goes on. "But, in San
Francisco the Italian Mafia doesn't have
room for anything big. He claims to have
changed his name to Mally from O'Mally
because, he proclaims 'I ain't no
bastard.'"

MARGIE pours more tea, first for TINA
then for herself.

"I went out with him once. That's
when he gave me a knock down on all the
boys. He said he'd bought this restaurant
and invited several of us to go visit.
When we got to the car, it was only me, and
him. But, lucky for me, the others showed
up right after we got there."

"Which restaurant?"

"No matter. A few months later, he
sold it."

"Oh," TINA dawns on the metropolitan
war game. "Just a lending game, I bet."

"He's certainly not a gourmand, just
a big eater."

"He seems to be in on fast money.
But it seems he has his hand in every
business deal that comes around. Through
the 'club,' right?"

"He would wish." MARGIE reluctant to
not be sure, recovers into facts, "I can
find out."

"If he's laundering money, then it's
cash he needs to flow; and nothing to do

with bookkeeping. He or his boys are no thieves."

"We don't think so," MARGIE hides the second shoe to drop, and does not say 'but.'

Like most nights everybody sees even in absentia, CITRUS walks into the gambling parlor, offers his swank top coat to the nearest employee by the door, and ambles through the crowd saying 'good evening' to certain few of the patrons.

"While Curtis is Davidal's partner, he certainly supports his own presence in a place where he's somebody, and without that place he would be nobody."

When he takes a drink at the bar, the barman knows what he likes, then discreetly he offers the BARTENDER a check.

The BARTENDER walks to the Baccarat DEALER and gives him the check, pointing to the bar and the large older man who sits there, engaged in conversation with an older, glamorous woman dripping in furs and diamonds. With jewels dripping off every hanging portage that makes her look some what like a department store display, her low cleavage reveals matronly bosoms and that is enough to occupy CURTIS' devoted attention. Occasionally his eyes drop with modesty to ogle the slit in her dress that fails to hide her garters at the top of dark silk stockings, for she uses the bar stool only as support to lean on at the bar. Her toes barely touch the ground, and as rich as she may be that seems both the reality and symbolically a portrait of her aged, slim line, presence.

"Curtis Deuitch is a conservative Jewish man brought into the arms brokerage game by East Coast finance who inspired his sense of patriotism." Margie continues while chewing, "He's an accountant who seems to have the best grasp of information regarding the commitment to fight by the Allies. It seems that he is forewarned on almost every major action, and his buying tactics are claimed to be directing the waves of munitions, hence attacks. Whether his is tipped or he is the tip, he can't be bought. It's East Coast contact with the 'word' before West Coast fact. He demonstrated principles and plays his investments close to his chest. Maybe a Wall Street Governor into industries. In San Francisco, he's into syndicated Real Estate. Everything he does is protected as confidential if not secret."

"Isn't everybody," says TINA between morsels.

CURTIS slides off the barstool, looking over the body of the DAME who coyly looks away to permit him to visually fondle her and all her exposures; and into him she redirects her gaze as he walks directly to the Baccarat table to a seat reserved for him alone.

There seems to be a semblance of 'G' men to watch over CURTIS DEUITCH, for he holds the West Coast tip.

TINA mentally sifts through all the characters, "They say they're all involved with the same company. It's one common cause, I guess; and you know the Jewish community loves causes. No self MARGIE snickers, "Yeah right." They both go for the same gem, MARGIE continues, TINA lets her have the morsel. "The game they play is control. You're right, it's a common cause and they all are included in the same profit. The competition is within, which one gets to call the price and manipulate the numbers. It seems that without competition men like this get bored."

Like he owns the place, SOL walks in, strides up the Baccarat table and with the aid of a CHINESE HOUSEBOY takes his top coast off before settling into his reserved chair. He motions to the DEALER who acknowledges in an intimate manner that his fortune is already on deposit.

"Sol Davidal seems to claim himself as the community leader," MARGIE adds another resume. "He makes all the deals close. He is the one who has the exact figure on all the men's interest and calls most of the shots for the whole community. His conversations with the Eastern financiers are usually before any pay off. His parties are the most lavish in the City. No one is barred, no one is left out. He's generous to a fault."

"They say his son owned Chen big, before he went off to fly bombers."

Always at the Baccarat table, AGNUS comes up to SOL and whispers something to which he responds by taking a few bills out of his pocket and handling them over. He looks around the room, gaze resets after falling upon DAVID in the background. She gives him a peck on the cheek, offers to repay. He holds up a hand saying 'No' with a tisk tisk of the tongue.

"His partner's son. A mild mannered man, but they say he'd kill for that son."

The WAITRESS comes up to the Dim Sum table signaling time to pay. "We both can pay," says TINA, "and get it back from my father separately."

"That's alright. I control the petty cash at the office."

"You sure about the money," TINA hides her surprise, "that's alright?"

MARGIE simply smiles and counts out some bills to pay the waitress who stands there tallying from a list and reviewing all the dishes over TINA's shoulder, for the list is done in Chinese.

Does TINA listen? "It may be Chen, all this time, trying to take more than his share."

MARGIE like TINA sips some tea, takes time to reflect for a second. ". . . to continue and find the slumming war lords, who are letting our soldiers crusade unarmed. Forsake and few baubles and some mysterious mistress' charms the winner on the books and with the jewelry does not have to be in the same game."

"And some big Real Estate deal."

Both together they say, "Big as Manhattan."

"Imagine buildings that tall in the City."

"Ugly isn't it."

"Murder."

"I think Chen has more at stake that what meets the eye, here." TINA roots by herself through her mind's eye, through the community. "He might have pulled off the robbery so he wouldn't have to pay. After all, he knows nobody's gonna pay for the dead bookkeeper."

"What did poor David tell us when he unloaded about the investment in the Pitt Engineering Company? And everyone became quiet? " "There's more to what's going on that what we see goin' on." Up the four steps to grope for the outdoors, TINA leads MARGIE out, having finished lunch and a run down on the case, pulling their coats on in the small plush lobby of the restaurant they drag up the few stairs from the sunken dining room full of good taste and girlie closeness.

"After all this work," TINA asks, "How's fun?"

"His name's Don Day. He's been through the war. He's sorting it all out." MARGIE looks up through the taller of the San Francisco buildings in this neighborhood. "But his sees it all through the amber light of scotch."

"But he's Irish?"

The sunlight slashes down on the two of them.

"The Irish in The City . . . they know all what's goin' on. I'm clever. I'll figure it all out."

When MARGIE enters the oak paneled office looking over the San Francisco Bay, DAVID looks up at her with his window and the light framing what is without doubt a successful, slick businessman.

"Margie! Hiya, there. You told my girl out front you were looking for a job?

But, . . . "

"I always wanted to be a mannequin, a
model . . . wear the finest clothes, don't
you know? Don't you have any connections
with Cartier to get me a position?"

"You came in here to ask a favor, but
I can't help you with Cartier. First off,
they're a jewelry house. Don't you need a
dress design house?"

"I heard the rumor, I guess you
invest in minerals. I thought of modeling
jewels and fine dresses. I thought Cartier
was into clothes too. Aren't you into
foreign investments? Isn't jewelry and
stuff that hot today?"

DAVID laughs, and says, "I'm a gun
runner."

She balks at his abrupt frank and
bold remark.

"No, I broker minerals for the
Browning company in Utah. They make hand
guns for the Army. Corporate funding for
contract fulfillment.

"They need metal and I dish it out
for the commodity. Not the speculation or
contracts but the rocks. The rocks that
they break down the ally into metal for the
gun parts. Nothing to do with fashion,
honey.

"Maybe that's what you heard.
Minerals, I mean."

They stare off. MARGIE wants him to
tell her about the Atomic Bomb and he sees
her as a beauty looking for an in to make
some money on her good looks.

"You give me more credit that I
deserve, I'm into Real Estate, here as

well. You want me to 'check it out' for
you? Is that it, Margie?"

"Oh, would you David? I mean they're
bringing a bit of Manhattan, I hear, it's
comin' out West. East coast fact, I mean.
If East Coast investments are going to
effect San Francisco, it has to be
clothing, don't you think so?" She leaves
the door open for another meeting.

"Well, if they're going to branch
out, they'll need commercial frontage.
There I can help them."

"You're such a sweetie."

With a nod and hugs, she leaves him,
without but a clue that the Manhattan
Project was on her mind and that it has
something to do with skyscrapers and not
bombs. And, that he has no idea about hot
jewels. She got something done.

With almost the same office, but
facing a window on the Bay, MARGIE walks up
to the blond PETER who quickly extends his
hand to her to greet her with a gentlemanly
hand shake.

She sits squirming in a leather chair
wanting to openly disclose her motive, now
in PETER's office.

"I came in on a pretext, Peter. I
have to confess, I want to know all you can
tell me about the 'hot' jewelry market in
The City."

"You say you want to talk about
investment and what I can tell
    you about the jewelry circulating
around this city is 'zip.' I
    don't know a thing."

"Didn't David call you? I told him

to scout around because I heard about a hot
jewel deal. Something that might get me
started in modeling."

"Sweetheart. If ever I hear a thing
about jewels, not David and his mining
ventures, I'll sort it out and tell you
first. But, I have to let you know . . . I
don't know what you're even talking about.
I'm into Real Estate and that's a syndicate
investment, anyway. That's what's got
David and me into business together."

"I heard about a jewelry house in New
York, Cartier or something looking for
'factors' to invest. Isn't that in
Manhattan terms a clothing line deal?" She
sighs in mock frustration.

"With an endorsement from the
investors, or like that, I could fulfill my
deepest desires to cover myself in
expensive jewels and be something. Like
Penny. In on a heist."

"What!?" he's stymied, "a heist?"
MARGIE looks dumb. "Huh?"
"Be what?"

"A fashion model, silly." Her
baiting of him didn't work and now she
plays the ditz.

"Whatever I can get you into, I'm
available. But I think you're better off
staying away from that kind of thing. I
mean . . . hot jewelry means strings and
strings attached to anything would make you
something other than your own person." He
knows what he wants of her, and it is
simply in her best interests. The boys
love playing the big brother, after all
they have seen overseas during the war.

It works on another level, his plutonic concern, one of innocence and they both relax.

"Oh," she says, and PETER falls for the ditz act. It puts him at ease.

In the early afternoon, the Tenderloin, San Francisco's wino district named for the inner thighs of the street walkers who followed the meat market and the place to buy 'that' cut of meat; the usually vicious and dangerous district is simply repulsive in this post roaring, bawdy days, in the afternoon.

The dirty wind up her hat and in her hair, TINA finds an old run down Tenderloin Hotel that she was looking for, and enters, past bums on the sidewalk, dead beats leaning against the walls.

Inside at a caged counter, desk where a skinny pock faced balding clerk sits with a pencil in his mouth, newspaper spread out in front of him, she gets a room number for JOHNNY MALLY.

Up the creaky stairs, wobbly, sticky banister that seems to make the climb more intimidating, TINA finds MALLY's room and knocks only to find the door falls open at the touch.

She steps inside and to her surprise the smell of hibiscus is calming, but Persian rugs leave the entrance looking clean, furniture while fake is splendid century French. A plush silence has settled the room once the door closed tight. The whole-make up of the room is so counter to the facade of the hotel itself, it disarms her and she begins to feel at home, taking off her gloves, looking around.

While the suite is 'plushed' up to the hilt, through the first bedroom door a MOLL in a satin robe and feather collar, nothing else but her mostly white skinned exposed body extended over a knobby spread, covered bed, and she eats chocolate cherry candies one at a time from a red satin square box, and talks in a monosyllabic high squeaky voice to an unheard third party seated with his back to the door; and also part of the conversation miming silent interjections this BOY type gunsel filing his nails and occasionally the tips of his fingers, nods and squawks too.

The type of girl to get in on it all first hand, MARGIE got it.

CHAPTER 13

Meanwhile, put two blocks and to the left at a sandwich bar, at Tommy's Joint serving with covered pickle dishes on the tables since 1921, a giant photo of Wally Berry above the bar, memorabilia graffiti all over the walls finds DAY, who sits with MARGIE on a date of his make-up.

"Is this model obsession a cover?" Day asks with a taint of jealousy in his voice with a slice of pickle between his teeth.

MARGIE looks at him without saying, but the noise from her mouth is sarcastic when she sucks an imaginary piece of something from between her teeth.

"They're all calling me to tell me in, about you. Why the visit, they wanna know."

She says, "Let's go to a nice place."

In the heart of downtown, the south east corner of Union Square where the young, socially dangerous Spreckles girl balances above the city as a sculpture on a pole, the Comtesse Dandini's department store of goods and nothing but imported goods of all sorts from France holds a lunch room in the basement. This is one of the San Francisco prides, The City of Paris.

Taking the filigree French cage of the largest French elevator to the floor below, open for the stairway down and all the way up to the multi-colored dome on the fifth floor above all. Like birds in a cage alone, together the couple descend into the pleasures of 'Franglified' San

Francisco.

One of the main features below in the cafe, sits behind refrigerated counters on plates of half sandwiches, cut and filled tomatoes, fruit tarts, puffy pastries with whipped cream or custard seeping out; and all service includes small dainty cups of coffee or etched glasses with milk and a row of flavored syrups in colorful labeled bottles with pour spouts propped up behind where the servers work. The service here supports little old ladies who hate to stay home, and the few in The City who know how to take 'high tea.' Seated at almost every table are little old ladies with lace veiled hats and white gloves. When DAY pulls out the chair for MARGIE to sit, she takes out her gloves which puts her more in place than without, even without her veiled hat the gloves at her finger tips seem to give her a permission for tea, here.

"Tina is inquiring in a manner to look for the immoral Chinese. It is those whom she lists in her notes, otherwise. We think the robbery is an inside job. I am suffering from a keen desire to be a model. I was half using the chance to get David and Peter interested . . . in me, I suppose. Half a chance, but to find out about their investments."

MARGIE's dreamy, far off look has DAY gasped at her painted, French style of haunting rouge and exciting beauty. Her off the side of the head Beret with a veil adds to the foreign touch as her dialogue begins to show effect he never saw in her before. Mostly, it seems the imported

French environment has transported them both.

"So, you always wanted to be a model?" DAY looks at her with worried joviality. "A figure model?"

"What kind of a girl do you think I am?"

"Oh, I know what kind of a girl you are." DAY brings her down to earth.

After all, they both look back to the night they met. Picked up, or bumped into in an alley. "Who knows what cats and kittens bump up out of alley ways during a war."

"I'm really a good girl." MARGIE briefly bores her look into his head.

"Excellent, in fact." He suddenly senses her vulnerability.

He glances at her partially eaten sandwich. "More mayonnaise?" She shakes her head. "Maybe an eclair, or Napoleon?

"Oh, Don," she begins to lament. "I want to have money, be admired and be pampered. I'm so tired of having to work, take 'crap' from those rich boys who think they can play us for suckers.

Those guys don't know what it takes to make a girl happy. They think you can get into a girl's life and her drawers and toss her off like a used banana."

"Peel," he interjects.

Then she, having become acrid with the visceral tirade, follows her anachronism. "They're always just so careful not to trip on the peel, goin' away."

In the posh café, the calm scene with

DON DAY where MARGIE tells him of her
driving passion to be a pampered model
because now she feels used by men without
recompense. This leaves him dashed.

'Figure model,' he asks his inner
self, seeing her in his mind,

in a flash as a classic French
postcard nude showing off in front of him
in her apartment at the end of her bed. He
looks at her, helpless, himself.

"The investor search thing is the
cover." Hapless she reveals herself,
"t'answer your question."

DAVID's office, again a paneled
affair with personal brick-a-brack and
certificates, private triumphs in photos on
the walls. His office faces the window
onto the San Francisco Bay.

Now DON sits across a large desk
facing DAVID, both with a crystal glass and
some amber liquid, so with DON turned they
both sit facing the Bay.

"I'm looking for the class of people
who might be into buying old guns." DON
has a unique way of prying. "The stolen
guns from last night's robbery on 3rd
Street go from office to office as an aid
to some bigger thing."

"If it's a crime to deal guns these
days, you'll have trouble finding anyone
doing it illegally. Immorally," DAVID
continues with a merchant's dedication,
"maybe even harder. No one looks down on
an arms dealer in this city. What with the
Navy on the streets, the Army, too, in
uniforms and selling their guns for 'rum'
as it were. There's hardly a man in this

'town' who's not connected with guns, Don."

He takes a reproachful break, a sip of whiskey, rattles the ice, and adds with a sort of futility.

"You're gonna have trouble."

"I know," DON says fruitlessly assertive, "I'm on the street." He looks at his friend, a far off critical eye unnoticed for the beauty of the high toned office view compelling their both attention.

"I'm the one who knows . . . the trouble."

In PETER's office, DON sits at a low table with a pair or drinks in front of them. The silence is meaningfully broken.

"I wouldn't know who would buy those kinds of guns. Seems like an Italian gangster style gun, but too big and there aren't many Italian gangsters in this city who would not bring an 'piece' in from Chicago, or New York." PETER's speculation sheds no new light on the subject.

"You think they might export?" DAY has no real idea of how to get into his real concern. The big bomb.

The two of them lapse into silence. PETER strokes his chin for a moment before answering and DAY has a chance to finish his drink in small, slow swallows. He has to wonder if his ideal to sell all the nations' armies the same bullets has merit.

"There's so many more things to get into here, in The City, in these times. There's an active slave trade that the Italian's are trying to stretch into from the Asians." He thinks out loud, "A stretch meaning they want it stopped, the Asians are trying to pay off to keep it going."

In DAY's mind, the pictures of the Robbery at Chen's, when the three CHINESE climbing down from the window with a black bag appears as DAY awoke from his drunk.

"You say the Chinese are the bad guys."

PETER continues, "There's a game called 'the mistress slide' where one 'power' tries to muscle in on another 'pole' and ploy is gang with a dame who he makes out to be crooked. He gets her to betray the guy, and polarizes his interest in her, with the interest in the 'game' -- that's for some profit -- they're playing out.

It's a mean street, I'll tell you. The gun trade is the most 'legit.'

"Sounds like 'Allies and Assholes.'" "You headin' back to Europe?"

DAY still has his head in the clouds, in the picture of the Robbery at Chen's and the three with the black bag climbing down from the window.

"It seems like the war is the most tame," says DAY in a daze. "Same thing," Peter stammers on, "but a voluntary service for the rich to 'stay' that way.

DAY comes back to life.

"What do you know about Penny laying out for Sol?"

"She's probably one in a million different from the rest who doesn't need to play on a slide for a guy, for all things. He's the best choice for her, rich, I guess. He owes the Italian community too much nothin' to be playing his mistress' jewels in a Chinese gambling parlor. Popped that bookkeeper over his partner's son's debt. You know, Chen sees his daughter, Marissa?

Yup! Davidal 'n his daughter caught up in Chen's web."

"Or fun and games. Like Penny played off a sapphire."

With that last thought, PETER's lost in his drink, half way to his mouth.

"I thought the Manhattan Project would make him out to be a rich slob."

"So, there is a big munitions deal behind that Manhattanization thing?"

"No. That's a Real Estate deal."

"But the big deal with the bomb . . . ?"

"That's our deal with the Big Bomb. Big as Manhattan and with

Sol dealing on East Coast group for a megaton. Or something.

"Hell, I dunno."

So, DAY pours himself a straight 'dump' and whacks it down with a smile before taking off. "Gotcha."

Rising from the club chair, DAY says, "I thought it was his daughter's necklace."

"And, I thought Margie was after bein' a model . . .

Both say "citizen." At the same time, and they laugh all the way to Pete's office door.

"What's makes for the doubt that Davidal's anything but a patriot?" "Well, he is Jewish."

Standing by the office door, DAY stops drinking, puts the glass on the table by the door.

"It all goes to show, until the investment pays off, we're all restricted . . . until the war's over."

Chinatown, as always on Grant Street shows store fronts littered with brick-a-brack, and small gift items. Though the day shows on their watch, the light filters through tall buildings close together and awnings over the sidewalk along the skinny one way street making TINA and MARGIE look like curio seekers, browsing.

Behind a small counter inside an overwhelmingly stocked store, they approach the salesman standing almost protecting an old hand carved, ornate cash register. The man has little to nothing on his schedule as though he owned the place, for any worker would be dusting, stocking, taking stock of merchandise. As the register tender, he stands there just tending the passing of time. A monument to the Chinese adage that the reward for patience is patience.

The two girls enter and approach with the one extra step to stand in front of the cash register from the doorway. In Chinese, TINA asks 'where's the real boss?' So, he motions for them to go upstairs.

At the top of the stairwell the room opens immediately into a Chinese family owned sewing, sweat shop. Dusk seems to have fallen during the early afternoon by the last step into the room with dusty windows.

From seemingly having operated the
controls of a time machine, TINA and MARGIE
look upon the business of older Chinese
MOMMAS doing hand work on brocade clothes.
Perceived as slaves, they stop talking, but
in a moment all smile, having stopped their
gossip, actually happily busy in their clan
of workmanship.

One at a time the older women
describe the two young women who
interrupted their hand work. Curiosity
builds into their dialogue and they, one at
a time, stop stitching clothes to assemble
their wits over tea, a break, and some
conversation.

It takes just a moment for them all
to assemble, take a relished break allowed
by etiquette with guests for their pause,
and to pull chairs up for their guests,
themselves and talk to the two younger
girls who relish what the old women have to
say.

"These men are picking their wives
pocket books and passing the family jewels
to their girlfriends while they make plenty
money off the War."

Both TINA and MARGIE cannot believe
how the gossip is ruled by what happens at
the seemingly private gambling parlor,
Chen's.

Suddenly, the activity at one
gambling parlor has become the center of
the world. Waverly Place in Chinatown, San
Francisco is a prophecy fulfilled as one
important, entrepreneurial landmark.

Belligerent, TINA remarks, "Makes you

wonder why the Chinese aren't in it?"

Unfazed by the young Chinese girl's attitude, they listen as MARGIE adds her round-eye remark.

"The Chinese are so <u>good</u> aren't they Mama San. At age nine they do 'red envelop' pick ups and learn about how to skim city ledgers. It's a fad, or what? Fast money at age eleven pays off Mama San's Gai Pai and sister's numbers, right?"

Without pause, no refusal about how the Chinese hold themselves outside the eccentric Culture of The City.

"It's true," the old Chinese WOMAN smiles. "Chinese have a problem with those who can't get into Medical School, or can't count on their connections for good jobs. It's more the boys who group together, and hold the family to stay together when all are poor and uneducated, they turn into Tong leaders."

"Or, they immerse themselves in their studies," adds one of the other old Chinese ladies. It just might pay off, in time."

"The unknown contribution to China to fight Japan is unknown, mostly hidden money, for the IRS and agents that snoop into OUR pocketbooks take it all for the big Army. We are seen and not heard."

"I know, it's a constant war from within the families." TINA knows for a fact.

"San Francisco offers little chances for a Chinese boy." MAMA SAN reflects on the dead Chinese bookkeeper pulled out of the Bay. "Some Jewish boy overseas worth more than a Chinese bookkeeper these days."

MARGIE comes back. "You might stick together and take over some day."

"They're buying a lot or property," MAMA SAN squints with an intensity of a sort of pride in their power of patient take-over. "Not investing in war?

"That, you don't know."

"So, who's the patriot?"

"Chinese not investing in war," and the old lady rolls her spit. "Chinese paying for guns and bandages."

The working ladies look up at the working girls, "Patriotism will come with ownership. Time will show them all, we're one in the same. Big time ownership in this city. When the war's over, you see."

Both girls are silently repentant, as they return to their office on foot through the maze of a straight street series in Chinatown now embraced in the natural grace of dusk.

"Those are the pawns?"

"They're all pawns."

MARGIE with a character reversal on TINA interjects a Chinese moral to her version of the story thus far.

CHAPTER 14

In China, kings are called Magi, or
Magots in French, and all gossip takes on
factual tones through them. In the Chinese
community, evening exterior things take on
personal perspectives.

For the general glow of The City is
too unexciting to have any
    sort of public appeal.

Slowly ambling through the back
streets, WON, directed by previous
knowledge, goes into the back of a hillside
commercial San Francisco dwelling.

Up the wooden stairway it appears
almost like a fire escape. He looks up and
also, carefully watches below.

WON enters a Chinese apartment where
beaded curtains hang motionless at side
doorways and incense is burning.

A CHINESE MAN enters wearing the silk
robes, Chinese box hat and long pig tail
straight behind him like an old world
Chinese. He opens a door to greet WON.

He greets WON with a polite bow,
hands clasped and hidden in the sleeves of
his frock. His name uncannily isn't
Chinese.

"My friend BOBBY PRESCOTT," says WON
in greeting.

"Ah so. Honorable Mr. Won has graced
my apartment all too infrequently. This is
an honorable pleasure. Tea for you?"

WON returns the bow. "My dear
friend. Ah so. It has been too seldom
that we come together to enjoy the song of
the swallow. I have come to listen to the
Mocking bird. Some tea would make the song

just that much more a pleasure."

PRESCOTT bids him to follow, on inside. His walk indicates that he is not so old as his wardrobe. His features are reassuringly Chinese. Apart from his staggered American speech, his action are comfortably western.

They enter another room through another beaded curtain and sit to face each other. They stare for a second.

WON speaks first. "I am set upon a task to curb a scandal."

"If there is anything I can do," PRESCOTT says. "I am always at your service. If there is someone who is bothering you, just tell us where to find this person. We can make it so silent even the secrets of the breezes will never know."

PRESCOTT announces his power in an offer as would any unrestricted wise guy.

"That is a comfort, Bobby PRESCOTT." WON plays into his staged cordiality. "I am in no danger myself but it is about something I am not able to find. Do you hear of any unusual items being offered?"

PRESCOTT responds without a second to think. "My 'bullets' have some new 'pieces.' You want something you can't get from the Italians? I have 45 automatics that are newly acquired and never been used."

"I am looking for a sapphire," WON begins. "Maybe some loose diamonds, or in a necklace. And, books that might exploit a family's worth, ledgers."

Just then a CHINESE BOY, from the

night of the black bag robbery, bursts into the room, from a glimpse behind him, it is a Chinese Laundry in the back ground where PRESCOTT lives. Without daylight to better disclose PRESCOTT's location no one may be the wiser that he fences stolen merchandise and harbors fugitives in the Chinese community.

An excited, scrawny CHINESE BOY, LEN CHEW stands in front of the two older Chinese men, and with baited breath tells PRESCOTT in Chinese, but LEN CHEW all the while looks at WON with precautions, respect, unable to hide in his language as is his habit in this clandestine habitat his urgency to evade the law.

LEN says in Chinese, "WE HAVE HIM HERE." He seems to just notice WON. "HE HAS THE *NEWS* AND THE VALUE AS PREDICTED. 'Frenchie Joe'" And, LEN glances at WON, but he continues in Chinese. . . . IS RELIABLE AS WE EXPECT. WE MUST GO TO THE SOURCE HE'S REVEALED."

PRESCOTT turns to WON to explain, in calm tones, a contrast to Len. "Frenchie Joe is an Italian, but with French habits for gossip."

Then to LEN in Chinese. "CAN'T YOU SEE THIS IS NOT THE TIME TO BRING ME INTO YOUR BLUNDERS." 'Frenchie Joe' GIVES YOU THE INFORMATION AND YOU ACT. WE PAY AS HE DIRECTS, GET WHAT IS IN THE OFFERING; OR THE SOURCE ENDS WITH HIS VERITABLE LIFE."

Acting from the back handed signal to leave from PRESCOTT, LEN exits.

"Frenchie Joe has information all the time, but not all the information is timely."

Almost as though PRESCOTT expects WON
to respect the secrecy, he continues with
WON. "Frenchie Joe is one of my sources
for information none the less. We pay and
Len Chew acts on my behalf. If we should
ever fail in finding what we're after, his
own mouth, will be terminated."

A finality of the word 'terminated'
simply expressed well in soft tones through
razor slit eyes that cut to the edge of
fact, which WON wonders for an instant.
'How mortally true are your facts?' "Humm."
WON wonders, "About your bullets, you might
let it be known it could be lucrative to
get hold of some jewels. That without the
Chinese it would be dangerous to deal in
sapphires or blue diamonds this season.
The guns are tools on the stage, but the
stones are the 'first properties.' You
tell, the stage could be a Chinese set?"

PRESCOTT, cool as dealing with the
sale of green tea. "And the ledgers? What
sort of boxes does this tool open?"

"YOU are crisp." WON appreciates
dealing with green tea. "A Chinese fortune
cookie company on Waverly Street --
'Company records.' It requires movement
with discretion. Report only to me about
them. The true value is there."

PRESCOTT who may have been clued in
on this commodity. The Ledgers Frenchie
Joe claimed were of value, but PRESCOTT had
no previous knowledge before this. He
glides onto the original point. "We can
talk about my 'bullets' at another time,
perhaps. 'On the books money' is big game.

Not worth a life?"

They stand, both as men determined.
PRESCOTT has a new edge. WON
realizes he never knew the ledgers had
value, so he now knows that. And by
revealing to PRESCOTT that the books are
important, PRESCOTT discloses to a
detective that the ledgers are within his
reach.

"You have been seen." PRESCOTT says,
"In that vein, you must come out the front
door. We don't want to arouse suspicion by
being unnecessarily secretive."

WON exits, lead by PRESCOTT through
the laundry onto the street side of the
building on the hill.

"We have tried for more than
information with Frenchie Joe." PRESCOTT
continues, "What he does ... for himself,
mostly. There was something about paste, a
'swicheroo.' It is a term which means
nothing to me. Is that something
valuable?"

"I don't know." WON asks, "Can a
'swicheroo' be bought or sold?" PRESCOTT
remains in control. "That is answered
first by an old Chinese question, Won. Can
it fit into a box?"

Once onto the street level with
PRESCOTT they bid farewell among the
passing pedestrian Chinese. It is not so
late after all.

"Can we keep Frenchie Joe out of a
box?" WON asks.

"Every puzzle has a key piece."
PRESCOTT remains evasive to the end. "And,
you know Chinese boxes can only be opened

when you know the key piece."

The city of San Francisco is established as one of rare architecture that sparkles after wet wether, for it's the end of windy winter and a mid Spring. The City has no idea about the rules for seasons, rain drips off trees and puddles dry on cracked sidewalks. The wind is like a broom.

Inside Won's office, a typical detective office of the times of war, personal at every turn with a display of personal pride, ego on the walls and in cabinets memorabilia on exhibit. His collection of files and memorabilia on the walls is very Chinese-American. A mixture of race relations in photography and brick-abrak in cabinet cubby holes.

Pictures of him accepting awards from the Mayor of Chinatown, formally dressed Chinese man with sash, he in a Brooks Brothers' suit and the both of them next to flags in a stand, some of organizations, some of other countries --all with the American flag included. The office glows warm in yellow tungsten light in the late PM. The Meeting of 'minds' over tea at Don Won's office is between father and daughter, whose strong feminine character not bowing but respectful of her father.

WON seems insistent, in his mild manner. "Again, I went to see PRESCOTT."

TINA expresses certain emotion, exclaims, "That fake Chinaman. Oh, why don't they see through him?"

"The Chinese come in many forms," says the father. "Like all the peoples are composed of separate individuals. They cannot be judged, as nobody can, as one big group.""You said that right. Big!" She says.

Ever the obedient secretary, MARGIE enters with papers for WON. TINA subtly changes appearances with a change in posture. She ceases to sarcastically react to her father's comments. She would never even hint of disrespect for her father, as a good Chinese girl.

"When magnates are thrown out onto the street, you attract many nails." WON leads them through his certain wisdom.

"Bobby Prescott is well secured inside." WON gets an idea.

"Tina, go out to the neighborhood and see what you can do to draw his bullets into action."

MARGIE sits to take notes.

"I knew of a woman who was looking for jewelry. Money was no object."

TINA tunes in quickly, says "I'll investigate what they think is 'no object.'"

The Chinatown exterior show store fronts, looking inside of a small neighborhood grocery Store. Transparent inside from the outside during early evening.

Outside under electric converted gas street lamps, TINA WON approaches the store front dressed in an overcoat and man's hat.

She presents a softly durable character as though she may be a native to the city, and furthermore a boy.

Just inside, five idle YOUNG CHINESE

BOYS gad about looking harmless. TINA WON
overhears something in English, expressed
as secretive because of the ALL CHINESE
dialogue and patronage, including her and
the STOREKEEPER.

BOY #1 says, "Now we got the guns, we
can take every liquor store in town."

Paying for a candy bar, -- Her small,
beautiful gun is exposed at the back of her
neck, from under the hat and behind the
collar.

TINA WON looks up from having
overheard, and with the boys attention when
she dramatically pulls off her hat.

A breathtaking beauty as well as a
gunsel further tantalizing, the boys she
lets the raincoat fall open, which
devastates the boys, capturing, in the
collar, her cascade of hair; and her daring
dress that shows in every way she's a woman
to . . .

. . . YOUTHS stunned with open mouths
and vulnerable to desires, disarmed by her
attractive, dramatically exposed femininity
in a store now steamed only partly by the
outside rain and fog, as the evening falls
into night.

Provocatively leaned backwards
against the counter, TINA exposes her
intentions.

"I'm interested in jewelry, at any
cost but not any price. It might be more
lucrative to get hold of some business
ledgers.

You might know Bobby PRESCOTT?"

One of the BOYs says, "We've tried
that with him. There's always a fake

necklace in the community. Now we've got
pistols. To hell with PRESCOTT's paste
sapphires."

TINA WON is suddenly bewildered. She
says, "Try for me. You look around for me
anyway."

They fumble all over themselves
agreeing to help her. While she pays for
the candy bar, she tosses them a business
card.

When she stands paused to open the
candy wrapper, the boys drool from her
sensuality or the appeal of the candy bar.
Either way, they slap fight hands over
possession, control of her card, as

she wraps herself up again against
the weather outside and leaves the store.

Amid DON WON's office of personal
glory, inside at night, DON WON sits
puzzled and concerned. Inside of his
office, he muses over his concerns, openly
to include TINA, MARGIE and . . .

. . . DON DAY, who sits slouched in a
chair with bottle in one hand and a glass
in the other.

TINA stares at DAY. "This is not
hard to uncover."

She motions courteously to Day, then
takes tongs to place a cube of ice in her
father's glass, first.

Showing life, DAY surprises everybody
and stands to add whiskey into everybody's
glass.

Then, TINA continues behind him
filling tea cups at a slow pace,
indifferent to DAY'S notable condition of
oft occasion glib fatigue, she follows him

and places ice in MARGIE'S glass, finally
her own ...

"The way I see it," DAY says while
pouring the whiskey, "the boys into Real
Estate finance need cash money and while
trying to stir up something to make easy
money, riled someone in the Chinese
community."

. . . Into his own glass, he pours
the most and downs all in one gulp.

"It seems one thing being offered is
some guns." TINA is clueless as to what
this means to DAY. "New and newly
acquired. Services next. Who'd engineer a
paste copy? Then, who'd assign bullets to
protect it? Or is it a revenge bullet?"

DAY, suddenly perked up, "What's
that? Newly acquired guns ... then you say
the robbery was a Chinese gang? That's
what we thought at the paper."

WON looks upon DAY. "Yes. Is that
helpful to you?"

"Heck yes!" DAY becomes excited.
"That's my story. I'm investigating a 3rd
Street gun shop robbery."

He holds up, not to expose his
informant who already told him about the
paste sapphire.

Precociously interjecting, TINA says,
"That's the Chinese gang. Different from a
Tong group protecting a family. A free
running group of Prescott's 'for hire'
gunmen. It's betrayal, I bet.

Paste those kids said, and a
sapphire, too. They know!"

Before WON can clarify that it was
CHEN who told them about MARISSA DAVIDAL's

necklace having been flung into the game.

"Fact Jack!" DAY says, "Thank you Tina. That means there's stories coming up about Davidal. If I can get to the police in time ..."

"The police?" This alarms WON.

"I work with them." DAY says, "You?"

"It would be highly unscrupulous, my son." WON says with a deathly calm. "They would put the finger, so to speak, right on me; and I would be of no use to anyone -- anymore."

This suddenly worries TINA.

"Oh, you mustn't go to the police," she says. "He means. They would kill him."

"Our game is business outside the police." MARGIE clarifies exactly what they do in The City.

There is a silence, all anticipate DAY to make a profound apology for the suggestion.

"Oh. Then, what?" He condolences without pause, "I just want my story."

WON breaks the tense silence.

"You didn't realize that the robbery you had witnessed was the door that could open on the biggest indiscretion in San Francisco. These men have all their money on ledgers, marked in blood mingled with the water of the San Francisco Bay; and tied with the fates of the United States itself. In the War that could be on the verge of economic disaster for the entire Western World, they put up real money, but borrow from the Chinese for games. This, some say pulled Japan into the war.

Americans holding out on Asian interests.
China a ripe apple to be plucked while the
West harbors all the coal. People, here
they say, discriminate against each other
for money. Fortunes to one, scandal makes
small change to another. Neither eccentric
without consideration for their
eccentricity over the lives of small ones."

"Wait a minute." DAY wakes to the
facts he knows. He perhaps is the only one
who knows all the facts. His mind working
as disjointed as the facts, but with WON's
clarity he knows it . . . all. "The coal
was for Japanese steel, and armament to
fight our allies. The Chinese!

"You're talking about necklaces and
ledgers in a gambling parlor ... hard to
imagine death to all of China and what you
guys are working on ... I thought ...
Davidal?"

They all begin to mentally abandon
him.

"Wait a minute." He says, "I mean,
you're talking about a necklace and I'm
into a big munitions scare. Davidal's
power cannot be that much of a 'muchness'
over fifteen thousand dollars in paste?"

In sudden burst of excitement
futility, DAY belts down another two
fingers of whiskey.

WON ever the wiser goes on. "Yes,
you must know. The police, here, have
their own code. Now, we have been hired by
Chen to find missing jewels, stolen from
the safe one night. It could bring great
misfortune upon San Francisco's financial
community that holds the supply of war toys

together. On Chen's ledgers, it becomes
not play but power. There is much
financial concern, moreover, Japan invaded
China."

     "They're our allies." And WON belts
his whiskey in one gulp, then chews on the
ice. "You are correct."

     Mentally closing in on the big bomb,
seen in private, secret news releases DAY
from collaboration, so he sits frozen with
wet sympathetic, drunk eyes.

     MARGIE leans into him, in the dark
about what pictures are running behind his
eyes.

     "Yes, sweetheart. You did see
something real. What will convince you it
was not just a dream?"

     DAY FLASHES in his seat, and it's not
the whiskey. on -

     The Alley, Waverly Place in
Chinatown, blue night, very dark.

     THREE MEN climbing down the wall with
a black bag.

     He cannot hear TINA talking, her
voice musical and haunting.

     "You, do understand. Duty?"

     DAY's flash is DEJA VUE, a FLASH
FORWARD. In his mind, under a sapphire
blue light, TINA and DAY are together in a
doorway pulled close together with her
dress hiked up as they are publicly making
love standing up.

     Suddenly they run off, holding hands
and together fly into the misty fog, clouds
surround them and lift into the dark sky.
It looks surreal, it looks true, but is it
actual? Emotionally DAY the Irishman with

this stunning Chinese girl?

DAY's FLASH RETURNS him to: In the smoke filled office, coy, TINA turns from DAY's glazed stare; but she has difficulty keeping her attention on the discussion. It appears he has had a fit of sorts.

She fondly looks at the befuddled DAY, as he has trouble following the discussion with his own mind confused by whisky.

By the psychic experience. Her sudden clarity accents her bright nature.

Accentuated by melancholy, TINA says, "There's a quiet greed creeping into the old Chinese women, too. You can tell with Chinese when they jump into detail."

Eagerly clarifying insights MARGIE says, "The real crime, they think is corruption in the investment community. While bank money is frozen ... With bard cash, somebody could gamble away the life of the whole country."

DAY's attention on MARGIE, then WON then TINA barely notices that MARGIE watches him at every emotional moment, notices that he is not focused on their discussion at hand.

"And Chicago or Detroit always trying to get a bite of San Francisco," TINA adds. "Margie's reports and the way the old Chinese women spilt it to her. Stealing's okay, private build up in the Tenderloin makes it look like poverty will become The City fad when the war's over."

Fidgeting with anxiety, MARGIE is upset over DAY's lack of attention as he follows TINA's every move. When they all

pause to reflect and simultaneously take a
drink, DAY follows but enveloped with his
own vision, he pours himself another
whiskey just a half beat late.

"I would say it has fallen to the
Chinese community to hold the city
together." WON offers solace, followed by
this insight. "PRESCOTT has not always
told me everything."

"He has often tried to mislead you,
father," TINA says.

"He's never led me." Her father
says, hefting his pride. "He might be
pointing the finger, and it might be that
he is after the 'rain on the grown tea'
that serves weight to his own interests.
He never tells me anything but what leaves
me to think and this time ... He said
'Frenchie Joe is not French.'"

They pause while DON WON reflects.

"We have the Chinese community," WON
thinks out of his mouth. "The investment
community and the Italians somehow held
together

by one piece of paste. Hummm. There
seems to be an odd Irishman in this
triangle. The stage is set, but who will
seduce the manager? Who is the manager?
What is the value in all of this?" TINA
gives it a try.

"Paste?! Johnnie Mally runs the
Italian mob ..."

DAY wakes up. "Fudge! Did you say,
Frenchie Joe?"

DAY seems foggy from his sudden
returned taste for liquor.

"Hold the line. I know him from

Saint 'I.' High. He's no more than a
cowboy, old San Francisco, Barbary Coast
family, Frenches Bank."

DAY leans back, satisfied with
himself, and passes out.

"Ah, so. Money and school ties,
both." WON takes over the lead. "We go to
Parlor of Chen. Tell everybody that we
know what is missing and there is a reward
for 'the properties;' and we see what comes
to play on stage. Who manages guns, books,
or little girls' sparkling things. Take
the powder out of this play and find some
actor with a smoking gun."

TINA hedges, looks over at Day. "Day
is out."

"It's night." Says MARGIE looking
out the window.

Just before they all leave, TINA
notices DAY having passed out, is about to
drop the glass he is holding. She reacts
quickly and catches it, fondly looks back
at him. He sleeps now, passed out in the
chair with his clothes on including the
overcoat.

They leave a light on in the office
and exit into the night. WON, TINA and
MARGIE who hang together going out the door
as if in a line for the school recess.
They go to Chen's.

Time passes. Inside DON WON'S
office, late night, DAY wakes up alone. He
picks up the phone, makes a call.

DAY speaks into the phone. "Penny.
You got any new info on Davidal? I'll
trade it for your pasted sapphire. I mean
Info. From behind your back."

CHAPTER 15

Suddenly, Day in his car pulls up to a curbside front of a dark Cow Hollow town house. Trick of the night! By DAY.

At the moment DAY pulls up to the curb, he shuts off the car engine and cuts his headlights. The door to what is revealed as Penny's house, opens. The black-out night exposes the street, darkness broken by inside light.

Standing inside the foyer, crowned by electric gaslight style globes, PENNY dressed in a satin robe faces a MAN softly talking to her at the stoop, which forces her to stand close to him. He gestures with emphatic implications. Smug, she only listens.

As he turns the light falls onto his face to reveal it is . . . SOL DAVIDAL. As he leaves . . .

. . . DAY quickly slumps down to hide below the car window to feign sleep as a shadow figure, waits as . . .

. . . SOL gets into his car and tunes in the radio.

Then, a moment as the MUSIC builds to a swing number SOL drives away with a clarinet and a saxophone dueling against a big band in musical triumph.

DAY exits his car and goes to the door of the house. Muted from inside the house on a seemingly large radio console, the same music fades but not out.

Penny's apartment sprawls with a lavish deco style interior, same radio music continues from the street and draws the socially clandestine outside scene inside.   Soft lights dangerously spill onto the curfew enforced street.

Inside, DAY is perked by the lavender sent.

"Come to pick up the lady.   Ready?"

"Oh you timed it right on the minute."   PENNY says with languid sensuality.   "Just let me put on some perfume and throw on a dress."

"Yeah, powder.   Forget the dress."

As she swings through the house, the flair of her silk Pajamas suddenly makes her disarray look formal.

"Do you know what you're doing?"

She tosses on a mink jacket that formalizes her get-up and justifies gutter-brain actions by gathering things to go into a small clutch-bag.

"I thought you knew a lot."   PENNY taunts him.   "You came to tell me, remember?"

She's barely awake after the end of sexual recreation and the preparation of stepping out.   Casually formal she shows lots 'a

flesh' to — DAY, who stands there as though be doesn't notice.

PENNY from out of her back room into the light, takes only a short look at him weaving and, she confident, believes he is too dazed to understand what he just witnessed.   Her with DAVIDAL.

She stands at the car, now outside, turns to him.

PENNY has come to her senses.   "Can you see well enough to drive?" "I can drive to China, the way I can see."   DAY sustains

with insight. "How 'bout you? You
satisfied, rested?"

She remains standing by the car door
for him to open it up.

PENNY becomes restless. "Then you
can pick up Marisa. She'll join us to
Chen's."

"Of course. Marisa Davidal, to
Chen's."

They drive off in the car.

The car cuts through the fog DAY
asks, "Didn't she go to Paris?" PENNY says
clearly though the fog, "Just got back.
Hang on to that info. We'll talk on it
later."

Parked in front of the Davidal
Pacific St. Apartment. Through the dark
night, PENNY, nervously fidgets. She
waits, looks up at the apartment and
without words she asks for a cigarette.

DAY hands her the cigarette.

DAY seems puzzled. "What is it with
you? What are you willing?"

"I'm on fire."

"First you wait, now you can't sit."

"I'll go up there." PENNY remains
seated, unlit cigarette poised. "I'm so
hot."

She looks over to him for a light,
but starts to exit the car before he can
respond.

"I'll go. No," she pauses. "I'll
stay."

DAY slowly fumbles for his lighter.
He looks at her with controlled lust.
"Don't tell, somebody's daddy didn't finish
the job."

PENNY ignores his crass remark.
"I'll go." She's restless.

"I'm on fire ... gimme a light."

Too impatient and without the light,
she's out the door and up the apartment
steps.

In seconds they come down together.

MARISA the gorgeous brunette and
PENNY a Jean Harlow blonde.

"I just had it on, just after
returning from Italy." MARISA concerned,
about having lost something. "And, that
was just last week."

"You have a lock on?" PENNY knows
what happened to the necklace. "Just got
back from Paris. What was the occasion
last before you left, Dinner with Chen?"

DAY perks up. CHEN with MARISSA
DAVIDAL.

MARISA reveals another tumbler in the
lock.

"Yeah, with Chen. I wore the black,
crepe draped Spanish dress. It was my
father's Opera night. He's never there.
He wouldn't miss me. I had the sapphire
necklace on that night. The night of the
Opera."

"I thought you only wore the sapphire
with that satin dress you wear with your
Chinese friends." PENNY has no trouble
forcing sincerity.

DAY adjusts the rear view mirror to
eye them in the back seat. "It's so
decadent." DAY says to himself.

MARISA DAVIDAL elongated in the car,
a white powdered face like a porcelain doll
PENNY a gold lame show stopper, gives DAY

'knife blade looks.'

"In to Paris and out again. During a war, I mean." DAY justifies his words.

PENNY says, back to her girl friend, "Maybe you lent it out?" DON mutters, offers MARISA something from a silver flask. MARISA takes it and says to Penny, "Is he alright?"

"He's blind ... quite handy." And, PENNY takes the flask.

His car slithers through the dark city under curfew into the Jackson Heights area.

PENNY coaches him. "Donald. Would you mind taking a right up there."

MARISA's thoughts are elsewhere.

"Shit!" MARISA says from out of the blue.

"Thinking about the sapphire necklace." DAY mutters.

PENNY says, "We looked all over." PENNY sits, uncommonly quiet.

The awkward silence breaks as she fishes in her small handbag for a 'stick' and the girls share it.

PENNY leans over to push DAY to go faster, to "get going, right, now."

The gambling parlor is hot inside.

When DAY arrives behind the girls, after parking the car, he finds MARGIE with the OTHER GIRLS in tow.

The crowd parts and the two women enter still smoking 'sticks.' Boozed, DAY pockets PENNY's flask.

DAY comments, much less woozy than he appears, "Marisa, over there, can't find her sapphire necklace. She may need help.

One of her boy friends saw it. Chen's favorite."

He looks into MARGIE's face. She looks back. Together they know something. They now know DAVIDAL took the necklace from his daughter, for sure. They see that PENNY is chummy with MARISA DAVIDAL, but has no idea that she corresponds with SOL.

"Wasn't Penny here when he played the necklace into the game?" DAY hides things. "Penny's playing dumb."

MARGIE is too honest to play hide and seek with facts.

"Yeah? Well, if I can help myself I'm always willing. Funny, no one wants to remember that night."

She looks across the room at MARISA.

"What are you willing, Don?" She asks.

"Sheeez!" Day acts awed. "She just got back from Paris, modeling. Can you believe it? I'm willing to call her a model ... citizen."

"Put that off." MARGIE says, "She looks like a Victim, to me." Mildly disgusted, she gets up off the stool by the vacant Gai Pai table, walks away from the GIRLS sharing a smoke.

MARGIE senses separation from DAY, she's upset. "Please! You gals all trying to slide the law? It's all who's who, here."

DAY appears at her side, Pulls her toward the big game.

"Come on by me, Margie." DAY grabs her. "They don't know who's what ... over here and help."

"I always told Penny, she needed help."

DAY to Marisa, "I told her you lost a necklace. She's a detective."

MARGIE covers modestly, "Well I work for one. I always wanted to be a model, though."

"Oh, you should be." MARISA says, "You're beautiful."

PETER comes up to MARISA's side and whispers something that makes her laugh. He interrupts her with MARGIE and MARISA goes off to gamble with him.

Watching his club, seeing WON and TINA circulate; and now MARGIE with DAY and MARISA, CHEN becomes more interactive with the club activity.

MARGIE says to DAY, "She doesn't seem too broken up about it." As the group now dispersed, it's CHEN who follows after MARISA and DAVID slides next to MARGIE, DAY follows.

"You sure know how." DAY says with DAVID in mind. "In this city (sarcastic) ... Everything that's going on."

DAVID sights in on TINA.

"That's a real China Doll. What's her name, Tina? Her father's
a real smart guy."

"Shoot it to her. She loves guns." DAY is in a sarcastic mood. MARGIE becomes caustic. "Why do we hang around this crooked Chinese 'pit.' Look," and she points to the Baccarat table.

"Davidal versus Deuitch, again."

"Right." DAY says. "Same boat and no new fish. Word's out, now about the

switch, so come on Margie, let's cut.
Izzy's Speak' on Jackson where it's
straight."

To avoid the tension building up at
the table, DAY quickly grabs her arm and
sweeps her away. He's stopped by a
BECKONING BARTENDER with a phone, call for
him.

The group splits up as PETER goes to
talk to DAVID. The all-alone, MARGIE sees
CHEN left standing next to MARISA.

"These Chinese don't know the power."
DAVID tells no one in the crowd. "There's
no gamble in 'war toys,' so I guess Chinese
play Davidal and Deuitch for sport. Funny,
no one else can profit more by trying to
get in through the basement."

CHEN hears him, and his face grows
stern.

PETER says, "At least we have a war."
And CHEN curls his lip.

The men disperse toward the big
Baccarat table past stoic, MARISA, who
turns to the gentle, stiff lipped CHEN.

"I love to wonder about the
mysterious Chinese." MARISA remarks. DAVID
shuffles back and Hovers near MARISA, CHEN
notices DAVID, and modestly looks down at
chips in his hand.

DAVID digs his grave deeper.

"The Chinese are such good book
keepers. I mean the way you're taking care
of accounts, and all. With the war, I
guess, ... the close proximity of fighting
to San Francisco, I mean. The gaming runs
high. With the Japanese in Long Beach . .
. they say."

MARISA tries to yank CHEN out of his
building rage.

"Look-it," she says. "I was just _in_
Europe; and that's far away." She hugs him
close. "They don't know."

Silently CHEN muses, the naive DAVID
plies a place at one of the tables.

DAVID tries to dig himself out.

"I mean Japan. Fighting in China."

And Chen coaxes a suddenly
sympathetic MARISA away. She stays back
and watches CHEN, her eyes glued onto him.
But she never follows him as he wanted.

All three stay together, and meander
to a roulette table. They play, randomly
throwing chips onto the table. Back by the
bar, DAY pulls MARGIE up close and whispers
something that stiffens her back with
suppressed glee. "Stay shut-up." DAY
whispers.

DAVID keeps plying Marisa. "What do
you know from Paris? Me being far away, I
mean. Marisa, during the occupation?"

"Most times, I don't know from
nothin'." MARISA says. She means him.

MARISA slides near the bar, to get
another drink, and in time to try and
overhear . . . .

Ambling in the group DAY and MARGIE,
who would rather not talk, cross over to
the roulette table. Reluctantly DAY let's
go of her arm so she can go to the Ladies
Room.

Like stacking a deck of cards, DAY
and his young boyfriends shuffle to another
table, avoid heavy "man talk," they see
CHEN nearby mostly eavesdropping. MARISA

falls into step with a fresh cocktail in hand.

"What you did in Paris," MARGIE asks, "Did it work? Get a lot done?"

Since MARGIE knows with MARISA what she was doing in Paris to save the Jewish families they move about like best friends.

At the bar with the boys, DAY stays on his case, and puts out a question. "There's a lot of action in this city. David, what do you know about big '45s?"

DAVID forever the wise guy, responds, "Are you asking me about strippers or guns?"

The boys laugh. CHEN leaves to put more distance between them in order to oversee other games. Looking to the side, he watches MARGIE and MARISA amble into the ladies room.

DAY, sarcastic, "Don't worry, the war's still 'over there.'" PETER seems to want to unload something, and he says, "Some of the 'collector's items' got out and with War blood still all over 'em -- our blood. Don't you read the papers?" He points with his thumb cocked at DAY.

"It's a big threat," PETER continues, "like it's coming over here. Right, Jack? Hitlerites are like cockroaches, and they'll keep coming back."

DAY watches MARISA, sway and support slightly crooked European black-market seamed silk stockings, as she returns to the big game tables with MARGIE following a few steps behind.

She follows just far enough to watch what attraction MARISA causes in the room.

The usual, and not much more from foreign visitors like MALLY.

DAVID, whose eyes bulge out. "You guys ever see anything like Davidal's accounts. Like one of those Colt 45 automatics. It's a big format, a threat just looking at it. Even a little guy holding one of those grows ten times. War's closing in on all levels." He looks hard at Day. "Think about that when you do your editorial, Day." He takes a swig, "It could all come down in some alley in The City. One shot. Boom!"

DAY returns his attention to his two rich friends.

"I hope they're watchin' you arms dealers."

"Hold on now." PETER says, "Did you see that erotic China doll that was in with her father? Now, there's a format, I'd want to watch."

DAY remains aloof, and MARGIE reappears, signals to leave.

DAY turns to PETER, "Talk to her about guns." Although standing close, DAY retains a distant intimacy, and as DAY, returns MARGIE's head gestures and winks a 'no.' He continues, "She loves guns, I tell you."

DAY signals to MARGIE 'not yet.' She sidles off to find MARISA and PENNY to start some trouble with them.

DAY and PETER sit at a low table with a pair of drinks served in front of them. The waiter leaves them with heavy smoky silence anticipated to be meaningfully broken as DAVID hangs back to overlook the room.

"So now What?" DAY continues, seated
though unsettled, "What! We're sittin'
here smokin' cigarettes and suckin' up the
juice for what? Spill!"

"We wouldn't know who would buy those
kinds of guns locally." PETER tries to
worm out of a confession, "Italian
gangsters in this city would bring a
'piece' in from Chicago, or Detroit.
Smith and Wesson, mostly."

"Forty-fives', Big format, huh?" DAY
keeps plying, "Banks can also get frozen
with Sol's size money. Makes 'em
'Pixelated.'
That it?!"

Silence. PETER strokes his chin for
a moment before he answers, and DAY has a
chance to finish his drink, but instead he
pushes the glass aside.

"No! There's more things to get into
here, in the 'every growing' City, in these
times." PETER holds his ground like a
child trying to act like an adult. "The
Italian's are trying to stretch from the
Asians."

DAY won't buy into that. "That's not
it. Give it up."

PETER tips in, no patience. "Okay,
so I'm in with Sol and his investors. New
York style. Real Estate's soft and our
money could help the cause, you know?
We're not bullet pushing criminals."

"Hard to tell, the way Sol treats
Curtis." DAY remains quietly disgusted.
"You guys are holding out."

"There's this game, called the

mistress slide." PETER finally has a
chance to unveil something. "The 'Big
Cheese; plays his mouse on the chutes and
ladders. She can steal but she just can't
rob." He snickers obnoxiously. "A crooked
skid from the 'heights.' While we're
playing out some sure thing money, and
control turns to manipulation. It's a mean
street, I'll tell you. No love at home and
it isn't about money. Lust for sex, sex
for baubles, a likely scenario for the
eternal . . . life or death struggle."

"Sounds like 'Allies and Assholes' to
me." DAY, defensive because he believes
PETER is talking about PENNY. "You two
both in on what's goin' on? It seems like
the war is a gentle bust." "Don't tell the
world, reporter, the war is about power."
PETER gets back on his own podium.
"According to Davidal, it's service for the
rich to stay that way. The bust? That's a
role for Marisa Davidal. She goes with a
Chink."

"At the same time she's in Paris to
save the Jews."

"You know that?" DAY reacts with
disdain to the inference about Chen. "You
into the Davidal deals? Like the one with
the Trotskiites, Peter?"

PETER takes a drink and taps DAY'S
glass, admitting to nothing, asking if he
wants another.

"What brings you to know about Penny
laying out for Sol and Davidal's daughter's
act in the basement?" DAY has the opening
and lances into it. "Know nothin' else?"

PETER shows he's effected by not

being affected.

    "Make no mistake. Penny can't rob.
We think it's just 'too

    much' to be playing with his
mistress' jewels in a Chinese gambling
parlor. What's that make the odds?
Between Davidal and his daughter. Chen
masters a real game of chance."

    He talked too much, as DAY makes that
mental note.

    DAY'S lost in thought, his drink half
way to his mouth before he puts it down in
disgust.

    PETER whacks his own drink down with
a smile and desire to put it all away,
before DAY pushes his chair back to take
off.

    "Funny thought." He gets up to leave
PETER in a mire of his own sweat. "Seems
like a small price to pay for a Jewish man
to let a Chinaman in. You in on it David?"

    Shocked, PETER stiffens looking up at
DAVID who looms overhead. DAVID sits down.
"I'm for freedom, baby!" He looks up with
open eyes. "For all. No restrictions,
palsy walsey."

    DAY remains on track. "We been
talking about the class of people buying
into some bigger 'dealie-bob' than 45's."

    DAVID seems to take the chance to
relieve himself. "If you think it's a
'big-wiz' crime to deal guns these days,
it'd be a crime just trying to find anybody
doing it illegally in this crowd. We
support the war, big time. No one's down
on munitions contractors in the City.
Here, the Nay's on the streets, the Army in

every bar ... all the uniforms with hardly
a man in this 'town' who's not connected
with guns, Don."

But, DAVID casts a reproachful eye.

"I know. I'm on the street." DAY
says, and MARGIE approaches and brightens
Day up. Come on. "I got the line on an
important suicide."

"Somethin's crackin' up in Berlin,
they say," says DAY as he

leaves with MARGIE on his arm.

They leave everybody behind with a
budding curiosity, overpowered by their own
morosity. To amuse MARGIE, DAY twists and
contorts his face.

MARGIE says into Day's eyes, "I don't
care what they say, I think your face is
cute. That the phone call, Don?"

"Them's always they what got no
taste." And, DAY looks back at the table
he left.

Behind a the small table, PETER
softly calls out to his friend. "Hey,
David. If you're into Sol's big project,
put your money on the table."

"Convince me that it's a good play,"
DAVID responds, "and convince me that the
war is almost over."

Both DAVID and PETER look hard at
each other, knowing something the other one
hopes he doesn't.

Slowly, with determination DAVID puts
his money on the table for the drinks.

PENNY approaches, looks down at the
two scoundrels.

DAVID, looking up at the not so daffy
blond, "Give up any keys, yet Penny?"

PENNY returns the look with fear on
her face.

Far from abandoning the general
cause, DAY, inside his car continues his
intent with his small, but most important
constituency, MARGIE. DAY sits, gloating
over something, keys in hand, inches from
the starter key hole.

DAY, paused and non-plused says,
"Suddenly, there's a hook for my story,
Margie. Who else hugs enough control over
the Manhattan project?" DAY is looking up
at the starry sky through San Francisco
slotted canyon, low city walls. "Contracts
big as God?" He looks at her bewildered
face. "Got the phone call. Berlin's
fallen. Hitler committed suicide."

Both sit mouth poised for a quip that
never comes.

DAY says softly, "War's over."

They kiss. Hard and longer than
typical.

He starts the car.

Bubbling with excitement, MARGIE
starts to unravel.

"Did I tell you Davidal threatened
me. Told me to keep away

from it, Don. Or, he'd make me a
skid on his slide."

"<u>Nothin'</u> personal, honey." DAY has
his headline, so what does he care for
anything else.

"WAR'S OVER! Though, there's still
Japan, they invaded China. Chen's still in
this. I mean, there's big money on his
ledgers.

I think he's only ... not the

'wiz-bang' gentleman in that club that we
see him to be. The more I get in the know,
I don't believe these guys."

She feels shattered, he's hyper and
that leaves her alone on the passenger side
of his car while he drives. DAY has a date
with his story. She's threatened to her
life. Now he wants the headline in red.

"What's it mean?" MARGIE searches
for her clues. "His slide?"

"A skid ..." DAY tells. "It's a girl
... someone Who's stopped your life.
Slide's the Life . . . like with chutes 'n
ladders.

"I'm through ... being a drunk." Day
continues with a sort of resolve. His
character has taken a change, though even
he knows nothing about what might come of
it. "This is big. The WAR's FUCKIN' over.
Now I got what's maybe a Jewish spy ring
story with what I get out of Washington
Davidal's exposed with his ass in a sling
by his own syndicate."

DAY is intense as he drives,-

The clacking keys of his typewriter
resound first in his head, from the
immediate future. He's a hack against the
dark night that rolls past outside his car
and that leaves MARGIE against the cold
window on the dark passenger side with her
own now empty plan.

CHAPTER 16

DAY has the story in his mind, and the clakity clack merely transfers to the action of moving his mind into print once he finally sits in his office.

"... now one Jewish family in New York ties up the war sentiments, and investments continue from San Francisco. East Coast Trotskiites exposed by San Francisco founding father's patriotism.

"With West Coast money pouring into frozen, hungry Russia and more money pledged at war's end, it is rumored American finance could energize allied troops on exit from the European theater.

"While at Potsdam, Stalin said a New York source, gave them American plans to develop an atom bomb as the give-away project for ordinance. Peace it seems is funded by War Incorporated West.

"East Coast Trotskiites could continue their protest, while sentiments in the government along with San Francisco investments support starving Russia and offer substance for a pressing end run that expects to halt the Japanese oppressors and to bring an end to war in both theaters.

"Entrepreneurs everyone, now dedicated to end the war. China has won our sentiments, as the Pacific Islands' war continues with growing optimism for a close well in sight."

The story writes itself in the news room out of his thoughts from the car, as DAY remains proud of himself for taking the secret of Hitler's suicide all the way to the office. He turns to MARGIE who looks distraught for she has no idea what he wrote, or what sentiments he sacrificed to bring the recall up and closer to print.

Suddenly, inside the news room V.E. Day -- Armistice with Germany, surrender May 7 1945 -- gives the newspaper activity that includes the whole staff, day and night shifts. Ecstatic, they all appear to become part of the grand finale.

A veritable conglomerate of fancy dressed society editors and their tipsters gossiping while typists type. Several men with blunt brimmed hats sit typing away. Collaborations between young and old, men and women typing away. The end of the war causes everybody to want to finish whatever they had going, and they want to start a new world. Each and every newspaperman and woman in the city seems to be at their desk typing away.

Day and Night, outside, inside East Coast West Coast as military officers, enlisted and the whole city population bursts in celebration.

DAY with MARGIE sitting on the edge, corner of his desk, in the news room, her legs crossed, and she filing her nails, as he's writing a story on his Underwood.

DAY talks while he writes, mostly to entertain MARGIE, so she will want to stay with him.

"Allied Liberation armies on the Russian front today pressed toward North-East Germany to see what had been rumored as concentration camps."
Typewriter clacking continues non stop, and DAY writes and talks. "Poles,

Czechoslovakians, Jews with relatives from all over Eastern Europe are on the edge of despair with an invested interest in these first days after the fall of Berlin."

In physical disarray, now DAY still in his tuxedo looks up, but keeps on writing.

"What does Won say?" DAY asks and keeps on clacking. Frustration builds as he digs for more details with his eyes, MARGIE, herself somehow refreshed simply looks at him. She knows he searches for the words, so she stops with her telling of self pity in spite of himself, who wants to know more.

DAY, who wants it all at once. Given a little of the big pie, he wants all the crumbs, too.

"The one about Davidal's deal ... sapphire was paste?"

And, MARGIE acknowledges him with the motion of her leg over the edge of the desk.

"This deal got both Peter and David riled ..." DAY continues, "the one card they played. Come on, Margie. The necklace! What'd I miss? What's the price of a necklace in a Chinese game of baccarat with these big blow-hards."

"I just like watchin' you and listening to you go on." MARGIE says with the dumb look on her face.

He smiles into her coy, sexy smirk. She files on her nails, re-crosses her legs.

DAY looks her up and down.

"You were right about wasting your

legs. There's the crime." The phone rings.
DAY picks it up. Passes it to MARGIE.

"It's Marisa. Remember the model who
came the other night --from Paris -- with
Penny?"

Oblique to his bombardment, MARGIE
answers the phone.

"Hello? You found out?" She
listens, "Yes War's Over. Don got the
call at Chen's. Sure, armistice party'd be
fun. Where?"

Day motions for it to be 'here.'

He sweeps his arm for her to look
around, the staff, their informants, their
friends; a melee in the middle of work and
happiness.

"What about you all coming over here?
To the newspaper."

The news room at the San Francisco
Chronicle is an all open single floor in a
south of Market stone brick building. Dark
wood floors and no barriers with open beam
ceiling to the effect that forced air ducts
and wiring to hang exposed. While there
are no spider webs, little dust in hard to
reach places, the ashtrays overflow and
sometimes the air hangs so thick it makes
privacy a given.

DAY chops away at the keyboard,
working on his stories.

COPYBOYS come and go to take away his
pages.

MARGIE keeps the tulip phone in her
hand, she pushes the lever to hang up, and
she says, "You said Marisa told you
something about

her necklace. You can ask <u>her</u> when

she gets here. We saw a necklace that
night, not a sapphire ... the game got
busted over diamonds. Davidal's rage,
remember?

     "First the gambling table, then on
the singer, finally in or out of Chen's
safe."

     "I was comin' through the alley.
Ring a bell?" DAY says and he points to
the typewriter. "War's over. That's hot.

     "And Marisa will be happy to learn of
the camps and the liberation of Jews,
Poles, collaborators . . . " He pauses,
"sadly mostly Jews. Fact Jack, no longer
just rumors."

     With a memory of the alley all his
own, MARGIE, ignorantly gets on the phone
shakes her head "no." DAY picks up the
other ringing phone.

     "Yes," she says into the phone.
"Rumors debunked. You did it, honey.
American Army're heroes to everybody."

     Phone piece on the desk, into the
speaker on the stand and DAY typing, hot on
his story, upset for having been
interrupted.

     "Yeah, Penny. Party here."

     Enveloping into his own work, his own
world begins to fold in on him. His world
and the real world have always been the
reporters' notebook. Now, it happens to
fall on the end of the World War, and for
DAY the numerous secretes begin to
overwhelm him while friends call in for the
social agenda.

     He hangs up and resumes typing.
MARGIE on the phone to WON.

MARGIE remarks into the phone. "It looks like a party <u>here</u>. Everything's comin' clean. We gave up the dope on a floating sapphire, so that could come out, too."

"Hi Tina." DAY on the phone again. "Yeah, she's here talking to your dad and everybody else in town."

MARGIE says, covering the mouthpiece in spite, to Day. "Don said a party might work to our advantage."

DAY back on <u>his</u> phone, says, "You come over. Seems like we might have the whole gang here in the light."

He resumes typing. MARGIE continues on the phone with WON.

DAY picks up the 2nd phone again, and talks. "Yes, Lieutenant. It might help for an Irish cop to come on over to the paper and manage the excitement. Silk stockings are gonna' show. By the way, I need that detail from your man in Washington. And, for you ... " He looks up to see Margie agree. "A Chinese clue might be here."

Just when DAY hangs up . . .

PAUL DEYOUNG, the newspaper's third generation publisher, also dressed in a Tuxedo, like DAY but fresh, comes up to the desk with some of DAY's pages in hand. His exasperated tone is modified by the sight of MARGIE sitting cross legged on top of the desk.

At seeing him, she brightens.

This newspaper publisher has made lots of money. A graduate of Towne School, a rich family gentleman's school of

extremely high college preparatory
reputation in the heart of The City, he
came from a family of money in the paper
business. He bought the newspaper out of
crisis and took the San Francisco Chronicle
to battle the Hearts' empire and the
Examiner. More than a social butterfly,
but a guy with a handsome square jaw whose
dedication to business pushed aside any and
all women friends. While the gals come for
his money and companionship, they leave
when the idea of something long term forces
them to see his absolute passion. None of
the women in his life have ever been
anything but privileged. None of the women
PAUL DEYOUNG takes out ever supported
themselves. To call them working girls
might confuse them with another sort, and
to call them all gold diggers would
discount the fact that most have their own
fortunes. PAUL is a dedicated news hound
who happens to own he keys to the whole
newspaper game for the upper crust of San
Francisco.

This member of the San Francisco
gentry has a good grip on what developments
make New Mexico the center of the Manhattan
Project. PAUL DEYOUNG knows that the
United States of America has plans for an
atomic bomb, because his family donates
tons of money to both the university and
the foundation by which Dr. Edward Teller
and J. Robert Openheimer completed research
on the fission theory. PAUL is a peer
amongst less than a dozen who know all
about the A-BOMB, but none but the
President of the United States is yet to

know what or when it will be used.

This one guy wants the American people to know all about it, but he has no idea of the treasonous shenanigans that have gone into motion about the plans for the bomb to end all world wars forever.

PAUL says, "Get onto the story of surrender, Day. And this Manhattan scandal you're preoccupied with has to be 'cracker jack' writing. But put it on a back burner before it burns the paper."

He turns to Margie. "Hello!"

"It was just notes you got." DAY justifies his writing.

"Margie, Paul deYoung, the publisher." He turns to Paul, "Margie, my girl of the hour, or off hours ..."

The sparks from that introduction are oblivious to all but MARGIE who cannot see how obvious she shows her romantic interest, and somewhat in surprise to PAUL. The reporter, DAY has tuned in to the end of the war in Europe, and that means more than enough 'noughness. The possible end of his romance evades him.

The second phone rings again, and MARGIE already listening to . . .

WON on one line, has only two hands for one phone. So DAY points
     at PAUL to pick it up.

PAUL takes the cue, "Yeah. I'm a friend of Don Day's. You're
     David? He's ..."

Hearing it from both sides, he stands paused; the girl on a phone next to him, and the guy on the phone in his hand. PAUL gets the point that he became the host to

an end of the war party he gets to agree to
invite the entire city of Gadabouts.

MARGIE goes on about the kindly host
PAUL the Publisher over the phone to WON.
PAUL gushes as he looks upon her, legs
dangling over the side of the desk and
skirt rising higher with every swing of her
knee. She has become as much an
advertisement for Hanes stockings with the
embroidered label showing against her pale
while thighs, as she is a flirt.

Meanwhile the other, third phone
rings as Paul, a guy used to composing
engraved invitations, AD LIBs an invitation
and hangs up with a blush on his face. DAY
only takes a second to look up from his
typing and motions again for PAUL to field
the call.

PAUL signs and with reluctance picks
up.

"Yes. I hear there is going to be a
party here? You can bring whomever you
wish. Uh, who are ... ?" He assumes his
position, "Oh, you mean who am I?" and
sternly affirmative remarks, "Yeah, I'm
sure it'll be alright."

He fields telephone calls all glib, a
new commanding personae giving way to
humble quests for the party gathering at
the paper. When the City Ed Scott Newhall
enters, he tunes in to the publishers' new
role, while never giving up his own onus of
responsibility.

"Day." City Ed Scott Newhall retains
control of the moment, "Refine these notes.
Looks like you finally got deYoung to work.

Be careful of the redlined stock it

might get us into trouble.

Our man Palomares did some leg work in Washington, so work that

in." He shuffles some of the papers in his hand. "Get me a story on Chinese gangs. Side bar on your robbery." Affirmative, he plops the pages onto Day's desk.

"And, this is a 'bio' on a San Francisco Chinese boy who's in Germany. Do another surrender side bar with him. We'll run the 'gang thing' on page three. Side bar on page two. Shit! We work our asses on local crime and the end of the war steals Page One."

"You said you'd give me the headlines in Red," Day says, as he tries to seize the moment.

PAUL defends his Editor, says "There's still Japan."

They both pause for a stare at -- PAUL who is on the phone talking to a woman, and MARGIE on the desk catches another ring.

That comment echoed through the huge news room and for a split second all typing, all breathing stopped and the sun shifted into dawn, or the lights spiked on a new electric spark. It seemed the whole world changed light bulbs.

City Ed Scott Newhall turns to PAUL, and head fakes toward DAY. "Looks like we got him where we want him. Now, Port Chicago explosion, munitions scandal like you thought. Facts still hidden about those 350 dead negro boys since 1941; and it's the end of the war, already." To Paul again, "He's right on top with it, prejudice, rumor and innuendo."

"What a cracker-jack."

The Port Chicago story was forced, glossed over about a weapons explosion in Oakland's Port Chicago where an all Negro enlisted men work force were killed, wiped out just before the war's end.

The conspiracy theorists have never stopped making up a story of prejudice and murder, but the real crime was the lack of investigation. Accusations fly in the face of no answers, found or sought, at those dockside bosses and superior officers who stood watch when the failure to save the dock or the shipment took prescient to any investigation over the loss of human lives.

"The Port Chicago deaths of Negro dock workers will remain a black hole in the west coast history of and beyond the end of World War II." Time taken to fill in the rarely seen publisher, DAY sketches his follow up assignment.

"The remains of almost 360 U.S. Navy and Merchant Marine workers were non existent, blew up, even the two ships involved were almost dissolved." NEWHALL adds, "Nearly 250 of the men were Negro and a few who survived were later tried for mutiny having refused to continue work and load munitions under proven unsafe conditions.

"Details over convictions, prejudice, slanted values over lives lost and accusations," NEWHALL justifies his reputation as one of a serious kind of editor.

Convictions made were only resolved by the end of the war, when the US Navy integrated.

Back at the pronouncement of Victory in Europe, PAUL ever with serious intent to match point, says quickly to the City Ed SCOTT NEWHALL, "There's still Japan."

Beating up his star editor, the publisher keeps even the City Ed SCOTT NEWHALL on track with super quick, low hype glib comment.

MARGIE watches the scene unfold, breathing into the phone while eyeing PAUL. "In the end it'd be best if you could come over here." She hangs up and DAY's busy hacking away at the typewriter, PAUL tries to catch up on a pleasant conversation with the very receptive MARGIE but the phone distracts him.

The incongruity of a dedicated news junkie, in a news room, at the end of the big war trying to flirt with a pretty girl who may be somebody else's girlfriend causes a jerk in time. Something moved in the ethers of human ties, when all of humanity is joined in a kingdom on earth and one of the pawns may be struck by cupid, that causes a quake. It happened here in The City. At the end of a war.

DAY stands up, casts a defiant look upon MARGIE as he pulls the just completed pages from his typewriter bale, and takes them to the City Ed SCOTT NEWHALL only to return to see MARGIE, breasts threatening to fall out of her blouse, who leans against the desk fondly listens to PAUL, her eyes glued to his mouth.

Edgy and beckoning her, DAY stands to show her the article and hovers closely over her shoulder to watch as she remains cold to him, reads and looks back. MARGIE has become no more than patronizing, hands the pages back. Apparently PAUL offers more than DAY. A new path through life at the end of a war.

PAUL off the phone, again, and DAY passes him three stories; and quick, it pacifies the CHIEF, who hovers in the background, behind the publisher. PAUL is temporarily diverted from MARGIE by the news. Fresh pages in his hand. This is why he owns it. Hot pages anytime he wants.

Spoiled child MARGIE, slighted at playing second fiddle to the news in a newspaper office, takes out her compact and lipstick, and she plays on herself instead of talking to DAY.

The personal forays in these small battles of interplay on the floor of the San Francisco Chronicle is on going, and nothing less dramatic continues than those Ak-Ak Guns, machine gun nests, charging grenade throwers, dive bombers, line up of charging tanks that had finally stopped. DAY lights a cigarette, and begins typing.

Again, MARGIE calls TINA and urges her to encourage WON to come over to the newspaper, to celebrate with her and the gang.

DAY stands up after a marathon of typing and smiles at her. MARGIE, still not more than patronizing, eyes the arriving crowd, some of the staff from

Chen's carrying bottles of booze that are
passed all around.

The crowd builds, comments and
COPYBOYS interrupt DAY's writing.

Not used to these gadabouts at party
pace, PAUL, exhausted, remarks into the
phone, "I'm looking forward to meeting You,
too, Marisa." He hangs up, says to Day
"Who's she?"

"It's someone you'd really want to
know." DAY says with false enthusiasm.
"Her daddy just bought Manhattan, or
something. From the Rosenberg's."

Not quite so DAY could hear,
"Davidal's daughter?!!"

Enter City Ed SCOTT NEWHALL. Just in
time, as PAUL's contemplating the
situation, glaring at wise-ass DAY.

City Ed SCOTT NEWHALL tries to induce
MARGIE. "Use your influence and get DAY
into the story about Chinese teen gangs.
Sew up loose ends."

DAY overhears. "Yeah? About my big
boom-boom, it's all over town. Now their
calling the A-Bomb a tip at Potsdam, a lead
into a spy ring story and it's a diplomatic
give-away. There's a glowing ember of
public interest in the atomic bomb."

"It's going public?" deYoung remarks
softly, "Some kid of a Jewish conspiracy."
Loud enough, "Gossip."

City Ed SCOTT NEWHALL turns to PAUL
and says, "He thinks he's got the story on
the sale of enough bomb power to stop the
war with Japan."

PAUL has now dedicated his interest,
here.

"It comes from John Law, now." Day realizes how silly that sounded after it left his mouth.

Enter DON WON and his gorgeous daughter TINA. The normally serious City Ed SCOTT NEWHALL almost drops his jaw over the presence of this exotic Chinese girl.

DAY looks up, "Good timing." He turns to the City Ed NEWHALL, "That Tong War. Feature story? It's Here. And it's got long legs wearing a high slit dress."

Somewhat distracted COPYBOYS pass news as it comes in off the teletype about the Armistice. Multiple releases, World Wide press.

Lot of COPYBOYS' activity takes City Ed NEWHALL's attention away from the glamour build around DAY's desk.

Like a bottle of syrup spilt at DAY's desk, the social regalia oozes through-out the news room floor in the form of beautifully dressed and gorgeous girls and boys drunk but still in control.

PAUL moves close to, but carefully not touching MARGIE. He whispers something personal that makes her smile, look skeptically at --DAY who tries not to notice, while he busies himself typing the story. The City Ed SCOTT NEWHALL sides up to WON.

At the same time TINA sides with Day. NEWHALL is not disappointed to be distracted by her with DAY.

City Ed is completely taken by the turn of events, current and social, remarks "Oh my God! What a day for the news!"

The non-press throw happiness and

booze, kisses all over the place. The
press personnel are all smiling with typing
at full tilt and each to finish their
pieces signaled by giving pages to the
running COPYBOYS then begin with the
festivities. The press, traditionally,
never among those to refuse a drink.

DAY kisses TINA, MARGIE kisses WON
and DAY kisses -- WON.

Behind them, -- PAUL can't seem to
plant kisses on MARGIE who's, surrounded.
The City Ed SCOTT NEWHALL is abandoned with
WON.

They shake hands.

Enter police, to 'join' DAY and the
newspaper people, and the girls and boys
from Chen's, who are now all gathered
together.

The tone subdues, members of the
press have blended in with the social
gadflys, subdued not only from stilled
typewriters, the room filled with joy; but
trench coat-ed visitors have arrived who
openly refuse the celebratory champagne.

MARGIE is a sympathetic 'goil,'
legging it at the side of DAY's desk in the
center of the glamorous nest of joyous fun
freaks, and cops. The TRENCHCOATS huddle
with FABER holding cigarettes and him with
his cigar.

PETER sneaks off to the side to make
a phone call in private. "Hell or high
water, Sol? War's almost over and I've got
to get the letters into your folio. It's
GOT TO BE in there. That big deal with
Russia was my in, Damnit! You said you
didn't want to go on record, so Truman will

give up the A-Bomb at Potsdam?

"So, Hear me! If my fifteen grand
isn't in <u>there</u>, your second million in bank
notes will have to cover me. There was no
offer from Virginia, and a necklace won't
do it across my table." He gets worked up,
excited, threatening. "Because, at five a
ton, you <u>promised</u> me five million, and now
the war's over." He has to catch a breath.
"I got bullets to ship from Europe, now."

"What'd 'ya' mean it's up to the
Rosenbergs? Who the hell are they?"

With a voice that cuts into personal
ears SOL says, "Listen, I don't want
ANYBODY in on this."

"Okay. You explain it, later. See
you at Chen's."

DAVID appears, snatches the phone
from him.

"God Damn, Sol! What does this
victory in Europe mean regarding our bank
paper?"

Over the phone, SOL says, "It's going
to remain a secret. They could have US on
spy charges. I took care of everything."

"And the other thing ... I'm not in
for any spy stuff. That's not our deal."
He tells Peter, cupping the phone with his
hand for secrecy. "It WAS fifteen 'g-s'
for an atomic bomb," he listens. "Oh, you
know a secret? Well, it's out about ...
the jewelry?"

DAVID swings away having been
disconnected.

PETER, frantic asks "What did the man
say?" Seeing a blank face, he assumes "He
hang up?"

"He wouldn't admit to anything.
Shit! Our investment's behind some Potsdam
secret."

"They're gonna blame everything on
the Jews."

By now slightly too long a distance,
LT FABER is tuning into what these two are
up to.

Suddenly, feebly nervous, DAVID
rushes back to the party.

LT FABER turns back to the reporter
of the hour.

"Day, what's the story?"

DAY, either not knowing or a great
secret keeper.

"The story's in the paper,
lieutenant. The facts? These guys are War
Incorporated, West. The men who finance
the war. What the bonds don't cover."

Across the office to the styled
PEOPLE and GIRLS who look more like a
fashion catalogue, a social collection of
'niners' guzzling champagne and eating
herring and caviar. The people, poised and
posed are different than the constant
shuffle and deal at Chen's.

A collection of working newspaper
personnel and the gadabouts and gadflys
shown in the small numbers that they are.

Less than two steps back into the
party, DAY turns and loudly comments.

"For the fact remains, there's still
Japan."

DAY's into the Ritz crackers, while
The TWO POLICEMEN stand alone, looking on
at San Francisco's low-life and inner world
gathering. Fear filters through the elite,

while celebration masks continuing concerns about the war in the Pacific.

LT FABER with his eye on PETER and DAVID.

"I think we found our motive. Some profit ... big format --guns." DAY approaches PETER standing with MARISA, she exits back through the crowd, DAVID joins them, which leaves MARGIE the only girl who suddenly locks looks with PAUL; and they leave DAY reproachful.

"Where is it?" PETER answers DAY's inquiring look. "Our money's tied in With it."

DAY remains naive.

"The mistress's necklace?"

MARGIE's attention's captured from not to far away by Day's question. MARISA is too far away to hear anything.

"No, you fool." DAVID responds, "Not Penny's necklace."

"You guys aren't going to believe this," DAY decides to spill a few clues, "but the necklace that caused the stink was Davidal's daughter's. Not Penny's sapphire or Deuitch's blue-white bank of diamonds. Read tomorrow's paper."

DAVID moves away from PETER.

"You were there. Wasn't the bet called with Penny's sapphire?" DAY sees their confusion and with his quick wit spoils their alibi. He changed the subject.

"I was there the night she came through the waves of Waverly Street," DAY makes an hourglass, woman's-figure with his hands.

MARGIE sits, listening in. "Took me by the behind, called me who I was and loved me in her own time. It was on a Murphy bed and we had a sheepskin."

MARGIE's unmoved, she looks at PAUL celebrating with some champagne in hand and the beautiful women at his side. She can tell they know, but don't know it was her in the story DAY tells.

"It isn't right to run that story," MARGIE implores him. "Yet." PETER, DAVID stand baffled. Behind them LT FABER listens.

DAY says, "That night, I was stopped outside in the alley by a crowd comin' out."

MARGIE, with PAUL mingles with the others.

With FABER too close to ignore, DAY volunteers, "Personal experience."

CHAPTER 17

Meanwhile, back inside Chen's gambling parlor. By the Ladies' Room where all circumstances unravel.

Making a slow exit from the ladies room, sneaking through her loose satin, full-length jacket PENNY bumps into FRENCHIE JOE with a stick she spontaneously offers for him to share, both nervous and him looking particularly shifty.

"Hangin' out with the wrong crowd," PENNY says.

FRENCHIE JOE seems startled, "What? What are you talking about?" "Davidal's stones seem to be part of a public offering and you're the only kinda pasty guy who'd know. 'Cause I gave 'em to ya. What's up scares me."

Still in the dark, FRENCHIE JOE acts dumb. "Whatduya mean?"

"To illuminate the picture for ya," PENNY begins, "Celebration's goin' on everybody's talkin' and you look like you're using the moment to 'case the place.'"

"Oh, yeah?" FRENCHIE JOE gets embarrassed. "Then, you got me, I'm cased." He changes direction. "Let's you and me get outta here. It's buy-sell influence comin' in from Detroit."

At the center of Chien's parlor, enter the ecstatic "GROUP" who continue their celebration from the newspaper.

PETER pipes in. "It's all over. It looks like the European Theater closed."

PENNY distances herself from FRENCHIE JOE. PENNY asks, "And Italy?"

"Even Africa," MARGIE says.

DAVID laughing, "Hot. Hot hot hot. The Chinese are the next heroes. Spotlight's on Japan."

"Read all about it." And sounds of a typewriter still resound in their happy heads, "We just got back from the newspaper." Celebration breaks out at Chen's where the global leaders are now a half step behind... . In the news.

CHAPTER 18

Someplace where wooden stairs secret and scary climb up to the dark where no light is revealing until daytime, because it has to be that place where you know only because you have been there before.

Inside Prescott's Chinese parlor it seems actually homey with somber light, and the sound and smell of rain outside.

Meanwhile, DAY heard in between the clackety clack of chips back in the gambling parlor, muttering behind the clickety-clack of his typewriter his details for the story. "I got work to add, Tina. There's still an eclectic motive ... the story I want." Sound muffled by the private parlor's soft carpets, and the rain. In everybody's mind click clack of Chips, laughter and loving all around the place; WON is heard within the walls of Prescott's reality because of his normal voice. He too resounds with the idea and with the voice of DON DAY, 'the story I want' that firms his conviction over an eclectic motive. Although they are much the same, the Jewish community and the Chinese are still separated by a largesse of wealth versus lots of money for individuals.

"Now, Bobby PRESCOTT, the plot thickens. Chinese motive takes secondary twist."

Inside the Chinese back room, WON is less pleasant company on this visit with PRESCOTT.

"Last time you were speaking of the rage of bulls. Be precise. Japan invaded to occupy my country. The big boys assets are frozen. Their ice could have bought food, medicine." PRESCOTT says without looking directly at WON.

"You have found a 'go-boy' and the position you want is an executioner. You have worthless paper books and precious properties who's the bookkeeper? ... guns are worth money as are jewels; so you have to pay a share and to do that you lower yourself to deal with the Jewish community, or become less an attractive magnate with smaller money against the Japanese. You would do neither of these things, Bobby PRESCOTT I know you.

Who's manager?"

PRESCOTT looks up at him. "What is it that makes you so unpleasant? Need an elimination?"

WON quickly puts it on the table. "No! A murder could complicate my robbery investigation. I would have to deal with the police. You must help me. It's to hold San Francisco together."

His desperation becomes attractive to PRESCOTT.

Pleased, PRESCOTT motions for WON to sit down. Obstinate, he stands, and continues.

"Put out the word that you want to talk to your 'bullets.' Let the whole community know that I shall be here also to interview them. The first person to become curious and invite one into his confidence, have them inform you of this 'first curiosity seeker.' Tell me. Then we will have one to interrogate. They will want to tell."

PRESCOTT still feels he holds the gavel in this meeting.

"That is so you will know who faked the jewelry. Frenchie Joe' is not yet in the box."

WON tries to agree and draw out the information he seeks. "Ah so. What's in the box, could it end the war? All the grime settles in the basement here in the city, Bobby PRESCOTT."

"In this city? East coast fact, west coast face," PRESCOTT steeps his dissertation in bitterness. " We're all looking for ... hard cash fact."

The sun has long set on The City with so many ethnic eccentricities in a way one might think would stitch them all together. Their separation remains of a sort of greed, an ambition to own and hold the power of lots of money. Even where the money is fabricated on chance and held on worthless, private ledger paper the power remains with whomever does the holding.

Even in this bowery coast, the immigrants of the East for San Francisco means Europe, or the Far East that means China where the powerful put the Chinese in the basement; and the Jews in the East Coast Banks. For the banks in San Francisco are ruled, since the Gold Rush by the Italians. In one rare case, there remains the French and the elite Bank of Paris with branches of personal names.

Back at Chen's where the atmosphere amid stoic CHINESE is partytime through-out the gambling parlor. Men with some CHINESE

GIRLS are passing paper money to them for their exotic acts in this private illegal club.

CHEN'S BOYS circulate and advise couples in the shadows to refrain, necking that leads to clothes parting, that might lead to more revealing acts, which are strictly forbidden. This is a gaming house, not one of ill repute in any way. A Chinese family upholds a moral influence.

MARGIE moves over to the 'big boys' at the gambling tables where their exciting cards are dealt. Despite the champagne and end of the European theater, post war happiness, the men taking cards from the shoe are made somber in the presence of real money.

MARGIE fishes, gambles with the stakes of human emotion at CURTIS' side.

"What's the matter, big boy?"

Without looking at her, CURTIS replies, "I'm worried."

MARGIE stays focused.

"Your debt's covered. Now it's the pay off, War's half over. Right? You're a bookkeeper. Aren't your balances paid in diamonds?"

CURTIS looks at his cards, not at the girl.

"I'm worried because I gave Davidal's girlfriend my daughter's opera seat."

"Big war profits position," MARGIE closes in. "Is that what you call it? A seat at the opera? Position?"

He looks up at her through red circles around watery eyes. CURTIS says, "Yeah? A dream. Our big bomb deals ... is an all together different opera."

MARGIE gets private up into his ear with her cheek, and SOL sees. "His necklaces' been on the slide."

He looks to the side, into her face and says, "Davidal's a manipulator."

Another gambling coup and another necklace is thrown into the pot at the Baccarat table. The emerald necklace sparkles against the greet felt.

MARGIE's mouth drops.

Sure enough, the recently talked about sapphire necklace and from the most intimate depths of San Francisco -

... MAGGIE THE BOOT'S emerald necklace sits on the gambling table. The boys at the gambling table are scared, face to face with real gangsters like Detroit's BILL MARKHAM. PENNY looks like her nose fell off.

The new man at the felt table has pulled a bauble from the depths of San Francisco's bowery. Nobody gets inside that far, that fast. And what else might he be in on in Our City?

Now with a chance to coup-up, the Detroit gangster BILL MARKHAM at the table chimes in.

"End of the war and we've all got a chance at fortunes here.

The west coast trend seems to be to throw in the family jewels." Somber and in control SOL says, "Can't get anyone else in, now Markham."

"That's not what I heard." BILL MARKHAM digs his pitchfork into the big Jewish man's heart. "You think I ain't got no booody."

He sings out of key.

"Around and about in Chicago, we
heard there's a portfolio open, a position
on some books, ledgers floatin' around
somewhere. You squawkin' about your
Manhattan sizing investments because
Detroit's movin' in?" He grinds his words
agonizingly slow. "Bein' in what I'm into.
Knowin' what I know."

Frightened, standing behind them
PETER says, "Go ahead, let them in. We
still have the Pacific theater."

Tipped with liquid courage, DAVID
adds, "I'll back his overtures. Gentlemen,
this is Bill Markham from Detroit. Now
it's Chinese pick-up sticks. We can use
their money, because, flash! Japanese are
still in China."

Among the faces of CHINESE, FILIPINO,
RICH MEXICANS, ITALIAN AMERICANS, and ALL
AMERICAN boys and girls, MARKHAM is a new
player to face an angry SOL DAVIDAL at the
Baccarat table, and CHEN's eyes follow as
all eyes fall on him.

DAVIDAL'S mouth is tied shut, afraid
because they all might go off about the
bomb, and DAVIDAL still has the grip on
that for himself. He remains calm, tense
but certain.

Dominant , BILL MARKHAM, is
respected by a side glance from -JOHNNIE
MALLY. CURTIS snickers at SOL's
diminishing role.

DAVID stands back with tall, thin
defiance. The meek CHINESE BOOKKEEPER
humbly rushes up to take the necklace. THE

BOOKKEEPER weighs it at the table, examines the stones with his loupe and casually shrugs, rolls his eyes in silent sarcasm to pass acceptance on the value.

He straightens his cashmere jacket, pulls at his filigree tie and BILL MARKHAM boasts a toast, glass tilted toward DAVIDAL.

Chen's BOOKKEEPER takes the jewelry away while bowing to the dealer approving his credit to a 'higher limit.' CHEN is worried, the sapphire, he signals to the dealer, "It's a real emerald?!"

Comes the reply all without words, cards pass out of the shoe. CHEN steps in all too fast, his moral display of annoyance hidden in Chinese stoicism.

MARGIE moves around the table where the action seems the main event. MARGIE leans in to make sure he knows she has seen the sapphire necklace elsewhere besides here, the other night, too. Frenchie Joe' hides out toward the back, pauses to make sure he's unnoticed by ... .

CHEN, who goes into the back room to place the jewels in his safe, as FRENCHIE JOE follows into the shadows of his office.

From back in the gambling parlor, MARGIE remarks, "'Deja vue, big fellah, imprevous!'"

MARKHAM's low and masculine voice replies to her, "What does that mean?"

"Seen it before. Be aware, impending danger."

Meanwhile, back at the gaming room, under the table, a note is slipped into CURTIS' hand.

Inside the office at the Safe in Chen's office, the dial turns, the safe is being cracked by FRENCHIE JOE, while at that very moment CHEN walks out into the light and smoke of the gambling parlor.

Little has changed there.

Before changing her position at CURTIS' side, MARGIE repeats herself, "If you think you've seen it before, be forewarned."

At the same table, MARKHAM overhears.

"Of what? Paste?"

Ignoring MARKHAM, MARGIE, concentrates on the gamblers, fades back into the group of SPECTATORS. Meanwhile CURTIS sneaks a peek at the note.

Boldly, having noticed CURTIS read the note, MARGIE says, "How well you know what!? Comin' in from Detroit just last week, too?" At the Baccarat table SOL contemplates his cards in tense silence, appreciative of the aggressive girl, MARGIE, and with a sneaky side glance at MARKHAM.

Again, the gaming room with people, like shuffling cards, change places around the table. CHEN returns into the main room and never notices FRENCHIE, now skulking in the shadows with the sapphire necklace sliding into his coat pocket, back near the office.

CURTIS passes the note to SOL over the table top. MARKHAM's face flushes in paralytic anger.

The cards showing a perfect nine belong to CURTIS DEUITCH.

The players table the cards, and with

head movements directing their action, take
MARKHAM away from the table, as they leave.
Assisted by CHAUFFEURS and BODYGUARDS just
the BIG 3 leave the room.

Seen watching are all the players
from the newspaper party, too.

TINA motions to MARGIE.

TINA talks close to her ear, "You go
up, and I'll cover down the alley."

DAY enters the parlor just as the Big
3 and followers leave with determination,
everyone ignores him. A mouse scurrying
around the big house cats.

He confronts PETER and DAVID in the
melee. Without acknowledgment of the force
that just passed him, he asks, "I gotta
know something. You guys into big
investments with Davidal?" Following in the
parade outside, PETER replies, "You already
know that, Day."

DAY lays it out in quiet tone, "You
into the atomic bomb?"

THE BOYS shove him aside and they go
back into the gambling parlor. He calls
out behind them.

"Would you buy into it if you had a
chance?"

They ignore DAY, return to their
gambling. The BIG TOTES and their MUSCLE
MEN have shoved past him.

DAY regains his balance, then follows
behind to try and find the girls outside.

He feels lost, abandoned by them so
he looks both ways and staggers, tired and
under delusions of lost friendships and all
the sleepless work, he mussels past the
grouping at the door. Without conscious

choice he goes toward the direction TINA took down the alley.

The rumble confirms that CURTIS now owns DAVIDAL's family jewels. Still inside by the front door, just standing inside the club entrance at the bottom of the stairs, the BIG BOYS, DAVIDAL, CURTIS and MARKHAM formally exit to a parked limousine. Their BODYGUARDS left behind.

Cut of a different cloth, each of the big men enter the same back seat of the limousine. Somewhat like a Mack Sennete comedy with big men almost a parody of the circus act with clowns into a small car, this is the big men piling into same back seat of a big car. Trying to feel safe inside the limousine parked in Chinatown's Waverly place on a corner.

CURTIS enters with some effort separated by BILL MARKHAM, who peers over at SOL, all three, now, packed in the back seat as the car opulently rolls a couple dozen feet down the alley where it turns around to roll back again, a dozen feet backwards altogether.

CURTIS speaks.

"'Whatda' you think?"

SOL sparks back, "Get wise, Kike. They want money for the jewels the mob robbed."

MARKHAM puffs up, sandwiched between the two San Franciscans.

"I thought it was fake.'

SOL, in calm fury rolls the paper note in his hand.

CURTIS blurts out. "Mob? We're dealing with what mob?" Looking out the window, SOL seems alone in the car.

"You must be out of it," SOL says softly.

He comes back with a hard look at MARKHAM, smug on the other end of the back seat.

Mobster or not, trapped between the two city boys MARKHAM tries to defend himself, squished in the back seat.

"That sapphire looked too good to be unique. My emerald was!" "This isn't Detroit." Outside the car, on Waverly Place and only a few feet from the Fortune Cookie Company, the mood inside is like the dark somber wet night just outside the car door.

Creaking leather from classy new shoes breaks the back alley silence as the men step out of the car.

Standing still by the limo without topcoats, SOL and CURTIS are met by a -

FIVE MAN CHINESE gang in topcoats waiting, already there down the Alley, now -- outside of the Limousine. A standoff.

CURTIS standing on the outside speaks with authority, while DAVIDAL stands on the other side of MARKHAM in the middle who stiffen when CURTIS makes the accusation to these thugs.

"Your note said the necklaces we used were stolen. It called for a meeting, said you had something for us. I want the diamonds, we want to recover our property."

CHEW looks back, cocky in his quarter length black leather coat. "The diamond's, gone." CHEW has a harsh voice for a small kid, threatening for a face off with three big men. "It seems they were fooled by the sapphire."

Back in shadows, MARGIE who has been trailing them hides, fades back in the shadow of an alcove.

An argument ensues because CURTIS is outraged that the 'bauble' was sold, after it was recovered -

Out of the shadows, awkward, DON DAY almost 'lurches' onto the scene and from the shadows, -

There is a timely distracting Spring lightning flash from the sky, and -

TINA jerks DAY back into a doorway where she was hiding also; afraid to be seen by sudden light, MARGIE jumps back too, into an alcove down the alley on the other side from where the men are gathered, closing in on the Chinese; now apprehensive looking up and down the dark alley. Three white faces, white with reasonable

fear and rain dotted moonlight.

SOL steps up, nervously outraged, interrupted by the thunder clap he looks up. "Damn, freak Spring showers! Get to the point!

I came here because I thought you had something for me."

Not wavering CHEW spits back, "Why was that sapphire paste?

You gonna cost Mr. Chen."

SOL, CURTIS seem stunned, speechless. The LIMO DRIVER leaves them, returns to the car with MARKHAM, nervous, out of his home court, at his side.

SOL looks at CURTIS, then looks back to the punks.

"Paste ... wha, wha. My sapphire?!

(dumbfounded) You haven't got a chance to find that necklace. You Chinese live in a 'soup bowl' here in this Chinatown -- version of Hong Kong. People hanging out on all street corners, hanging out of the windows." CURTIS, not willing to have DAVIDAL out maneuver him.

"When are you Chinese going to come out of the basement and get behind this country's War effort?"

"We're not the ones with a Chinaman in the basement," CHEW remarks. "When you let me tell you, at least we're not throwing bad debts and good money to be blown up like paste, powder only for the celebration of the fourth of July. We're not picking our wives purses and paying our daughters boyfriends to blow people up," he adds with malice.

Badly withholding outrage SOL opens up. "You're talking paste. I'm a genuine asset to this country's war effort and you are toying with the 'powder' to blow us all into the beyond. You haven't got a chance in Hell of finding that sapphire you claim I owe you. When they play the 'jew's harp' you listen and like it ... you haven't got a Chinaman's chance of pinning that on me."

CHEW cuts him with sharp eyes. "Mr. Davidal, I am a Chinaman." BAM!

A gun goes off and SOL DAVIDAL is pasted dead.

Exposed amongst the gang of the FIVE MAN CHINESE GANG, only the barrel tip of a smoking gun peeks out of the folds in tell-tale topcoats.

Suddenly, rains come down in buckets.

The GANG MEMBERS run. Chinese boy CHEW is left with a large 45 automatic pulled out and pointed out from his waist. It's a turn around, as CURTIS shuffles closer and MARKHAM steps closer -- both are more frozen by the downpour than any threat of devious recriminations.

Bent over, shocked as he eyeballs.

SOL's dead body that lies flat out on the street.

The CHEW boy flees.

Without looking back, sideways or even forward, he runs past DAY and TINA in the doorway. The GANG, however, spots them.

DAY quickly pulls TINA close to him and starts to smother her with kisses. -

Afraid they're about to be victimized by the killers, for a distraction he pulls her dress up flashing, her bare behind, her beautiful legs taut -

Fascinated and seduced by the scene as the Chinese Boys pause to look, threaten with the gun. They see it is a Chinese girl, and -

-- as TINA, who immediately catches on, unbuckles DAY's pants the passion, in the sapphire blue light of illusion works. The same vision enacted from DAY's flash inside Won's office.

Although MARKHAM has called hits, seen men slain in streets all over Chicago, with the refined CURTIS DEUITCH next to him in the pouring rain, the caper has gone all too sour.

Inside the Limousine, shaken with fear, claustrophobic by the coal black

rainy night, CURTIS squirms next to MARKHAM
in the back seat. Both pale with fear, the
driver up front, nervously gets the car
into gear; and they're out of there as
tires squeal, smoky, even on the wet
street.

Noteworthy, the wet street glistens
with each flash of lightning and those slim
alleyways shake with shafts of thunder that
seem

to recall the old days of feeble
structures that made Chinatown

home for so many, so quickly. The
place of dreams, shattered in

a war with the patriarch slain in its
place of symbolic prosperity.

Outside through Waverly Place into
the open mouth growls of rainy Chinatown
night, a different night. Outside this
rainy night is one without comfort.

Additionally discouraged by the
downpour, the CHINESE boys momentarily
seduced by the sexual detour, decide in a
split second that the shooting went unseen
by these two who continue lewd loving even
after -

Up the other end of the alley - The
Limo, DEUITCH and MARKHAM have gone right
past them.

From alcove to alcove, and taking
advantage of the shadows, MARGIE, although
remarkably upset, having seen TINA and DON
in full sexual regalia, follows the CHINESE
boys dedicated in her silent chase through
wet, mysterious Chinatown.

Dedicated to follow the case, and
with tears mingled with the raindrops, she

follows them into the night, reluctantly looking back.

The night rain washes more than the cobblestones of hope and streets of dark camouflaged city night. This time the night rain paints the alley with a blood stain of that hope for the war's quick end. The man who claimed leverage to end the war could certainly never compete with the governments that truly pay for the war to sustain liberty. The man who supported the chains of freedom in the form of laws to support liberty lay under that rain in that alley, which held the stitches on the crazy quilt of two ethnic victims of the war in Europe and the war with Japan.

Inside an apartment above the laundry, Chinese hallway, looking into a dingy, smoky place full of the CHINESE TOUGHS hanging just outside the door peering inside stands FRENCHIE JOE. Under FRENCHIE's arm, the ledgers show he has a bargaining chip as he enters the den of thieves . . . and murderers.

Taking unknown chances FRENCHIE JOE speaks. "What are these books? A kiss-off? I see what's the value here."

They back him out.

FRENCHIE JOE makes a plea through the crack in the door. Through mean slanted eyes CHEW says, "We don't need no books. A real sapphire! And besides, to see what matters to us, you don't have the eyes."

CHEW closes the door. FRENCHIE JOE's outside helplessly protesting.

As if uncovered, some fact of value or another bank uncovered that still has a fortune to recover after the war, the rain breaks to leave FRENCHIE and everybody with a new albeit not so clean city.

CHAPTER 19

Two detectives out of the three are gathered inside Won's office. The light seeps in from a wet morning.

Forever his daughter, but for now in the role of one of his assistants, WON with TINA go over lists of names in the office.

He is searching for a file in his cabinet, pulls one particular file and shows her photos from it one at a time.

WON says, "Our investigation tells me there is one more leader of raging bulls who are always drawn by the same color cape. Nowa-days in San Francisco, it's become a crazy quilt. But always threads are documented."

He goes back through more files and looks in his other cabinet drawers, as TINA patiently sits and attentively chews on the eraser of a pencil. Forever the little girl.

Enter MARGIE returned from her chase, worn and frazzled but excited.

Still gasping for air, MARGIE begins the story, "I followed the boys to an apartment above the laundry."

WON pulls a chair for her.

Acting like the comforting father with his other assistant, WON makes her comfortable.

"You look like a starved tiger, my number one girl Friday."

TINA says, "Sit down, catch your breath. Let me fix you some tea."

Repressing spite, MARGIE tries comforting herself.

"That was some diversion, Tina. It

worked. Are you ever lucky." Warily, the two girls watch each other as TINA fixes more tea and MARGIE unfolds her story. While her story unravels some clue not yet found, she watches TINA for a clue to her true emotional tie to her man and their sexual encounter she witnessed, forgetful that what saved their lives.

"The boys converged near the laundry. The Italian they called Frenchie Joe interrupted them protesting about the scene in the alley ... they were all excited"

Her wild looks at TINA no way interrupt her story.

"And this guy Frenchie Joe wanted to know something quickly.

He was very impatient. He had ledgers."

TINA modestly serves her tea.

WON both a good father of a beautiful daughter and insightful detective.

"I heard, it was a close call in the alley. You are brave women, why was Frenchie Joe there?"

"He was in the alley, too." MARGIE continues.

"He was with them all along." She pauses for tea and a reaction. "The boys insisted they paid in 'bullets' and that was that.

"Unless I miss my bet, they appeared to try to get the ledgers from Frenchie Joe, but he held onto them. He thinks he has something bankable. It seems he's the one on the spot for the sapphire, though."

She sips tea again, picks up some photos, recognizes three of the Chinese gang.

"At first they rejected him."

WON stops his searching and sits.

"They pulled him inside," MARGIE goes on. "He wouldn't leave and he called them fools." She sips to bring on some calm. "Then they took the books and all went into the laundry. I could see when the door opened."

Looking up at the ceiling, WON reveals in wonder, "I know who opened the door for them?"

"Through the keyhole I could also hear, and see a little bit. Mystified, MARGIE says, "Only a little bit. It was all very mysterious, and the door seemed to open by itself for them." "Mysterious, sure," WON continues in his daze. "That Bobby PRESCOTT! He knows how to mark books, and he's got them."

WON storms out of the office.

The City mists with brown tears, because the seaside dusk is filled with signs of a brown out, as lights come on in some places because The City slowly wakes to the change in International Affairs. Just as The City gives up to familiarity, the scope of its involvement in the world that envelopes it to squeeze out any sort of weakness in the individual residents. It can be a lonely place, or with strength a place to fortify courage.

Even though the murder of SOL DAVIDAL makes for big interest in The City, the whole world seems to have entered inside the Movie Theater Movietone News, which shows: Hiroshima bomb film and the first

famous mushroom clouds pictures released to
the public.

The movie ANNOUNCER introduces
history as he says, "President Truman made
this statement:"

On the screen, President TRUMAN sits
behind his desk.

"The world will note that the first
atomic bomb was dropped on Hiroshima, a
military base factory where components for
armaments were manufactured."

Sometimes history makes men, because
when men die they rarely make history in
the face of bigger events. The weather,
the wars, the criminal acts overshadow the
death of even the greatest pioneers in the
world.

The Pope should know, the boys of
Boys Town might not even be able to know
about one man in an alley so far away from
any form of a true light.

While the syndicate leader might be
gone, the syndicate will continue to see
The City rise to heights beyond
expectations. Even rise beyond
Manhattanization.

Inside BOBBY PRESCOTT's back room, in
somber light, WON is standing and BOBBY is
seated. Both hold teacups.

WON speaks severely. "All has
changed. The scandal not worth taking to
the police in the darkness of murder has
hit the streets. You have had time to call
me and yet I appear by myself. Wonder as I
do to solve crimes without anyone knowing
makes for a curious discovery on this one.
You said the ledgers would come even if it

cost. A life, whose responsibility will survive though the innocent power has been killed and the books are still in the wrong hands scalds the streets and alleys of our city."

PRESCOTT, unflappable, responds. "The scandal is not over money, Don Won, but over love. Even when the war is over, the profits will be shared; but now without love forlorn. Surely, Don Won you can appreciate that the innocents are still among us. The married boyfriend has left his nightingale and the song of the widow will be blue but sweet without the mistress and her sapphire of paste."

"The master of which mistress and her sapphire will not suffer the most?"

He gets up from his chair and goes to a cabinet, but turns when WON speaks.

"The accomplice of the criminal who pulled the attack on the financier was also the robber who stole the books and the jewels.

You know I now have a murder to contend with, and you throw in love."

In one motion PRESCOTT pulls them out of a cabinet and offering the ledgers to WON says, "The suggestion is here. No Chinese Boy would dare steal from the house of Lai. Wealthy tall mountain supports a salon of Chen, gambling cannot be subject to attack Chen by a gang of mere Chew boys."

Now up going toward the door WON, after PRESCOTT gives him the package at the door. He accepts the ledgers PRESCOTT has taken out of the cabinet, but he knows the case is not resolved.

WON adds, "There remains a sapphire necklace. Stones to pay the price of chance in the face of war debt."

To justify motive, PRESCOTT says, "The families of China have never put their wives in debt, gambled their sons against mistresses dreams. That, my dear Don Won, is a Greek tragedy."

"It's all Greek to me." WON surprises PRESCOTT in Chinese, saying "HOW DO WE MAKE IT UNDERSTOOD THE WAR DEBT IS NOT TO HIT THE STREETS OF San Francisco? SO NEAR, the Japanese FLEW OVERHEAD AT Huntington Beach!"

"Never OUR friends," PRESCOTT responds in English. "I understand San Francisco. Hidden is about China. Diamonds bought food, commodities. The rest is safe in this American, Vaudeville comedy. Japanese invade China, Don Won! We have not found a box to fit that one into."

WON takes his jacket off in anticipation of meeting the warm night. "But you do have a bank?" As he leaves in profound wonder, with the ledgers covered under his jacket, he stops to remark with a distant gaze outside.

"Frenchie Joe's nothing for money but a cheep tout." PRESCOTT interrupts WON's warm thought as the comfort of having regained the ledgers for his client is unbroken, but not for trying by Bobby PRESCOTT.

To make things smooth, WON turns, "Summer time brings kids out onto the street, Bobby PRESCOTT. Let them learn to play kick the can with everybody else. A child's happiness cannot be put in a box or found in a fortune cookie. True power resides in all of man. The City through the many facets of different glasses sometimes holds danger."

"Our bank is the Hong Kong Shanghai Bank." PRESCOTT wants to come to a point of sensibility in this finality as the war that effects them all comes to an end.

"Don't get Shanghai-ed by the Hong Kong Shanghai Bank."

With his head in clouds of pensive clues and few answers, WON scuffs his step as he walks to his car. He feels like he got answers, not the direct conversation that a detective would be able to cash in with as satisfactory to his client. With ledgers firmly under his arm, he feels good about having completed some service to his client, in any case. Enough to continue without the police, and that is his contract as much as it might just play into the plot of his enemies.

With his director, the client Mr. CHEN to be satisfied, the short list of enemies has begun without him even knowing it. To contend with the unknown, unsolved are the unseen Chew Boys.

They put themselves out to get jewels and got nothing but paste, and now that the subterfuge of war is lifting, they will be pushed into something irrational.

Along Waverly Place possibly seen from Sacramento Street, during the day from a not too distant corner, CHINA BOY CHEW eyeballs

WON who leaves a parked car with TINA who waits inside of it.

Into his pants pocket, CHEW ...

Replaces the big 45 Colt automatic he had in his hand, tucked inside his black leather coat, then he steps back into a doorway to join TWO of the BOYS waiting to witness the hit.

Reluctantly CHEW tells them, "Can't do it. They've got the line on the sapphire."

He pushes the BOYS toward WON and TINA down the street.

When ... WON and TINA move, so do the boys as they act in such parallel they appear in simultaneous timing like a wolf pack following a dear.

With reluctant memory, CHEW mutters, "Frenchie Joe's nothing for money but a cheep tout." He scratches his cheek and wonders about what he overheard, "What's that mean? Does he have money?" CHEW BOYS follow the WONS without one idea as to why, amongst them.

CHAPTER 20

In the world, the war in Europe is finished and the war in the Pacific appears to be over for an elite who know what few others could only imagine. For, in both closing theaters, organized crime rules and a post war black market gives birth to an underground of mostly the down trodden. None the less, different senses are piqued in San Francisco, as dangerous battles continue in The City, at every strata.

Outside Waverly Place, the premier Chinatown street in front of the Happiness Fortune Cookie Company, danger lurks in the plain of day.

WON with TINA and MARGIE stand on the curb with CHEN. KIDS in tee shirts chase one another around the streets nearby, playing tag on summer sunshine streets between cramped buildings just like city children play all over. Hopefully war will never come again.

To the prominent man in broad white stripes on his blue suit, who stands with irrefutable claims of respect, the end of war will bring results. Chen listens as WON delivers.

"You have the books again, but greed still rages over sights of more fortunes, ruthless now that blood has been drawn. Are you satisfied?"

With reserve CHEN responds. "The balance of debts knows nothing of bloodshed, only greed --and prejudice."

"Is rage still a secret?" WON pushes. "Can you sell power for paste, or find a needle in the haystack to bring happiness?"

TINA simply cannot stand still.

"Ask him this, father. Does he know who owned the sapphire?" Undaunted WON continues, "More like a sapphire in the soup.

Can we pick it out in the War Won Ton, Chen Lai?"

"The war is black and white. In the crimson and gold Chinese community they only think of the family." CHEN cannot hide his bitterness. A bitterness, perhaps resolved. "That's how Marisa explains differences to me."

TINA still just does not get it.

"Ask him this. Does he know whose necklace it was to begin with?" WON plays the father card. "The family who plays together, stays together. Doesn't the family that owns this sapphire come together at Your gaming house?"

CHEN mentally staggers up to the aerial act of a conscience trapeze feat that suspends the emotions of a powerful Jewish family with his grasp of an ethnic community that holds all the answers with none of the power. DAVIDAL's death had been sad, but he emotionally prospered, his love may be fulfilled without him and no struggle over DAVIDAL's daughter. He would not like to fall, for in this kind of high flyer act that he has engaged himself, there is no net.

"All the rich families of San Francisco come through my parlor." Chen says withholding a sigh. "The bait and switch takes many forms, character is tested in many ways. I see chance challenge all men."

Trapped into an ethnic nostalgia for the Chinese troubles, CHEN thinks out loud. "Of the murdered bookkeeper who insisted SAX's son pay his gambling debts. A friend of DAVIDAL, Mr. SAX had only to suggest his remorse that caused him grief, and especially while his son was in Brussels where the Germans held the upper hand, at that time. He did under no circumstances wish to recognize his son had been gambling, none the less recognize he had been in the Chinese gambling parlor.

"Since DAVIDAL had invited the boy into our den of inequity, a den whose equities would never invoke any value to SAX; he laid it down to DAVIDAL that he would like him to 'take care of it.' The bookkeeper was 'taken care of,' but in a manner that SAX would never know or approve if he did. Even if he did care, it had come to LT FABER to cover the incident, and cover the incident was his deed for the war effort. But that becomes FABER's conscience and the Irish in The City who know everything that goes on, who knows of the many laws here, which becomes their reward in the self restricted catacombs of San Francisco? Is it the secret or some resolve?"

WON knows he holds the secret, but what CHEN wants is the resolution.

Sensing CHEN's nostalgia as a mitigation of his determination, not willing to break his reserve, WON soothes the hostility with consolation. "Isn't love the ruler of every house, any way it can be found? Sweet, whether paste or a sweet naive thing made into a tart that gets passed around. But, death? Sensing WON can read his thoughts, CHEN changes his tact.

"You seem skilled at this knowledge of love, Don Won. Can you find the burglars without bungling my life?"

TINA becomes agitated by the dance.

"Ask him if he's seen anyone wearing the sapphire necklace ... in the parlor." She fidgets not taking notice of what goes on around her in the neighborhood.

But WON is a knower.

"My girl Friday tells of a new friend who has asked that she help find her missing necklace. Maybe lost in a drawer of panache and panties, or perhaps dropped in a plate of gai pan while stooping low to serve a guest at her home. She is Marisa Davidal whose father threw the piece on the table that night. This suggests the crime remains in the Chinese community. If they would only recognize love where it burns with a passion that when unfulfilled can only leave scars without cuts. They do gossip, Chen Lai."

TINA ever persistent.

"Ask him this, honorable father ..."

CHEN now irrationally excited.

"Through Penny I got word about the loss. I cannot tell you what I was thinking when I saw it on the Baccarat table. I wanted the girl, and her necklace meant nothing to me but the sentiment I felt for the girl. You know what it is to find a woman of the world? Don Won, you know what that is?!"

"It's the lives of innocent people," WON says.

Surprised TINA remarks, "Chen Lai, do you know about Marisa's necklace?"

"Not that to kill the father." CHEN continues with a sobbing whine. "Yes! It was faked. Fast bucks by cheep girls diffuse the all powerful."

"I believe what you do, Chen Lai," then WON makes an offer.

"The books of scandal have yet to be resurrected, and their significance, my dear friend Chen Lai, is what I am willing to pursue."

Hiding deep in shadows, CHEW BOYS hear the offer, residuals of following TINA and WON and listening to them with CHEN; and they profit by following some more they become undaunted in their blind pursuit. The danger becomes, not what the CHEW BOYS might do, but that they know not what they are doing.

Family rites always making news in The City that dozes but rarely sleeps. Sometimes a father knows what might be building behind their daughters indiscretions, and those times might call for a retention of confidences. WON knows, DAVIDAL knew.

Intimacy is rare in the News room at night.

TINA brings Chinese take out to DAY at his desk. He stops to look appreciatively into her eyes and take a few bites before going back to his writing.

The reporters writing with no others in the news room never seems to pause.

Daylight doesn't interrupt his writing, so TINA reappears with coffee in a covered cup, which is a relief without pause to recognize gratitude. He writes, and she feeds him with chop-sticks.

DAY continues to write. His tux jacket wilts over the back of his chair and musk turns to soot on his collar, sleeves, his cuffs.

Nine days DAY writes. TINA remains attentively present as she brings him variations of sandwiches, take-out and coffee in paper cups, and ...

Revised copy brought to him by COPY BOYS. Busy as hell, DAY stops only to nap on a cot, with an Army blanket there in place for any dedicated newspaper reporters coming back from the field with stories burning in their fiber.

On DAY's desk photographs build in piles that fall to the floor, and more than enough of them are of the big bomb blast, the mushroom cloud that DAY occasionally glances over in a knowing pride that keeps him writing.

Soot falling on the Mission Street below makes the neighborhood look unwelcome. Strictly work spaces, industrial district with no real value for life with no walk in business in the area apart from the occasional sandwich or coffee shop. Cars pass with no regard for pedestrians, because there are no pedestrians. Just soot on the sidewalks.

The other side of urban San Francisco, at Clay between Polk and Leavenworth this dark, dark night is somehow more civilized.

Here The City's lower Mission district survives at best inhabited by white collar workers. The dedicated kind who will no longer miss ration books.

WON steps out onto Leavenworth at Mission Street, hidden in the darkness of the shadows of tall buildings, two CHINA BOYS dart backward out of sight. They still follow WON. Dangerous, CHINA BOYS easily dodge recognition, disguised into too much foot traffic and cars. The end of war has changed The City habits. The CHEW BOYS pocket large 45 Colt Automatics, clips checked before moving along the street, in and out of the shadows again.

The game around neighborhoods lower than Nob Hill made clandestine by the laws of the brown out that hangs in The City as war habits are hard to break. Here the sneaky Chinese bandits take subterfuge in strictly business activity that begins to close the day.

At this location they might stand out, for the blue collar crowd is leaving the streets and the CHINESE BOYS are simply not part of the white collar crowd returning home with loosened ties and brown briefcases.

Inside the newspaper's City Room TINA is always there, at the newspaper desk near DAY in a fresh dress, clean hair ribbon, bright smile to contrast the dedicated DAY, becoming more ragged, unshaven working on his end of war story. His own version of a tuxedo now DAY, stays busy at his typewriter. Into the secure workplace of

the newspaper WON enters, MARGIE comes up
behind him without taking notice of TINA at
rest on the cot nearby.

Without looking up DAY says, "This is
a piece a' cake. With these headlines, the
news practically writes itself."

WON looks around at the remnants of
the ritual to get a newspaper out and onto
the streets.

MARGIE startles DAY, remarks, "That
tuxedo could write your story for you, at
this point. You haven't been home?"

In sight, by the nearby day-cot
stands TINA suddenly, making her emotional
presence known. The desk overflows from
days of paper from the wire, photos, and
DAY's writing. He turns to MARGIE his eyes
red, lids droop in energized fatigue.

"Nine days, war's over." DAY says,
"And there's another story -the Boom-Boom
and no local pay-off. Now, Davidal's
dead."

WON starts, a little bit worried.
"Might is right. Isn't that the deal?
Don?"

They smile and DAY sober, brings out
a bottle of perfume spray from his desk
drawer. He makes the air cleaner, in his
own mind and tries a distraction.

DAY recites his words, "Another
diversion, but eventually everything
becomes clear. The Manhattan Project is
more than Real Estate."

From romantic self pity to news
interest, he continues, "Davidal's big bomb
deal revealed with Hiroshima. The pay-off
still unfinished in the West Coast

community. The mystery is not over.
Chinese might come out of their basement,
but will the bankers ever come out of their
bank boxes? You're with us! And the
Chinese community with a stake in this
rallies with the rest of the whole of San
Francisco and in fact the west coast."

WON remains unsure of the story.

"I can't stop talking like
headlines."

"Maybe it's time for another drink.
Do you have any of those little umbrellas?"

DAY shakes his head 'no,' pours
whiskey into glasses for MARGIE and WON but
none for himself. But, MARGIE is looking
around, for deYoung, perhaps.

DAY says, "I gave it up, among other
things."

Noticing MARGIE's distraction,
noticing that she missed DAY's last comment
spoken with exasperation, it fosters
disgust toward TINA. And from TINA toward
her father, as WON drinks anyway, these
emotional trials are too petty for him and
unknown as a choice, maybe.

TINA slips next to WON, who with an
all together different concern goes to
another desk and picks up a phone to make a
call. MARGIE without drinking puts her
glass down to level herself with DAY.

MARGIE wants to capture his
attention, be sincere with him. "Do you
think I can find someone to lean on?"

DAY polite. "We all stand alone. We
just blend in, Margie." "All too often I
find I'm trying to match green and blue.
Does that blend, Don?"

"What you're after is a new mode --a quick form tie-in."

They both pause for emotions to register. A passing COPYBOY drops and takes new pages without pause, as he sees something personal in development.

MARGIE goes on. "What is it we're all after, Reporter? Answers, answers? Pull the answers out of gum wrappers, then spit the gum on the sidewalk?"

"You're full of riddles because you can't face your emotions. You have choices, here, just like the whole world, now." With his heart opening, DAY says, "We've shared a lot. Now, it's different, an atomic age ... and now it looks like Paul for you?" Lean, hungry suspicion reeks out of his look at her. Stifling jealousy, MARGIE says, "Is this about a maniacal affair, Day? How is your report going to read? Tina's version?"

Looking around, the emptiness pervades, because TINA is gone. Back into the story DAY remarks, "Just looking for an end.

This War story's gone on too long, already."

Attempted intimacy reeks all the way into the back of the news room -- the couple continues in intimate arbitration, as the COPYBOYS tread softly.

DAY, with excitement looks at the copy just handed to him, and passes it, open mouthed stunned silent to MARGIE.

"All that work, and the story is the pay-off, baby."

Outside the world continues.

Inside the movie theater, Movietone News Clip explains: Nagasaki bombed Aug 9th 1945, with aerial views for News clips that causes ripples of confusion, elation, shock in the audience.

People celebrating on the streets. With fear dissipated, it

becomes joy that directs the social action in The City.

While dark, in friendly San Francisco, Mission district streets remain shady.

Down the street, around the corner from the newspaper building, and three alley turns off Market St., CHEW weaves his men's attention toward the Newspaper building.

Out of a car around the corner from the Mission Street newspaper building, TINA had disappeared into an alley coffee shop.

From the shadows cast partly from late service coffee and sandwich shops, CHINESE BOYS follow, suddenly because it's WON continuing toward the party at the newspaper, perceived through the celebrating crowds as a ray of hope brightens the scene South of Market Street, the CHINESE BOYS have a redirected quest. Under their own cloud of destruction, the TWO CHINA BOYS try to head WON off. TINA seems to have been left out.

Propitious trailing by the now diverted CHINESE BOYS, in the back of the newspaper building where TINA comes out of the coffee shop. Secretly noticing the CHINESE BOYS, TINA watches them follow her father and goes the other way, while ...

The GANG continues, now with guns drawn, inconspicuous amongst the whole city of loud celebration, as they follow down an industrious section of wide Mission Street, they remain in pursuit of WON.

WON suddenly disappears in shadows off tall buildings.

One of the BOYS fires off a round into that shadow, sound muffled by sirens and horns of celebration.

Himself bold, CHEW steps out of the dark and fires into the shadow. All seems to stop. Some coincidence has caused a pause in the sonorous city-wide celebration.

From out of the shadow, one CHINA BOY CHEW staggers into the light, but not hit. Swaggered by a DRUNKEN SAILOR and his TART who bumped him. CHEW darts along the sidewalk, quick again to regain his balance, and into the newspaper building far behind WON.

Apprehensive, CHEW looking around the street at the GANG by the front door of the newspaper building before he goes inside. He stops to give them his orders.

CHEW tells them, "Take her out without me."

He exists, by going inside the building.

Filled with self importance, the BOYS meander off back into the shadows of the alley.

CHAPTER 21

Night breaks to dawn. While CHEW
goes up into the News Room. The City Ed
SCOTT NEWHALL comes over to the desk with a
front page headline in red that he hands to
DAY.

Still and dominant, City Ed Scott
Newhall says, "You're a psychic? Look at
this! Headlines in red! Nagasaki bombed.

"Japs surrender. Start writing about
VJ Day, Day; and don't leave out the
Manhattan project, this time. Fat Man and
Big Boy. West Coast fact meets East Coast
fact. Not our story. Yet."

He tosses a telegram on DAY's desk
and grabs Margie's discarded glass, swigs a
drink.

Joy in a newspaper office is mostly
controlled. The staff becomes more blaze
with years of exposure to events, character
developments, the news as it makes history
as time develops their stories senses, and
its value. Hardened to the facts is not
the true picture of the newspaper man,
though serious and job before all makes for
more of a truism when making a picture of
the newspaper man and women.

"Let the East Coast try this part of
the story." City Ed SCOTT NEWHALL
swaggers, "You're the only one with the
true answer to THAT one, Day."

They all toast, but -

Outside the people in The City see
only joy, resolution and relief for the end
of sacrifice and for some, squandered lives
full of reckless experiences.

Brief Movietone News cuts of

Americans, tortured prisoners of war, being released feed pain onto the streets of The City when the cinema empties. A painful summary in clips, years of clips that make a detailed display of atrocities our U.S. Troops had endured is meant to offer justification and pride to our citizens. The ANNOUNCER booms inside the theater.

"The president's office issued a statement that described it as a decision to save lives. It was the ultimate effect that might stop the war and any more vicious killing."

PRESIDENT TRUMAN's likeness shows on the big screen with his statement in his own words.

"It was immediate and necessary."

The ANNOUNCER talks over pictures.

"The Japanese immediately pulled back even from their invasion of China by the diversion of the atomic bomb.

"In some places on the island of Japan, there are people who still don't know what that was. That great light over their heads. There are still many who don't know that the atomic bomb was just used for the first time."

Any celebration outside continues with mostly young people on the streets. The young Chinese, as few as the young uniformed Italians, Irish, Jews, Protestants, Catholic kids in their school uniforms who entered the theater in the light, come out brighter even with The City in the dark of evening.

Inside the News Room despite low yield lights, night breaking the scarlet sky of sunset pervades continuing awareness with the story of this complicated end game.

Still adamant over responsibilities of his job, the City Ed SCOTT NEWHALL grimaces through the strong drink. MARGIE smiles, but seems nervous, looks expectantly around the room. No where to be seen, TINA's absence is noticed in tense silence.

Remaining in charge, City Ed NEWHALL comments, "Everyone's out. You should see the streets, everybody's goin' nuts."

The City Ed leaves his conciliatory stand against DAY's desk. WON appears and makes TINA's absence noticeable to everybody.

DAY looks into MARGIE's eyes, but he seems to be baiting something more out of her as WON looks on, paternally. In his dazzled mind, TINA had appeared, now disappeared from the back of the news room. Suddenly worried, DON notices TINA's clutch purse on the office cot, day bed.

Even through the usually abandoned Mission Street, celebration populates the sidewalks, danger lurks outside the minds of men.

The unlikely truth of crime during the end of a war even at home, remains an unforeseen truth about the aftermath of war. Women worry about the fate of fatherless children, the rubble of bombed out urban centers, public works, services and the simple things taken for granted during times of peace after war. Concerns like milk, bread and staples in sparse

supply even after the shooting stops.
Nobody thinks of the ideological criminal
conscious that follows war, everywhere and
not just in the theaters of military
activity. Nobody thinks of the looting,
black market supply chains that breed
organized crime.

Inside the Newspaper building lobby
as the gang of pals from Chen's gather --
for another party, they cannot ignore that
behind them The City is lit with noise of
gladness.

From inside the newspaper lobby, the
CHINA BOYS plunge back into the street in
front of the Newspaper building following
TINA, whom they sighted, they watch her
with their guns drawn as ...

Down the street from the old
building, TINA has to exit from a cab,
paused she noticed that she's forgotten her
purse.

Still out of sight, the CHINESE BOYS
lower their bead on TINA -She goes back
inside the newspaper building.

Upstairs and in a buzz over another
headline, and DAY, many days growth of
beard on his face still works at his desk.
PALS have begun to surround him.

Concentrating on the story, DAY
barely glances up at them.

Smile on his face as his mind places
him at the center of attention, he says to
MARGIE, "News never stops coming. I was
here before you picked my pocket, don't you
know."

Enter the City Ed SCOTT NEWHALL in
serious fervor to beat the news with the

best paper around.

"Got a scoop for ya' Latest word on the Editorial wire, it's about prejudice. JAPS SURRENDER? Not yet! Page two."

DAY puts the phone down.

"Got a scoop for you! There's something more to the Trotskiite spy ring theory. Seems Davidal's a hero. He tipped the FBI to Rosenbergs right away. Never did put the money down on any A-Bomb investment."

WON perks up. He looks over the top of a tear sheet.

City Ed SCOTT NEWHALL hands the bedraggled DAY a wire release. Excited, however, DAY keeps talking.

"The Manhattan Project, meant an atomic bomb big enough to blow up all of Manhattan. Without Davidal, it's another East Coast 'bit,' they said. Play it Out, the FBI said, and they'd see who else Rosenberg's would go to. Just another West Coast deal?!!"

"No pay off?" WON stymied, asks "Then no money was tied up." "Naw, it was a spy story." DAY is back on the keyboard, putting down words, letter at a time. "All the time it was Davidal playin' the boards for to maintain secretes and smoke out any culprits and bite down on the East Coast fact."

"He put his family on the line." WON sits and stares in silent awe at DAVIDAL's secret patriotism.

Beneath the biggest guns on any ship in any navy, enough to dwarf the little Japanese men more than ever, as diplomats

in striped trousers and tails on board the
mighty US Navy battleship, Missouri where
a primitive card table is unfolded with a
deliberate precision that forces the
surrendering enemy to wait in spontaneous,
formal humility.

At attention along the Missouri deck,
US Navy sailors in their dress blue bell
bottom, mitty shirts and white 'Dixie cup'
hats and officers in signal caps wearing
the tan uniform in casual dismissal of
formality in their hour of finality.

VJ Day on board the Missouri Sept 2nd
1945, photographed by the AFART whose clips
will illuminate history and ensure no
successful revisionists would ever change
the fact.

City Ed SCOTT NEWHALL shakes his
head, skeptical that the Japanese will
understand what will show to humiliate them
without inflicting physical pain.

"Being the government!? For now, I
got some quotes from the Pacific theater.
The final acts are closing that theater as
a comedy."

"There is surrender." NEWHALL quotes:

He mocks Gen. MacArthur's voice: I'm
throwing a party. I don't care what the
Emperor's doing, tell him to get his ass
over here! The group of news paper
reporters mimic GI talk that overshadows
DAY's scoop on Davidal's heroics.

One of the COPYBOYS had turned up a
short wave radio and enlisted men's voices
boom into the activity over the short wave
radio now over speakers in the newsroom.

City Ed SCOTT NEWHALL tries to

lighten up the room, waves the line-o-type copy.

"Word by the operators over the wire, MacArthur's thrown' a party, and the Emperor's got no clothes."

Laughter, ripples through the busy room. Elation has made it unnecessary to cater to the boss; easy to make jokes on this day of days. VJ day in San Francisco makes for a release of tension and constraint. The fears all gone, the social mop-up will merely just begin. Speculation peppers the conversations about why the Emperor cannot attend.

Rumor holds that it was not his war, that the Japanese generals wanted war and the Emperor wanted no part of it. So, he refuses to come sit at the table.

"Rumor is that he never admitted to any declaration of war." NEWHALL struts through the newsroom picking up copy, reading and making some comments, here and there.

Those lurking CHINA BOYS outside the building are pushed to the side by the crowd that builds at the newspaper office inside, with the party to begin in celebration at night.

Gamblers, all creatures of habit, who gathered at the scene of one victory party come together to participate in another. From
the Chinatown club the first to arrive at the newspaper building is PETER with DORIS and DAVID with AGNUS in tow.

Following are the characters from Chen's, some of the Filipino men and their

Asian women. A pair of the Chinese servers
from the club enter carrying a couple cases
of champagne, each; and when PENNY follows,
FRENCHIE JOE sneaks into the newsroom, too.

With the onslaught, and after another
few cases of champagne arrive in the arms
of Chen's personnel, CHEN arrives; as all
the arrivals of this social registry have
pushed the CHINA BOYS and CHEW to the side
as they too become guests in this party.

The mood swells from overt happiness
to blind joy. CHEN lights up with a smile
when MARISSA enters. DEUITCH follows and
his daughter with some tall wavy red head
young man in blazer and tan pants with
heavy wing tips that cannot hide his every
movement. Kisses and hugs are had by all,
but the CHINA BOYS who sneak around looking
for something, someone who might stand out
with their stern, serious faces and sharp
movements seeking that one. No one cares
about them.

Enter LT FABER and his INSPECTOR.
MARISA, dressed in black, hides in CHEN's
shadow.

"That piece you did on Chinese gangs
opened a 'can of worms,' Day." LT FABER
standing over the reporter at his
typewriter asks. "You got a chance to name
names, for me?! I got you everything out
of Washington on the Rosenbergs."

While DAY acquiesces, because he had
his heart on the line for this. "The
police want to think they're entitled."

"You're right about who opened the
case on them."

"So, it's on the record that Davidal

opened the case on the traitors of the east coast."

"I don't know from record, but . . . ." FABER is cut off by the newspaper owner who stops any kind of traffic when his presence becomes him.

Silently and with elegance, PAUL in his clean, svelte suit comes up to MARGIE and motions for her to join him. MARGIE responds to his beck and call, obediently turns quickly and shows PAUL her respect, emotional and nervous, she jumps when accidentally he touches her. They both present signs of a new, mutually admiring relationship.

Looking on at the love tension forming just at his elbow, FABER is stalled while DAY goes back to work, as TINA pulls out chopsticks, holds a white box with take-out in one hand.

Coy, MARGIE tries to put forth a reserved attraction. Immediately, she has fallen for him, however. Consider: her boyfriend sits front row center to this play, being literally hand served by a tall, knock-out Chinese girl with chopsticks some gai pai out of a little white box. He wears the same tux he had on since they met. After ten days at his desk without pause his presence is sensed across the room; and finally his multimillionaire boss is ferputzed over her and her rival, friend and bosses daughter. "Paul, you have to meet my boss, Don Won."

PAUL and WON are softly introduced by MARGIE. She notices DAY's madly typing, tries to be discreet. He makes it hard to dislike a handsome guy that dedicated. PAUL conservatively opens up to WON in a manner to extend hospitality. This, his place of business begins to compete with the social activity from an outside world rarely brought into a corporation like this newspaper, and especially the sacred newsroom.

"You have to invite some of your Chinese friends to the party, Won." PAUL deYOUNG with a patronizing attitude when he would rather not have one, broadens the concept of 'the whole city in one room.'

Wanting to approach a solution to many crimes LT FABER, a tall well groomed man seems smarmy at this moment, as he comes up to WON from behind.

"Yes, Won." LT FABER sneaks in. "You have to invite some of your Chinese friends. I was just asking Day, here, what it is."

CHAPTER 22

Mission Street has always been the white collar strip between retail San Francisco and industry. Near the newspaper, foot traffic is mostly poor underworld at night, lunch counter crowd during the weekday.

Back outside, TINA winds through alleys off Mission Street, keeping close to the walls, trying to get back into the Newspaper building with a pot for tea, a building that has a revolving front door, which is wide open, open to the street. The cold marble, tiled floor makes for a starkly imposing secure lobby whose demeanor alone protects the newspaper. Security officers who pass unscheduled and stand in on each floor periodically lend to that security, too.

With society gathering by MARGIE with DAY, invitations from them who have both built their own crowd of social gadabouts, a crowd builds at the newspaper, their crowd for the party of parties . . . the end of war party continues.

"Part two," someone says, "there's no longer Japan."

With his eye on FABER, WON moves to the phone, silently. MARGIE senses something strained between her boss and the law. In response to WON'S head movements, she follows WON to the phone near DAY's desk.

WON whispers secretive, "Call Prescott. Remind him simply that I am here."

While WON acts as though he holds the

controls on all criminal activity, in reality his plan is nothing short of an experiment.

He holds his composure well, and keeps the plan secret, for in truth he cannot be sure that what he has in mind will work.

She dials and talks while WON stands there guarding his position between her and the LT FABER. Acting as the good cop, he watches over the party.

Mission Street and especially near the newspaper building when night falls deeper into the darkness of night, it becomes colder than under the sun. In this season, The City is cold, even though a sun might shine above it. While this is true of The City, it may be true of all port cities on the Pacific Rim.

The lunch counters closed. Soup kitchens, hamburger places done for the night, even pizza places closed up tight. All this known to TINA who had ventured out to bring back a tea pot, some snacks.

On this long night, TINA heads back to the party at the newspaper having failed to find any food counters open, makes a rush for the building, and TWO CHINESE BOYS, guns drawn, silently make the rush toward her from opposite directions making her into a sandwich between the both of them.

TINA abruptly drops to her knees on the sidewalk with such a dash, both CHINESE BOYS are startled and reflexively fire their 45's and shoot each other dead.

Even through the cold MISSION Street

atmosphere of a working neighborhood, at THE NEWSPAPER building front door TINA is paused, sweating but soon breathing naturally.

When TINA enters the building she seems taller, more steady but shaken with a steely edge of forced nature. Only due to her quick wit and love of life can TINA hold her own character together.

Her love for one other is no doubt just as directed.

Inside at the back of the newsroom the lights are low for sake of economy. The war is over so with few people working in the large writing area, only the lights over DAY and his party need be lit.

Within that interior dusk, PENNY, her eyes shifting all around the room suddenly at the sound of shots outside; and with glamorous self consciousness as only afforded by PENNY, herself indulged and currently enveloped with some TUXEDOED GUY who self consciously melts into the small crowd of couples discreetly necking. She stands in agile fragility, and each one alone, and together tied with a champagne bottle being passed around for refills that eventually reaches her, too. It has become a real party. While ... Business of the unfunny kind persist.

The ever serious City Ed SCOTT NEWHALL saunters into the melee, and says to DAY, "What's going on, here?"

Signaling the presence of PAUL deYOUNG with his head, DAY replies, "Seems our publisher's found the city's society, Chief. What-a bang, bash."

The two of them take a moment to look over the crowd. City Ed NEWHALL looks down at Day's typewriter and stack of pages.

DAY follows his gaze to the work on the desk.

"We have an unhealed wound of prejudice in the bank world." Nearby, so the City Ed NEWHALL can hear, MARGIE turns from PAUL'S side to tell WON about her last phone call.

"Not much to say, but the Chinese sage Prescott got your message." Adding, not distracted, from his own mental pile of stories, City Ed says, "Yeah ... Port Chicago, still a book on prejudice left open, too."

MARGIE back to business turns to WON. "Talked to Tina. Said Dad'll know ... just say, 'Chew.' Dad'll know, she lined up the bullets, she said. So I did. I told him that."

With his chin in his hand, elbow on his knee WON shows he knows what she meant. City Ed SCOTT NEWHALL chews more gum as though trying to get that story of what he overheard but will never inquire about, out of the candy in his mouth.

DAY tries his joyous irony out loud. "Hey! It's a newspaper, right? Everybody, everything comes to us."

The CHINA BOY CHEW, then FRENCHIE JOE and THREE ITALIAN MOBSTERS, MALLY with MARKHAM now tipped off as to what might be going on, and by confirming whispers among themselves enter the room cause the sound to dampen with curiosity about them. From the back of the huge room, enter TINA,

distraught from a narrow shooting escape.
Hardly anyone notices her.

The toughs, however stare at each
other, amazed TINA escapes any social
interrogation, as she weaves through the
group that has crowded around DAY's desk.

TUXEDOED BOYS and FANCY GIRLS are all
making out with the GIRLS in the fringe
areas where the lights are low, and with
booze in the crowded room in activity that
remains peppered with newspaper business
it's like salt on greasy-spoon french fries
that makes the spontaneous black-tie scene
sizzle. Burnt edges ignored with the
gangsters on the scene. One anchovy on the
plate as CHEW circulates in advance of
PRESCOTT, perhaps.

Suddenly, PENNY comes out of the
newspaper dark room with PETER wrapped over
her arm. Her lipstick is all smeared. She
is laughing, a wet, newly processed photo
in her hand.

She waves the photo, everyone can see
it shows the mushroom cloud of the recently
revealed Atomic Bomb, and she says in a
normal voice, "Boom"

Her laughter stops as she sees
everyone staring at her. Actually, they
only stare in her direction, at TINA. The
living serene, floatatious one, TINA who
entered from the street, wove through the
crowd, landed like a butterfly at DAY's
desk virtually unnoticed until her
intention got the crowd's attention.

LT FABER turns to WON.

"You have been undertaking an
investigation, now all the players are

here. You want to let me in on it, Mr. Won?"

WON slyly turns to him, "Mr. Won has a ton of things to sort out in this soup. The main dumpling has not risen to the surface, yet."

At his desk, finished with writing, DAY looks at MARGIE and PAUL, who with all his power remains frustrated, because with only two people between them, he can't seem to get close to her in the crowd.

From his chair at the desk, looking up at LT FABER, DAY full of confidence begins his dissertation.

"Sol wanted in on an East Coast deal so bad, he went around financial captain Bernard Barouche. Almost sold the local investment group into a megaton bomb plan with a government contracted mechanic named Greenglass and a Trotskiite named Rosenberg. Megatons at a 'dixie' per ton meant big bucks and to Davidal to control the whole war finances meant going outside the captain. See, in this case he thought he was being cut out. West Coast fact, he wanted more money for the West Coast deals. Secretly tipped the FBI. Rightfully wouldn't believe the government didn't pay for its own bombs. A real patriot. It fractured the City's ethnic bonds, because Old San Francisco, Barbary Coast banking families only saw syndicated profits from a simple, crooked munitions deal outside the captain. Secretes divided the ethnic fault lines. East Coast fact. To build up? Real Estate be damned, but not this Manhattan project. With no ready cash,

free guns on the street made Davidal
subject for hair trigger decisions.
Suspicions fostered by Chinese rumors about
treason, and Sol got it over a bad gambling
debt, before anybody could know. Revenge
maybe, all over a paste copy of a sapphire
gift to a two timing blond capped him off."

LT FABER chimes. "Not the only one,
got his just due."

Unable to release any tears, TINA
says, "Paste and powder all go Boom! That
right, Daddy?"

WON stands with LT FABER pacing
within a few square yards. All eyes from
the local gangsters including PRESCOTT who
had materialized through the cigarette
smoke like a mystic, to stand still for WON
to speak.

"Somebody lit the light of love with
a sapphire. The boys dealing arms only
angered small fry with big guns over a fake
stone and promise for very big on the-books
money froze all the banks. Spite and
anger, revenge if you wish, yes.
Boom-bang, royal flush!"

The crowd shifts into a gallery, as
the Chinese detective holds everybody's
interest.

"It was going to be Chinese or
Italians, organized crime for cash profit
either way, because this city was wide
open. Whose ever love this woman of prey
was, no matter. Small fish draw out big
pelicans diving for stones, nonetheless.
More stones, not paste this time, Detroit
Racketeers found a way in to what they
always thought was a soft City."

LT FABER narrates. "In-fighting at the bank, then. Chinese against the Italians on the streets, but a Jewish man with a big pouch got it. Makes for a hard, rock fight."

TINA hugs DAY, MARGIE sees her. The crowd shifts into cliques. TINA mentions to DAY, "If only Bobby PRESCOTT would come in." WON keeps focus. "The Chinese had the goods, I put a call onto the street for the books; and only got one headman too confused, himself. Big money on books. What value for the only books he knew? No one stepped forward. But, I did see who in gangs got interested."

Eager to squeal, FRENCHIE JOE takes a step toward the two detectives.

WON sees that and gives off more with a sign below his waist signal, to slow FRENCHIE JOE and allow all the facts in, first.

"The message of fear, hate. It told of War Incorporated West in trouble. Men stealing their wives and daughter's jewels can't get by in secret. Hot story runs rampant in this city. Thirst bigger than for gossip grew for real currency with some small China boys to maybe have some 'Big Deal' and couldn't bank what the big dealer knew. Too secret, too bad. Guns to paste to powder. One Chinese bookkeeper in the bay and one necklace gone to paste. Little men who think small is big.

"And who thinks about China with Japan killing on that soil?" LT FABER interjects again. "With word out about the war's end, money gets tight even in an

arena of organized crime." Protectively,
PAUL pulls MARGE to his side. MARISSA
becomes enveloped in CHEN's embrace.
Dramatically, BOBBY PRESCOTT enters the
circle from behind in the fringes.
Standing firm, wearing his elegant Chinese
robes, he gives pause to speculation.
Those in the crowd who don't gasp, swallow
some champagne. They sense that all that
is unknown will be known.

WON sees him.

"Enter criminal mind. Scare came to
the whole city ... Detroit moving in,
here."

Having diffused their worst fears of
MOFIA infusion, WON continues with his eyes
to cut PRESCOTT's scalp off and throws
daggers to pinpoint the China boy CHEW, who
suddenly appears with a step forward in the
crowd.

"Number One China Boy had to bring
headman some profit. Self directed
obligation. What good would East Coast
deal do China Boy? The number One, didn't
know enough. Loose face? Fix books? Blow
safe, again? Gets too complicated. They
can't wait, maybe Japan destroys China.
Number one China boy had to end bank lock-
out over revenge, and with only Davidal's
books, and sapphire of paste in gambling
parlor safe. No cash to him meant insult
to his headman. To him, a local power ploy
and no money for the Chinese. No law for
them. Tense situation, Chinese anger and
World blows up in his hot face. In Japan,
too. Chinese powder. Paste, damn it.
Americans of all kinds forget the Chinese

are besieged by Japan, too."

WON draws his finger across his throat.

"How could one China Boy know about an atom bomb deal, with our City in pieces over Real Estate and card games? Now even criminals threatened by organized crime."

The China boy CHEW sees BOBBY PRESCOTT looking at him, and even LT FABER becomes restless, CHEW becomes guiltily uneasy and tries to move out of the shifting crowd.

At the moment CHINA BOY crosses the now stilled room, like a frog that jumps out of the still water; and WON whose words spark motion.

WON cues the law. "For, who grabs the bodies floating in the bay?"

It is the INSPECTOR, LT FABER who grabs China boy CHEW by the collar, "Ak, ak!" And PETER with DAVID hold him from running away. Fearful, PENNY skirts the crowd.

What she does not know, she may never know. That shows how out she stays.

Definitely effected, a Chinese man, a gentleman, a father, WON continues in decided vengeance. "There's your China Boy, key to the murderer who called alley meeting for big call-in big debt money. Big paste for small money showed Davidal's fortune's gone East. Who'd know, 'Boom;' investment's gone . . . West and war's over. Just like that. West Coast fact. Dead man fact."

DAY can't hold back, says, "There goes East Coast fact."

CHEW gags 'Ak, ak!' Protest as the two POLICEMEN take him away, pull his gun out of his pocket. DAVID and PETER Standing all too near, turn dismally pale, and they begin to exit, remain enraptured too.

WON like a street side story teller goes on with it.

"Didn't get any necklaces. Poor China boy, Chew."

PRESCOTT remains firm and silent. TINA stands with MARGIE, DAY and PAUL at their sides look fondly at her father. They smile and toast a silent partner above them. MARGIE looks up to the sky for salvation.

Almost for a diversion, WON continues, "For a small sum, big books money means little to boys whose bigness is enough to fill their two hands."

'Frenchie Joe' who stands behind WON as the undisclosed connection, provides last minute evidence into WON's pocket. As WON looks across the room at BOBBY PRESCOTT, WON drops a hand

into his jacket pocket and pulls out the sapphire necklace.

BOBBY PRESCOTT and CHEN look on at WON with the necklace in his two hands, eyes open in awe, as -

DON WON crushes the paste in his one hand.

WON without flinching, "The headman attracts only a 'Maggot,' here meaning a Chinese king."

MARISA laughs in relief. PENNY moves close to PETER. FRENCHIE JOE sweats

surreptitiously in the background as he
secretly tries to pass WON the real jewelry
he fingers in his own pocket.

From his pocket, WON then produces
two more necklaces. THE GROUP snickers, as
this serious scene becomes amusing.

DAY tries to lift the attitude.

"There was a reason Bill Markham came
into town ... Bring in a new library . . .
make use of all the paste."

WON crumbles the paste stones, again,
and again. PENNY is pressed, comforting
herself against PETER but watching FRENCHIE
JOE.

DAY realized his joke fell flat. He
continues with his report. "Fenced a
sapphire and found a weakness in the city
that left an open door for his Detroit
organization. Fraud among thieves." DAVID
and PETER have their girls, DORIS and PENNY
near, holding them tight as all listen when
DAY, with their attention pipes up louder.

DAY has their attention.

"Like I said, Davidal had to control
it all by himself, because the one great
arms-deal of the age was a fake. Finance
foiled by paste -- arms trade foiled by
deception. His real deal was a tip to the
FBI about Rosenberg and in the end got
nothin' for himself." DAVID and PETER look
inward, each with different signs of
relief. DAY pitches the last strike.

"-- except a bullet."

Sweating profusely now, while
attention remains on DAY, FRENCHIE JOE
slips the -

"Even the banks got betrayed, caught

breathless on the same side of the fence as
treason, all for the price of a sapphire
necklace."

-- Real sapphire necklace out of his
pocket along with a Smith and Wesson 38
that he quickly hides, and secretly --
Passes the stones to WON. Finally done, he
sighs in relief.

None too pleased DAY with grinding
teeth unfolds more.

"Who'd believe the cost of seduction
here. What a patriot. Davidal, who fooled
us all with promises of an investment that
never would be. Who's ever to know what
power what possibilities in the City?"

WON finds a moment to slant the story
to love.

"I think the widow's daughter will
just want to see that justice is done."

WON takes the real necklace out of
his pocket and hands it to MARISA to
everybody's relief at the sounds of real
stones grinding together.

WON looks to the lawmen. "I don't
think the women are going to want to press
charges."

With paradoxical little girl tones
from an elegant gal, TINA says, "I got in
on another scoop. Everybody! Chen Lai and
Marisa Davidal are going to get married."

DON DAY turns to TINA WON.

With a flood of emotion and general
confusion all around, TINA aggressively
kisses DAY full on the mouth. Then, DAY,
tenderly returns the affection perceived in
the glimmer of her father's eye as the
celebration bursts into social confusion.

WON whose smile has closed his eyes.
"As I suspect: It would be our
'Dawn-Won-Day.'"

As DON WON stands looking at the
action, -- FRENCHIE JOE slips into the
hallway and down the elevator.

While DAY retreats back to his desk,
then hands his article, last page taken out
of the typewriter, to the COPY BOY, who
rushes it back to the City Ed SCOTT
NEWHALL, PAUL escorts MARGIE out.

With obvious pleasure, DAY
approaches a grinning TINA.

BOBBY PRESCOTT comes to WON, looks at
him with piercing eyes. "Aren't you
forgetting something?" PRESCOTT asks
without a glimmer of false confidence.

WON sees right through him like the
negligee of a Chinese stripper. "I
recovered jewels and the ledgers which I
was hired to do. I wonder why anybody
would need the use of a Bobby PRESCOTT,"
and his eyes slant as sharp as a knife.

BOBBY PRESCOTT has a self redeeming
comment of rational.

"Everybody has a Bobby PRESCOTT to
call out sometime or another." PRESCOTT
stands face to face with WON, who shakes
his bead in disgust. CHEN and MARISA
leave, embraced as though shaken, and
follows them with his eyes while holding
fast near PRESCOTT.

WON says, "I'm happy not to have to
be 'an everybody.'"

BOBBY PRESCOTT, whose reserve has not
chipped, tells WON, "Then I'm happy to tell
You, I'm the not headman. It's Chen Lai."

Marisa's trench coat swishes out of WON's view as she with CHEN disappear through closing doors of the down elevator. CHEN seems to have the girl, and the last laugh.

Inside the creaky wood paneled building, there's almost a fatherly comfort for the exiting gang.

Outside in the harsh cold air in front of the newspaper building it has become the end of the evening.

They all exit from the building, MARGIE with PAUL outside, his arm around her waist. While the formal, tuxedos and slinky dresses, disperse into the fog filtering through city streets mostly by taxi the taste of an end of the Great War is lacking some kind of just dessert in The City.

Standing at the grey curb, PAUL finally gets to kiss MARGIE and passing headlights flicker their romantic future down the road.

He leaves her to go get his car.

The fog closes in on DON DAY with TINA. MARGIE and WON stand together by the curb pleased, outside the landmark San Francisco building as they both silently look into the fog.

The City Ed SCOTT NEWHALL appears at the doorway with Day's last page in his hand, mouth open in wordless amazement, -

As LT FABER and the INSPECTOR materialize out of the fog and City Ed NEWHALL can see them nab -

FRENCHIE JOE, casually nervous, curbside waiting for the last taxi.

LT. FABER tries to steal the last

line in this end of war story. "You're a
real piece, Joey ... . A real San
Francisco banker's boy, alright."

FABER with his boys disarm him,
reaching into his jacket, and find his,
which is the barrel tip of the smoking gun
from the alley murder of Saul Davidal, 38
Special.

LT. FABER adds insult. "Worst thing
is, Joey, you knew about a pay-off to the
Rosenbergs and didn't tell anybody."

"I'm not one to dip my dick in that
swatch of prejudice," says FRENCHIE JOE.

City Ed SCOTT NEWHALL and WON watch
'the collar' through the fog. CHEN and
MARISA disappear as WON's paternal Chinese
smile broadens at the additional sight of
TINA, who affectionately fluffs Day's hair
while they go toward his car.

DAY turns away from TINA to see City
Ed SCOTT NEWHALL behind them wave. Last
page in hand. City Ed kisses the pages
that DAY had already written, pleased he
reenters the building. PAUL pulls up in
his car to take MARGIE away having missed
the national end to the international
finale, lustily deYOUNG begins his own
local curtain call.

As the police car, with lights
flashing pulls away carrying FRENCHIE JOE,
DAY and TINA drive away into the fog in his
car with 'brown out' headlight covers still
fixed in place.

LT. FABER comes up to WON. These
last two close the city. WON speaks with
soft confidence.

They both look up at a very dark

sunset sky, one to die for, mostly orange
in the high clouds of red and yellow.

"So you got the secret, when I said
China boy Chew was 'key.'" WON and the LT.
turn and walk together into the fog.

Still walking side by side with WON,
LT FABER says, "Yeah! I got it all. Chew
hit the bookkeeper for the Jewish family,
and squealed on Frenchie for Davidal's
murder in the Alley. It was over the
money. It's about Davidal's investment and
what went through Frenchie's family bank.
Nothin'!

"They call Joe Frenchie because he
never liked bein' Italian. The Jewish
syndicate never used his father's bank, so
stealin' from Davidal was no gymnastic
event of conscience. He had no affiliation
with anybody.

"But, when he stopped the payment to
the Chew gang forsake of making paste on
the sapphire, he had another minder bender
event to deal with. And he became the easy
gymnastic event to deal with."

They walk, FABER fiddles with a
cigar. Soon, WON has a box of matches in
his hand making sounds like a brush on a
snare drum while they walk toward the
street lights and a single car parked on
the street.

"There's little goin' on that we
Irish haven't managed or to be knowin'
about in San Francisco amongst all the
restrictions from all the laws.

"Whatever else is there in the world
to know?"

WON in Caucasian clarity says, "Just

between us friends, there are some things
we may never know."

He looks to the side at his police
detective friend. "The Irish," he says as
FABER draws smoke from his lit cigar,
"Lucky stiffs."

END

The font chosen for this book is the same for that of the newspapers of the day in the 1940's, Times Roman.